ABSENT VICTIM

David Roy

HOBART BOOKS

ABSENT VICTIM

First Published in 2021
by
Hobart Books, Oxfordshire, England
hobartbooks.com

Printed and bound in Great Britain by Biddles Ltd

Prologue

There is something out there in the Universe, some fragment or a fragment of a fragment that makes us who we are and when it is discovered it will change our view of life forever. That thing, whatever it is, will enable us to study the very structure of every living item on the planet and to explain how we came to be and how we continue to exist. We never really die, you see. Our essence lives on, perhaps diluted, and never truly dying like a beam of light that attenuates but never quite comes to an end no matter how faint it might become.

Josef Ankoplar, London 1897

Chapter One

The rain fell in torrents but I didn't even notice; there was so much more going on in the world and anyway it always rained in this neck of the woods. I just smiled as I wrote this because my friend, accomplice and useful idiot Billy always said, 'neck of the world'. It was one of his stock phrases, the use of which was either intentionally or unintentionally humorous since I was never sure just how dumb he really was. He certainly knew how to appear stupid but often there were deep currents of sense and perception flowing beneath the surface. Not always but often. He spoke so much crap that over the years I had just filtered it out, but his strange utterances came as a shock to those who didn't know him.

In between those times when I wanted to strangle him, Billy was a great ally whose stock in trade was to have rare moments of unusual brilliance which shone from the darkness of his idiocy like a searchlight. He wasn't in the office today; it was just me, but I had kept him on a retainer and he was on the other end of the phone when I needed him. This was at the time of the great plague, the Covid-19 epidemic that crippled society for most of 2020. I was able to go to work as a one-man band, but the truth was that I could easily have worked from home and often did. I was accountable to no one but myself and didn't have to 'social distance' because there was no one else around

I had my life more or less sorted by then. My house was detached and paid for. My car was paid for and most of the things in my house worked adequately, with the exception of the washing machine that was nearing the end of its useful life and staring oblivion in the face. My job – my security business – was ticking over, paying the bills and allowing me to set a little aside each month for the holiday I never took. All in all, things were… average.

The plague had its good points. One of these was that the gym that occupied the floor beneath my office – Strainers – was now shut, which saved me from having to listen to the sweaty efforts of the gym bunnies and men of muscle each day as they put their gorgeous bodies through enough exercise to kill a rhino. They all worked in offices, drove, and lived in considerable luxury. They didn't need to be as hard as iron. Maybe I shouldn't mock. They were doing their best, I suppose, in the absence of doing any real work. You never see a farm labourer in the gym.

The office used to have a great big chrome coffee machine, the sort of thing you have in fancy cafés that can make espressos, cappuccinos (with and without froth), Americanos, lattes and all the other derivations of coffee that you can imagine. One day it broke and I toyed with the idea of getting it fixed until I learned how much this would cost. I came up with a better idea. With Billy's help we bundled it into my car and fly-tipped it onto a country road near the airport.

I'll leave you with that sentence for a moment.

We didn't really. Billy and I took the machine to the tip and asked if they would like it. I had a fair idea that they 'recycled' items and was happy to get rid of the great, noisy beast. For some reason, Billy came with me to Argos to buy the replacement which was only, in my mind, ever going to be one of those white plastic kettles. I came out with a chrome kettle with some safety feature that I didn't quite understand. That was Billy's fault; he didn't want a white plastic kettle and I gave in to his demands just to shut him up. I didn't want him to make a scene. Anyway, my point was that it was much quieter without the gurgling, rasping monster in the office and since my staff had shrunk to just the two of us, there was no need for such industrial scale hot drink production. It must have saved me a fortune too.

But honestly, if you were on the phone as someone made themselves a cappuccino, you could barely hear what the person on the other end was trying to say, which was both frustrating and bad for business. But talking of that, things had scaled back over the years; the customers just weren't out there in the same numbers these days. With the wage bill much reduced I got by perfectly well.

Naturally when the plague hit, I was expecting a major downturn. After all, who really cares about a cheating wife or the drug den next door when humanity faces the prospect of a cull brought on by a tiny, unthinking, unyielding enemy that hit even the diehard cynics who barged their way through life without incident? It didn't matter if you were in the SAS or the frailest baby, this thing could get you. But luckily for me, the downturn didn't come. Things stayed the same.

Until they didn't. Then I got a job that consumed all of my time. It was the weirdest job, with a peculiar pretext and a situation outside my experience, or that of anyone really. But she turned to me, and I said I would do my best to help. I'm like that.

And she was paying.

***

5

In times of crisis and stress I used to head to a café called Della's which was owned and run, logically enough, by a woman named Della. Since the onslaught of the great plague she had been forced to close her doors and so I had to rely on my own cooking skills at work and the chrome kettle that Billy had forced me to buy. It wasn't the same by a long chalk. You see, Della was one of those people who you never fully know but who becomes part of your routine and who is always there. She wasn't someone to mess with, but she was tough and resourceful, and she made food just the way you asked for it. If you wanted your steak well done, it came out well done, not running with fresh blood like a prop from a horror film.

But her café or deli – *Della's Deli?* – was shut for now, so it was just me, the kettle and the silence: no clanging weights in the gym, very little traffic down below in the street and no inane office chatter.

I had a few bits to do. For one thing, I was chasing up business in Hong Kong and New Zealand, both unrelated cases but both pertaining to people who had gone missing. The first was a soldier, the second a railwayman. For another thing, I was looking at taxes: how much I should be paying and how much I should be deducting from Billy's wages. Billy had an army pension so the wages he collected from me were just beer money for him, but he still had to be taxed. He once said to me that he didn't mind paying his taxes, calling it his main contribution to society. That is a rarely expressed viewpoint.

I digress. I was busy with these things when the phone rang and made me start slightly, such was the paucity of telephonic communication events (Billy's term) that I was involved in. I mean, *I made calls*, but received few out of the blue, so to speak.

'Hello', I said.

'Hello. I need your help.'

'Okay, what is the problem?'

That's how it started. *I need your help.* This was the basic premise behind the new contracts I took on, so the words in isolation didn't surprise me, although what came next did. She gave me the details which spewed out in a stream of words, the like of which I had rarely heard from a sober person and which made me think that there were certain other difficulties in this lady's life on top of those she was talking about now. The exact words are lost to the shock of the call, but some are unforgettable.

'I have killed someone.'

My immediate thought was that I had a crank on the other end of the phone, although if this was a trick, why were they bothering with me? But it was irrelevant; I didn't really believe them.

'If that is the case, then you need to speak to the police', I said calmly. That was the top and bottom of it really.

'I have. They don't want to know.'

'Perhaps if you show them the body of the person you killed, they might.'

'Bring it into the police station?'

Now I knew she was taking the piss.

'Tell them where it is. Presumably you told them where to find the deceased person?'

'There isn't one', she said at which I rolled my eyes. I was about to put the phone back in its little slot on my desk when she saved the day for herself. 'I mean there is. Obviously, there *is* a body. But I don't know where to find it. Look, it's easier if I come in and speak to you in person; that's really why I rang up.'

'Well, we have this social distancing thing…'

'I can keep two metres away from you, you know. It isn't impossible.'

To put her off I said, 'and I will be charging you for my time from the outset.'

'I can pay. Look, I know where your office is. Can I just come in and speak to you? If you don't want to take it on, that's fine but at least let me explain.'

I agreed to that and half an hour later the bell rang downstairs.

***

It was a short walk down the stairwell to the communal front doors of the block, which I shared with Strainer's Gym, Horsehead Solicitors and an empty office. I picked up a handful of junk mail for myself and my fellow occupants and unlocked the door, pulling it open and standing back as required in these strange times. The little hallway was a bit cramped and I would estimate the distance between us as one metre, eighty-five centimetres, rather than two full metres. Was I putting myself in range of that virus? Could it leap that far? Who knew? I didn't subscribe to any of the hoax theories that were doing the rounds at the time: those people were dying of something.

'Hello. My office is upstairs.'

'Hello.'

I pushed two letters through the letterbox of Strainers and then led my guest upstairs, setting another letter outside Horseheads and then opening the office door.

She passed me at a non-regulation distance as she went in and I followed her to our executive seating area, as Billy always called it.

'Have a seat', I said, pointing to one of our low-slung uncomfy chairs. You might have guessed that *uncomfy* was another Billy-ism. He had millions of them, so many that he was well on his way to inventing and using a new language all of his own.

She sat and I filled the kettle to make coffee, which it turned out that she didn't want. This woman was not what I had expected, based on my semi-hysterical telephone conversation with her. She was mid-thirties, well-dressed for the spring and fairly well-heeled judging by her appearance. She was English and spoke like a well-educated southerner, but not too plummy. Her blonde hair was pulled back in a ponytail which accentuated her good cheekbones and complexion.

'Is there anything I can get you, since you don't drink coffee?'

'No thank you. I just need to explain my situation to you. I know how it sounds. I must sound like a lunatic.'

'Not at all', I said, but, in fact, she had sounded exactly like a lunatic, certainly on the phone. She was calmer now, as if she had managed to compose herself on the way over.

9

'Thank you for seeing me. Things have come to a head for me. Maybe it is because I am cooped up all day, but I need to get this sorted.'

I smiled sympathetically, all the while thinking, *'if you're paying, I'll sort it.'* It wasn't a nice way of viewing events, but I had bills to pay, modest though they were. Also, I didn't owe this woman anything. This was a business arrangement we were entering into and nothing more, and if she had the money to hire me to do a job, then why not? If the job was nonsense, then that was not my problem. If I had thought that she was vulnerable in some way, I might have spent time dissuading her, but she came across as confident, intelligent and fully aware of what she was saying. You could say that she was talking utter crap but in a logical, convincing manner that begged further investigation. Okay, she had sounded a bit peculiar on the phone, but not now. Now she was sense personified.

'What you said on the phone did sound a bit strange', I said.

'I know. Let me explain better.'

We were sitting two metres apart. Her voice was smooth and intelligent. I suppose she could be described as persuasive and I didn't find it hard to imagine her getting her own way in any number of situations, from speeding tickets to free drinks. That is an uncharitable view to take on her character, but it was the one that positively leapt into my mind. The truth was much more involved than that and much stranger.

I took a sip of my coffee. It tasted adequate. Billy had got me into the habit of describing things as *adequate, or average for the time of year, or below average*. He just didn't talk like anyone

10

else that I knew, and his bizarre linguistic technique had partially rubbed off on me.

'Well, take your time and start from the beginning.'

'Am I on the clock, like a taxi?'

I laughed.

'Not really. I need all the background that you can give me.'

She nodded and then said, 'well, in that case, make yourself comfortable. I have killed someone. I already mentioned this on the telephone. I have been to the police and they aren't prepared to investigate because there is no body. Obviously, there *is* a body. But I know that I have killed someone and so I need you to investigate for me. I will give you all the details that I can, and I will pay the going rate for your time.'

I nodded and began with the obvious question. 'Where is the body?'

'I don't know. I mean, that sounds stupid, but I just don't know.'

'Okay then, *who* did you kill?'

'I don't know that either.'

Now, at this early stage I was starting to have some sympathy for the police. I had never been a police officer but I think that if I was a CID detective with a loads of burglaries, assaults and fraud cases to deal with, I would be less than impressed with someone turning up and telling me that they had killed someone but didn't know who or where. How can I put this? It sounded like bollocks but for the sake of getting paid, I kept the incredulous look off my face.

'The next thing to ask is, how do you know that you killed someone?'

'I can just feel it. I know what it feels like to have murdered someone. I can feel the emotions of looking down at the dead body and knowing that you caused it to be there, that you killed that person.'

None of this was helping of course but as these words were being delivered in a sincere and logical manner by a well-dressed, intelligent, attractive woman and not by some slobbering armhole with flip-flops, leggings and hair pulled back in a bun so tight it made her eyes slanted, I felt compelled to listen.

I nodded in a sage manner and put a pen to my lips. I had probably seen someone do this on Quincy or some other programme that I watched in my childhood. Next, I took a short walk to my desk and retrieved a notepad from a drawer. When I sat again, I began taking details.

'Can I make a note of your name, please?'

'Stephanie Kuler. K.U.L.E.R.'

'Unusual name', I commented.

'My husband was American. Ex-husband, that is.'

She gave me her address and a few other personal details, for contact purposes mainly, and then I decided that we should talk about her and her background. Initially, she seemed reluctant, but she warmed to the subject of herself as time went on. Most people like talking about themselves, especially if they think they're interesting in some way, despite masses of evidence to the contrary. Some people of my acquaintance talk almost *exclusively* about temselves and often at great length, which is nowhere near as fascinating as they imagine. Stephanie Kuler did not fall into that category. She kept to the point.

'I met my husband at university. I did a year in Boston as an exchange student, met him there, blah-de-blah. When we graduated, we stayed in the US, he got a well-paid job, I got a less well-paid job. Things were fine but we eventually grew apart. He was rich when we divorced so I got a very handsome settlement. I stayed out there for a while but then came home and started a new life. No kids, good job, no mortgage… and I don't know what else you want to know.'

'When did you first start to think that you had killed someone?', I asked. I was aware that I sounded like a TV psychiatrist now.

Tell me about your childhood.

There isn't much to tell. Grew up in a cardboard box, abused by my stepfather, bullied at school but overcame all this adversity to become what I am today - a drug addict and prostitute.

'In a way, I have always known it…' She paused and frowned as if that simple statement didn't sound correct once spoken out loud. 'As time went on, the feeling became more distinct. It became more real, so that instead of being just a feeling it became a fact, a sort of vague fact, if you know what I mean.'

I had no idea what she meant.

'I understand.'

'So, in time it has just become more and more part of me. I am more certain every day that I did it.'

'Do more details come to you as you grow more certain?'

'Well, that's the thing. No, they don't. You would think that I would remember more about it but I don't. I become more certain, but the details are…'

'Just a blur?'

She shook her head, troubled.

'Missing. The details are totally missing. I can't remember one damn thing about the incident. I only know that it happened.'

By saying this, she had just brutally amputated my next line of enquiry, but I felt compelled to ask anyway for want of an alternative course of action, I suppose.

'Did you kill a man or a woman?'

'I don't know.'

'Did you kill a child?'

'I don't know.'

'Was it someone you knew?'

'I don't know.'

'Was it recent or was it long ago?'

'I don't know.'

'Was it in this country or was it in the USA?'

'I don't know.'

'Was it raining?'

'I don't know.'

'Were you outside or in?'

'I don't know.'

'In what way did you kill them? Was it a gun, a knife or something else?'

'I don't know.'

'Was it definitely murder, or could it have been an accident or manslaughter?'

'I don't know.'

From this line of questioning I concluded that she didn't know. I was tempted to ask if she had actually been present when she murdered this unknown person, but it would have sounded facetious to do so. I still wanted to be paid, so I gave her the benefit of the doubt, even though I was more certain than ever that this was utter nonsense. I blew air from my cheeks, which she interpreted correctly as early onset frustration (EOF). She must have read my mind.

'It isn't much to go on', she said, with mastery of understatement to the fore.

'Erm… I can see why the cops didn't want to take it on. This is like the opposite of a crime; I have the perpetrator but not the crime, or the victim. It's all back-to-front. You have come forward, thus saving anyone the effort of catching you, but you can't be charged, or sentenced, because there is no sign of your crime. I'm surprised they didn't get you to own up to some other crime, just to make use of your admission of guilt. I mean, you've confessed to murder and they didn't even have to beat it out of you with lengths of rubber hose.'

'Is that what they do?', she asked.

'Not if you have already confessed.'

I was veering off in the direction of stupefied disbelief and it was showing in my language and mannerisms but I still wanted to take the case because she was paying me and, let's be honest, she was rich and attractive. Who doesn't want to rescue a damsel in distress?

She sighed and pulled a face as if she had blown her chances of getting me to take the job. This was not true at all but there was something else that I had to mention, just in case she had overlooked this seemingly obvious fact.

'If you did kill someone, and if we find out who, and how, and why, and all the rest of it, you do realise that you are going to go to jail for many years? You will spend your best years, possibly your remaining years, behind bars?'

'Yes.'

'Why are you confessing? If you killed someone, then you have actually got away with it. If it was me, I wouldn't say anything.'

'I just can't live with the guilt', she said, plainly. That assertion – that she just couldn't live with the guilt – made perfect sense until you put it into the context of a crime which, by any normal measure of these things, had not happened. She seemed perfectly sane, but for a moment or two the thought crossed my mind that she was suffering from some sort of delusion, a mental illness. It was something I should ask her about: did she suffer from mental illness?

I should have asked but I just couldn't bring myself to, and not just for the sake of the money she was going to pay me to investigate this crime that never was.

'Do you have more questions?', she asked me.

'I suppose I should. Let me think. You have thrown me now. I can take this case on if you like and I am more than willing to do so, but it feels as if I have precisely nothing to go on. Like I said, I have the perpetrator but not the crime. There is no victim. You want justice but there is no evidence of a crime having been committed. Can this be linked to any missing persons?'

'Not that I know of.'

'Are there any unsolved murders that could be your doing?'

'The police don't seem to think so.'

'I have connections in the police, so I could ask around. But even then, it sounds bloody weird. *I have a murderer here; do you have any unsolved murders you'd like to pin on her?* I don't quite know how to phrase it. You might get prosecuted for a murder that you didn't commit but not the one that you... feel... you have *actually* committed. Then again, they would need evidence to link you to the crime, so if there were no witnesses and no DNA, then you wouldn't get the blame even if you confessed to it.'

'Will you take it on?', she asked. Her voice was suddenly emotionless as though the act of me connecting her to a murder was just a perfectly routine transaction like buying school uniform or depositing money in a bank. This was the *least* routine thing I'd ever done in my life, but the truth was that I probably could make a useful start just by calling in a few favours, exploiting the goodwill I had established with various people over the years and through over-use of unwarranted flattery.

I could do all these things.

I could justify the wage she would pay me.

But I could not *ever* envisage a time when I connected Stephanie Kuler with the crime of murder.

With the thought of ultimate and unavoidable failure uppermost in my mind, I said,

'Yep, I'll take you on as my client.'

Chapter Two

'Food for thought', you might say. I was intrigued but that might not have been enough to keep me going had it not been for the wage it would generate. Put it like this, what was there to investigate exactly? I would find *something* because she was paying me to do so but without that incentive what was there? Where would I start? She had read and signed a basic contract, but she seemed uninterested in the actual ins and outs of what she had signed up to. I suppose she *was* interested in the result rather than the means by which it was obtained, which was fair enough.

Once she had gone, I did the usual thing and 'Googled' her. Billy always said '*Gongled*', for reasons of his own. Her name brought up various Stephanies on Facebook, Twitter and Instagram but none of them had the surname Kuler. LinkedIn had a Brent Kuler from the USA, who might or might not have been her ex-husband. I made a note of the name and his contact details in case he made it onto my list of people to interview. I could start by asking him if his ex-wife was a lunatic. He might well answer in the affirmative.

Other than that single possible connection, the internet was a Stephanie Kuler-free zone, as if she had scrubbed the entire ethereal entity of her identity. If that was so, then it somehow fitted: why wouldn't someone who had committed an undetectable crime be themselves undetectable? Perhaps I had dreamt the whole thing. Perhaps, indeed, I would never see her again.

I locked up and walked home, pondering this strange meeting and thinking about the things I should have asked her. What about her childhood and her family? Could any of them shed any light on these untraceable events perhaps? She may well have talked to them already but it would have done no harm to ask them in person, even if only to discover that some childhood trauma had caused this worrying but fictional event to become trapped in her head. The idea that she suffered from some type of recurring delusion came to me again.

I paused and stood to one side, although the street was almost empty, and put a few of these questions into my phone as reminders for the next time I spoke with her. I already knew that my next port of call was Billy, with his superb, instinctive detective abilities. Once he was up and running he was unstoppable, but sometimes it took a bit of persuasion to overcome his natural inertia.

There was one other thing, which in all likelihood had no bearing upon this investigation; what had brought her to Northern Ireland? She had spoken about her marriage to Mr Kuler (Brent?) and that she had returned to the UK when that had failed, but why Northern Ireland, for she clearly wasn't a local?

I paused again and put this question into my phone. I would ask her but not before I had compiled a list of other questions to go with it.

The streets were almost empty, more so the closer to my house I got. A bus passed me, with its 'Not in Service' sign illuminated. A single car followed, then a truck and finally a police car, a white Mondeo. It was a zombie-less apocalypse, and no one really knew if this spelt the end of mankind.

I watched the PM's briefing that night and was comforted by the fact that the government was acting in accordance with the scientific advice on hand. As time went on, some commentators became dissatisfied with the manner in which the pandemic was being dealt with. Some of these, it became clear, were still just bitter about Brexit, some were just Tory haters, some just loved to complain, spread fear and discontent, and a great many others were self-appointed epidemiologists.

I was not an expert. The government said wash your hands, so I washed my hands. They said stay two metres away from other people, so I stayed two metres away from other people. I didn't find any of it much of a hardship. There were plenty of people who I was only too glad to stay two metres away from. I would have stayed further from them if required. Up to twelve miles in some cases. I wondered if life would ever go back to normal and if what we had considered to be normal was worth having again. It seemed to me that if the virus didn't kill us all, it had actually brought with it some good and had made people connect with their own lives even as they temporarily disconnected from the lives of other people. Social distancing, shopping for essentials, preparing meals at home, looking after your family, tidying the garden, exercising… Of course, that optimistic view didn't hold up too well if you were trying to run a business and watching it wither and die before your eyes.

I made a simple tea that night, read, pondered, watched Netflix pondered some more. In normal circumstances my street was quiet but now it was utterly bereft of life. My neighbours, most of whom I wouldn't have recognised in any

21

circumstances, were good, respectable people who stayed indoors as requested and, like me, did all the things the government asked of them. I didn't know if they were Catholic or Protestant, where they worked, how old they were, or what their interests were. It suited me fine and obviously it suited them fine too, because there were no breaches of this anonymous arrangement in all the time I'd lived there. I wasn't living in the midst of drug dealers and prostitutes and no one was giving me a hard time with late night parties, car doors being slammed or anything else. They were like little mice and I was happy to be a little mouse also.

I checked my phone for an update on the latest casualty figures. It had come down, but not by much and it seemed that we were not yet approaching the end of the crisis, despite some people's natural impatience. I avoided looking at my phone now since it seemed full to brimming with your actual *bona fide*, one hundred percent, guaranteed fake news. The only thing you could rely on was the fact that you couldn't rely on it. Every news outlet had their own spin. The good old BBC, staffed by wealthy socialists and still smarting from Brexit, was, according to some commentators, edging towards being an anti-government propaganda tool. They knew what was best for us it seemed, and it wasn't Brexit and it definitely wasn't the Tory party in government. Democracy was an ass as far as they were concerned.

I had just given up on the news. The papers too, never reliable at the best of times, just made it hard to get to the truth. They just did their own thing as usual and printed whatever they wanted. They were still filled with page after page of advertisements for Mediterranean cruises that would never happen and since none of them ran stories about Pippa Middleton's bottom anymore, things had really got intolerable.

In the morning I was going to ring Billy and enlist his help. Billy had contacts, some of them dubious in nature with a somewhat criminal outlook, just bordering on suitable for imprisonment. I didn't ask about them and since I used Billy as an intermediary, no personal connection to these people could ever be made. My deputy and I both understood the nature of this arrangement and he never questioned my need to distance myself from his group of helpers. My own contacts tended to be firmly on the right side of the law. If they knew of Billy's dealings then nothing was ever said. Everything just ticked along in that respect and no harm came to anyone who didn't deserve it.

I think you could say that I was a bit old school in some respects, and I had the freedom to get the job done in whatever way was most effective. I didn't have much to do with health and safety since there was only really me at work, with occasional input from Billy, and then often only by telephone. Sometimes in the office he would pretend to trip or burn himself on the kettle so that he could sue me. He wanted a warning label on the kettle saying that it might be hot, but I refused to give in.

My taxes were as straightforward as these things could ever be and my management style was unhindered by the need to communicate and ensure the wellbeing of my staff; Billy could look after himself in other words. Of course, if he had a problem, he could come to see me, but I doubted if that eventuality would ever arise; Billy was independent by nature, self-contained, resourceful, bloody-minded and stubborn. If something needed sorting then he would do it himself. I knew him so well and yet I barely knew him at all. He was a one-off, a child of the Universe no less.

I slept well that night – out like the proverbial light with no night-time trips to the bathroom required – and awoke in good time, feeling refreshed. I had intended to mull over the strange case of Stephanie Kuler as I drifted off, but it just hadn't been possible for sleep came too swiftly. That was one of the strange side-effects of the lock-down; I slept as if I didn't have a care in the world and awoke at the same time every morning, practically raring to go in a manner that I had never previously experienced in my entire working life. Maybe the air was cleaner, or maybe the normal worries of plain old life had receded, lost in the greater, global worry of the pandemic. Whatever it was, I felt great.

I lay in bed for a moment or two running through what she had told me, and although I was going to hand over some of the legwork to Billy, I still wanted a better understanding of the situation she had brought to my desk. It didn't take long to summarise. She had killed someone but didn't know who, when, why or where. She had supplied me with a complete set of unanswered questions, the sort of thing that Agatha Christie must have had sitting before her as she penned her mystery novels. Perhaps the who, when, why and where could have been replaced by a single 'if'. I could maybe answer the questions *if* she had actually killed somebody. Whatever the truth, I was going to get paid for finding out and, with that fact strengthening my resolve, I got out of bed, shaved and showered and then made breakfast prior to a day spent working at home.

Life was good.

'Yo, Bilbo', I began. It was my usual greeting to him, in the Belfast/Harlem street slang we had created specifically to wind each other up. 'How are things in the 'hood?'

'Not bad. A few zombie issues last night but otherwise everything is ticking along nicely.'

'Zombies?'

'Covid 19 zombies', he explained. 'It's a new thing. They're not too bad but they're knocking on the door and that sort of thing.'

'What about the security at your place?', I asked. Billy lived in a flat, part of a block with a permanent security guard, CCTV and intercom system.

'I didn't let 'em in. They wait until someone else is coming out and then sneak through the doors. It happens all the time. Not zombies usually but drug dealers and general criminals.'

'I see. Well, just keep your door locked', I recommended.

'I do. I've got a peep hole too, so I can check the corridor before I go out.'

Billy, by the sound of it, had completely zombie-proofed himself. I had never been to his flat and only had a vague idea where it was. Billy was very private and that was fine with me. He lived by himself and wanted no trouble, which could in part be explained by his upbringing and early life in this most troubled of cities. Billy could have ended up in a gang or one of the many terrorist organisations that proliferated in the seventies and eighties, almost like youth clubs for crime, but he had steered clear and always done the right thing. Along the way, he had made loads of dubious acquaintances. Billy, however, stayed on the straight and narrow. He was accepted by these dodgy characters but remained aloof. That was Billy: owned by nobody.

'So how can I help you?', he asked.

'I need you to do a bit of digging around for me. Have you got a pen and paper?'

He did of course. He kept these items next to the phone. Billy was on it.

'Okay. The name is Stephanie Kuler. K.U.L.E.R. Not much on the internet. American husband. Ex-husband, that is. Probably about thirty-five. Very attractive.'

I paused for a second as he scribbled down the details.

'How do you know her husband is very attractive?'

'Not him, her', I explained

'So, he's not very attractive?'

'Fer fuck's sake…'

'Okay. What does she want?'

'She has murdered someone but doesn't know who, when, where or why.'

At this point I thought that my friend and esteemed associate might say something but instead he scribbled down the details I had given him.

'Okay.'

'Okay? Is that all you are going to say?'

'What is it you want me to find out?'

I shook my head. This was Billy deliberately playing down his astonishment. He was keeping his natural reaction from me, just out of mischief.

'Hold on. You don't find any aspect of this peculiar?'

'The world is a strange place.'

I sighed. A world inhabited by people like Billy was indeed strange.

He spoke again.

'To start with I will get onto the interweb machine and see what I can find out. Then, I shall ring round my special contacts and find out more about her.'

Interweb machine was another Billy-ism. You're starting to get the picture, I'm sure. For a man of his generation he was, in fact, very proficient with the old interweb machine. He seemed to know all the tricks; things he had explained to me and which I did not understand at all. He wasn't remotely bothered that I didn't understand, and I think he was trying to make sure that I always needed him. As things stood there was no chance that I could dispense with his services.

'Anything else you can tell me? Maiden name, address, relatives?'

I passed over what I knew but I didn't have her maiden name. I would ask for these details later and send them on via the texting machine... you see what I mean about Billy-isms?

And that was it. Now, I had to find a way to fill my day, and my intention was to ring my new client and take it from there.

She answered after a few rings as if she were waiting next to the phone for someone to ring. Stephanie Kuler sounded alert but calm.

'I just had a few other things to ask you, things that occurred to me after you had gone.'

'That's fine', she said. 'Ask away.'

'Has anything come back to you about this event? Anything at all?'

'No.'

'Do you ever have… I don't know what you'd call them… flashbacks, anything like that?'

'No. Sorry.'

'It's just that you said that you didn't always think you had done this. I think you said that the feeling you'd murdered someone came to you later in life.'

'Yes, I suppose that's right.'

I was getting nowhere.

'You hinted yesterday that you'd always felt that something was wrong, so if that was the case then why did this, at some point, become the feeling that you had murdered someone? What I mean is, if you felt that something was wrong when you were say, five, then that didn't relate to a murder, did it? Not many people carry out a murder at that age. So how do you know that this feeling isn't just an extension of some type of latent paranoia that you were born with?'

'You mean, am I a nut?'

I strenuously denied this but, essentially, she was correct. Lunacy would explain the 'facts' she had presented more easily than any other reason.

'Not at all but why do you think that you always felt that something was amiss?'

'Maybe it was because I always felt that I was going to murder someone and then one day I did it. Maybe I blotted out the actual act afterwards and for a while thought that my guilt was just an extension of the feelings I had always suffered from.'

This sounded like utter horseshit to me but now was not the time to say so.

'Okay. What about your family? What do they think? I presume you have spoken to them about it.'

'I was brought up in care.'

'Oh. I'm sorry. From what age?'

'Birth.'

'So, did you ever meet up with your parents or any siblings, later on?'

'No, nothing like that.'

'Did you ever try to track them down?'

'Never.'

'Weren't you curious about them?

'No.'

She wasn't being unfriendly, but her answers were curt. Maybe she just liked getting to the point.

'Have you ever felt so angry that you felt you could kill somebody?'

'No. What I mean, I suppose, is *not that I remember*. Maybe when I did it, I felt that degree of anger, but I have no recollection of it.'

29

As she spoke, it occurred to me that the victim might be her husband. I tried to push this thought away and continue with my questioning but an image of him slain, lying in the kitchen of their expensive house in… wherever it was… and her making her hurried way onto the first plane out of America became fixed in my head. Hopefully Billy would be able to find out one way or the other.

'Hello?'

'Yes, sorry. I was just making a couple of notes', I lied. 'Just a couple more things and then I will leave you alone. Can you tell me your maiden name?'

'Patterson.'

I wrote that down and thanked her.

'Any other names you have been known by?'

'None.'

I wrote 'nun', in my notebook. Very funny.

'And lastly, why did you come to Belfast?'

'Work. I am a university lecturer. History. There was a job here, I was a free agent…'

'So, this is quite a recent move?'

'September.'

'Right, sorry, one last question. Do you think you killed this person here, or in England, or in America? It was Boston, wasn't it?'

'I couldn't say. It could be any of those places. It could be Germany, France or Belgium; I have visited them all. But the place that I have spent the most time is England. I think you can rule out Belfast because I already felt this way when I arrived at the end of August.'

'Why would you have killed someone?'

'I thought that was my final, final question?'

'Sorry, things keep occurring to me.'

'It's fine. I'm joking. I can't think of a reason. I am a fairly laid-back type of person. Slow to anger, mostly content. No one would really think I was a murderer, but I know I am.'

'Okay. That is definitely it for now, Ms Kuler.'

'Steph.'

'Steph. I already have someone working on it for me. If anything else occurs to you, even if it seems inconsequential, then just ring me. We'll get to the bottom of it.'

'Thank you.'

'But if you ever want me to stop let me know, preferably sooner rather than later. You know how much there is at stake.'

She agreed to do that and we ended the call. I had some more information but was no further on. The veracity of what she had just told me would come out once Billy had done his thing. I didn't think she was lying, of course, for what would be the point in that? She was already trying to get me to prove she was guilty of the worst crime. Had she been *trying to put me off*, then yes – lying made sense. I was confused. I sincerely hoped that Billy, though beleaguered by zombies, would come up with something for me, something that would be a starting point if nothing else.

Chapter Three

Over the years, Belfast had become a bit of an identikit British city, with a high street like any other, corporate pubs and ordinary crime. The things that had once made the old place unique – Primark, knee-cappings, bombs and drive-by shootings – had either become UK-wide or had gone away entirely. Primark, for instance, once an almost exclusively Belfast fashion emporium, was now to be found everywhere in the UK, even as a concession within Selfridges in the Trafford Centre. By contrast, bombings, shootings and knee-cappings had gone more or less completely out of fashion now that the Troubles had ended.

Few missed the Troubles, a complex near-civil war which had caused the deaths of well over three thousand people. The conflict had brought about a fairer society but at terrible cost, and it would be wrong to think that the people now lived in universal harmony. Bitterness and division still existed but it was tolerable simply because a return to the death and destruction of the Troubles was unthinkable. The price paid was the release of hundreds of criminals from jail and allowing men with blood on their hands to become politicians who would govern the country they had once tried to destroy. But if you could bear that, then fine. The alternative was more years of bloodshed and despair.

The city was looking much better. It wasn't stretching a point too much to say that it had healed, the old bomb sites gone and new, modern buildings growing from the soil like the shoots of spring bulbs, a rebirth, an affirmation of hope, the natural reward for years of forbearance or some such shit.

But if you wanted to see the divided city of the seventies, eighties and nineties, you didn't have to look hard or travel far, for there still existed those old communities whose frontier-town mentality and sense of isolation meant more than any false promises of reconciliation. Some people just didn't want to be reconciled. In fact, some people missed the battle they had fought. You might say that they represented something that had otherwise been consigned to history, but that was not strictly true because these communities flourished and perhaps just waited for their moment to come. The conflict had been paused but the wounds hadn't fully healed. That which had been fought over – and it wasn't religion despite what many might think – still existed as an open wound but one which was largely hidden.

Simply put, there was no middle ground. One side wanted to be Irish and the other wanted to be British. No one wanted this compromise state – a Republic of Northern Ireland – but it was better than war.

I remembered the bad old days and so did Billy. He could have got involved, but Billy had other ideas. At sixteen he gave Belfast two fingers and left to join the army. When he returned, the city had changed. Had it not done so I don't think he would have come back. My situation was different, but I had joined the army, stayed for six years and came back. The difference between Billy and me back then? There had never been any chance of me getting mixed up with paramilitaries; it just was not on the cards at any point of my childhood. It all depended on where you were born really and who you were surrounded by as you picked up your views on life.

So many things, good and bad, are accidents of birth and nothing more. People go to jail sometimes simply because they have acted upon the instincts and views they picked up from their parents and peers. In some cases, you could practically draw a road map of how their life was likely to pan out from birth to the point where they might radically change their minds about how and who they wanted to be. For many the road map might soon come to a fork junction where one question temporarily halted their progress: caught/not caught? Billy never got to that place but set off on a different road entirely. Personally, I didn't just set off on a different road, I set off from a different place too.

Billy rang me that evening to say that he had made progress, but he wanted another day for phone calls to be returned. What he actually said was that he was *waiting for some fish to come home to roost*, which not only misquoted the original phrase but used it inappropriately. I think this was one of his deliberate Billy-isms but you could never be sure, for the line between genius and idiocy was but fine with him.

I had filled my day with things other than the investigation into the untraceable murder. I had been for a run which had done me good, and then sent a few emails to people I knew in Hong Kong who might be able to help me find the missing soldier. My contacts out there included a friend who I had known in the army and a former HK police officer, both of whom had stayed on after the colony was handed back to the Chinese. As far as I could make out, they were rather sanguine about their new situation and really not too bothered about their new masters. Over the years, as letters had given way to emails, I thought that I detected a note of caution in their communication, as if the state authorities were listening in, or reading their texts. For instance, I had asked my ex-army bud how the lockdown was going in Hong Kong and he told me it was great and they could all wear shorts. I didn't get it. If it was a code, the meaning was lost on me.

Shorts?

My other Hong Kong case was the missing soldier. His name was Curt Johnson and his career in the Royal Engineers was cut short when he seemed to desert, a very peculiar move for a man of twenty-eight who had reached the rank of sergeant, was married and was expecting his first child. Sergeant Johnson just disappeared. The police were informed of course, and I dare say the Military Police stuck their oar in too, but all attempts at finding the missing soldier came to nothing; it was as if he had never existed. There was one tiny lead and it was this: at various points during his marriage he had expressed a wish to visit his father, who, as you might have guessed, lived in Hong Kong having served there with the RAF. When the marriage between the sergeant's parents had broken up, Johnson senior had headed back to his old stomping ground in the far east, a place where he had, he said, enjoyed the best years of his life.

The two men hadn't seen each other in years as a result and father, it seemed, never really expressed any desire to see his son. Son – Sergeant Johnson – felt differently. The lack of a father was an itch he couldn't scratch. When he went missing and could not otherwise be found, that left only a trip to Hong Kong as an explanation. The police couldn't investigate any more, for no new evidence turned up. No one had seen him leave, get on a plane, pick up a bag, get in or out of a taxi. The one thing he had done – or someone had done – was to buy air tickets to Hong Kong. Johnson's passport had gone, and some money had been withdrawn from his account, but there was no indication that he had bought currency and no record of him boarding his plane, or setting foot in Hong Kong.

It was possible, but highly unlikely, that he had got to the former colony, but with nothing else to go on it seemed like the last possibility to explore. In part I was going over ground that had already been covered by CID or whoever, but in amongst the small mound of information his disappearance had created there might be some important fact to be teased out. I didn't actually think there was, but I was being paid to look, so I looked...

So far, my two sub-contractors in Hong Kong had turned up absolutely nothing. There was nothing to indicate that Johnson had made it this far. Not one thing. There were enough loose ends to knit a rug with. Chief amongst these was the fact that he could easily have discussed his intended visit with his wife. According to her, she would have had no problem with him making the trip.

Was she telling the truth? Since there was nothing linking her to his disappearance and since she was paying me to find him, I just accepted that she was being honest. She had grounds for not being happy with him visiting his father at this time, however. For one thing she was pregnant with his child and for another his father had been a poor excuse for a parent so why did it suddenly become so important that he find him now? Had a pregnant woman killed her husband, staged his trip to foreign shores, disposed of his body and left no trace? Possible but scarcely credible.

You always check the obvious things first. His father was tracked down and was able to confirm that his son had not visited. Apparently, father had not even sounded concerned that his son had gone missing. You can't make someone love their own child I suppose. If Curt Johnson ever had found his pop he would surely have been disappointed by the reconciliation.

I wasn't judging. My own parents hadn't wanted me, and I had opted out of having children of my own. I was an expert in not caring.

Asking around, checking CCTV, and examining hotel records had turned up not one single trace. I had never been, but both my associates told me, more than once, that Hong Kong was an easy place in which to get lost. That was fair enough, but the object of the exercise for Curt Johnson was not to *lose* himself but rather to *find* his father. That being the case hinged entirely on his wife's explanation of events as she understood them. None of his mates in the army, when questioned, knew anything about this desire to meet up with his old man. He had booked no leave and had spoken to no one about this compulsion that apparently had overcome him and put his career and marriage at risk.

The wife could have booked the tickets using his bank account to make it look as though he had fled. The tickets could have been a red herring, as could her subsequent desire for me to track her husband down. If that was the case then she must have been confident that I wasn't going to find him and wasn't going to link her to a murder.

I'm sure you're getting a feel for the sort of work I did and the cases I took on. I was the last chance. When all hope was gone and every other course of action had been taken, when every stone had been turned, and light shone in every dark corner, that's when you came to me. I took the cases that the police could do nothing more with or hadn't touched in the first place. Sometimes I got results and sometimes I didn't; a large part of it was luck.

Billy rang that evening and suggested we meet in the office the following day.

'You have to stay two metres away from me', I said.

'My pleasure. I'll be taking the corporate transport module in. It'll be interesting to see how they keep everyone two metres apart on the CTM'

I should point out that the *corporate transport module* was the bus. More Billy-speak. And *individual transport module*, often shortened to ITM was a car. The *linked corporate transport module* was the train. Linked because the modules were connected to each other. You got used to his manner of speech but he drew some peculiar looks from clients.

'I'm sure they have a system. But seriously keep safe.'

'I'll be fine.'

'This virus can kill *you* just as easily as anyone else. It doesn't care that you are Billy.'

'I get it. Seriously, I get it. I understand the whole thing and I am being careful. When I have a whore round she is completely disinfected before we get started.'

He was joking of course. I'm pretty sure.

'We can do this over the phoning machine', I said, adopting his favoured terminology to save time.

'Face to face is better. Should I bring a picnic?'

'An office picnic?'

'Aye. Sandwiches, scotch eggs, little bottles of lemonade, salad.'

'Sounds disgusting. Just bring yourself. Anything I should be looking at in the meantime?'

'I don't think so. You realise that she's a fuckin' fruit loop, don't ya?'

'I think it is possible.'

'More than possible. This woman has some form, let me tell ya. More details tomorrow. So, until then Kemosabe…'

He was gone. I was left holding the phoning mach… phone and looking at it as if he had never been on the other end at all.

***

I was at the office for nine and the kettle was on the boil when he arrived.

'Just in time for a coffee', I said.

'Not for me. No drugs.'

'It's coffee…'

The truth was he just didn't want coffee. I don't think he did drugs of any other sort by the way, although he drank but not heavily as far as I knew.

'How was the CTM?'

'Yeah, it was fine. They have a big screen up round the driver so that you can't sneeze on him.'

'Nice.'

'He was IRA.'

'IRA? How do you know?'

'I just know. In jail, let out, the usual. Found God probably. Nice job sitting on his arse.'

'So, what can you tell me about Stephanie Kuler?'

We sat at our desks, slightly more than two metres apart. It was one of those rare plague days when it rained; droplets of water fairly lashed against the window but it wasn't cold and the forecast had suggested that the following day would be sunny, just as we had come to expect for our plague. The weather forecast was just about the only thing I still believed in the media, which was odd considering how unreliable it used to be. Anyone remember the hurricane of 1987? The Met Office didn't see that coming at all.

But the weather now? It was almost always as predicted.

'Are you actually going to listen?', asked Billy, his tone solicitous as if he worried about me.

'I am listening. Or I was ready to listen.'

'You were miles away.'

'Okay. I'm listening now. All ears. Aural reception devices at the ready…'

'What?'

'Nothing. Get on with it or I'll sack you.'

'Stephanie Kuler nee Patterson. Born in Oxford 1987. Married Brent Kuler. Lived in Boston. Divorced. Returned to Britain with a generous settlement to start a new life. Got a job at the uni, teaching history, which is what brought her to Belfast.'

'I'm pretty sure that I told you all this already.'

'I don't think so', he said firmly. 'Does that all ring true, so far?'

'Yep.'

'Good. She was brought up in care. Never knew her family and never sought them out. Never been in trouble with the police, never been sacked, hardly ever been to hospital as a patient. Never had a speeding ticket or parking ticket as far as I can tell. Not in this country anyway. She has worked in various universities in Europe. A year here and a year there. Liked and respected wherever she went. Small group of friends – I haven't spoken to any of them yet, always tricky to pull off – not on Facebook or any other social media bollocks.'

'Okay.'

Billy had done nothing other than confirm what I already knew but this was the start of a process for him and it wasn't something I was going to question. How he found things out was his business.

'So, what I am getting onto is tracking down her family and seeing if any of them have been killed. I want to find out about any siblings and how they have turned out and I want to talk to Brent Kuler. There is very little to go on.'

'I know. You sound apologetic, Bilbo and there is no need. This is all so bloody weird but she is paying us, so we do it.'

He nodded.

'What are your initial thoughts, Bill? Apart from you think she is a nut – if you meet her, she seems more or less sane, although she sounded a bit off on the telephone one time.'

'Initial thoughts are that she has a mental health condition. Having recently completed an online certificate in Lunacy

Studies from the University of Dundrum, I am qualified to make diagnoses of such based on third hand information, rumour and hearsay.'

'Are you a doctor, then?'

'More of a professor.'

'Right. She's a nut?'

'The facts fit that diagnosis.'

'If she wasn't a nut, what would be your thoughts in that case?'

Professor Billy, *Cert. Lun.*, blew air from his cheeks.

'The same really, except that she really did kill someone and then her mind has blocked it out. Trauma? I don't know. It stills requires a body turning up if that is true.'

'Can trauma do that, Professor?'

'I don't know. I missed that module. I had the shits.'

'Billy, that is no excuse. You can still do an online course sitting on the toilet.'

He closed his eyes and inclined his head slightly in a familiar gesture which meant, 'if you say so.'

'What else?'

'I dunno. Some sort of double-bluff. If she really did kill someone then she has got away with it. That being the case, why would she pay someone to figure out that she is actually guilty?'

'That isn't how she sees it. Or so she says. Her view is that she has done this thing and can't live with the guilt, or the uncertainty, or something. It is driving her nuts and she wants the truth. When you said double-bluff, what do you mean? How would that work?'

'Just say that she has killed someone. The body isn't found, the crime isn't detected and so on, which is pretty much the state of affairs. She tells the cops and gets them to investigate but they don't really want to know, so she gets us to do the same thing. Then someday a body does turn up and she can distance herself from it by saying that she has already tried to get the matter investigated...' Billy's voice tailed off as he reached the end of his sentence.

'That doesn't quite work.'

'No.'

'There is some logic there but...'

'It's as if we can officially exonerate her of any crime and declare her innocent. Then if someone tries to prosecute her, she has that as a fallback. The slight problem is that it would never work. We are her *get out of jail free card*, but actually we're not.'

'We take the money and run, Billy.'

'A cynical way of looking at it.'

'Maybe but what else is there for it? She wants us and we need money. We aren't responsible for what has happened. She is glad to have us on board.'

'I suppose you're right.'

'Thing is Billy, this is a company. She wants us to do this thing...'

Billy nodded.

'I wish we could go to Della's', he said, completely changing the subject.

'Hmm. Bacon bagel and cappuccino.'

'It's not just the food. It's the noise and the décor and Della herself', he said wistfully.

'You like her don't ya?', I teased.

'Yeah. What's not to like? Lovely woman, attractive, own business, unattached, gun.'

'Ask her out.'

'Lockdown.'

'I mean when this is all finished. Take her to a decent pub with some music. She always has music on.'

'I don't know. I don't think there's a spark there.'

'You have to provide the spark. She doesn't even know you're interested. You're still young, you have your own place, a job, an army pension and a season ticket on the buses.'

'When you put it like that…'

'What about the Variety? Great bands in there. I saw a band called Dea Matrona; three girls doin' Led Zeppelin, Fleetwood Mac. Brilliant. Della'd love it.'

'Maybe. We're gettin' ahead of ourselves. This whole thing might never end', he warned.

'The plague?'

Billy nodded and said, 'they aren't even close to getting a vaccine, so until they do, how can we get back to normal?'

'Some people have natural immunity now. They got it and recovered.'

'But it isn't beaten, and these virus things mutate, and once they have done that, the vaccine doesn't work. We don't even have the vaccine yet, but it might be out of date by the time it comes along.'

'You're taking a grim view.'

'But I might be right. What we're doing now might be the way we lead our lives from now on. We might just have to accept a certain number of deaths each year and try our best not to catch it. And all these countries who are coming out of it, who knows if it will come back in a second wave later on.'

I didn't know what to say. I'd had similar thoughts on the matter myself, but I had no answers and wasn't sure if Billy was looking to me for reassurance. I had none to give.

'You sure I can't tempt you with that coffee? It's Colombian super-strength and the milk is organic from Nepalese yak.'

'The sugar?'

'Jamaican sugar cane, hand-refined in earthenware pots by skilled artisans and then gently baked in the sun on the slopes of Slieve Muck.'

'Go on then.'

I smiled and made my way to the kettle.

'Which bit of that description got you?'

'Nepalese yak. I once worked with the Gherkins in Kenya.'

I had my back to him now as I prepared some bog-standard supermarket coffee from a jar. Gherkins? Then I realised that this was just more Billy-talk. Gherkins were Gurkhas of course. I couldn't give him the satisfaction of appearing confused, not after all these years.

'Fine men', I agreed. I added a spoonful of brown sugar to each mug. 'Do you want a cappuccino?'

'Depends on how you make the froth', he replied warily.

'Better not then. Flat white, it is.'

We sat for a while sipping coffee and saying almost nothing but that was fine. I didn't have to fill every waking moment with words and in Billy's case it took him time to formulate the verbal bollocks he used routinely. It was not quite as spontaneous as he made out, or not always.

'What was the traffic like out there?', I asked him.

'Quiet. A few ITMs, cop cars, vans, trucks. Still plenty of people off to work and what have you, but quieter than usual.'

'Tough if you run a hotel or something.'

'The government is helping out with money. Everything will recover. We might just have to wear masks and keep apart like we do now. That might just become everyday life.'

'That'll make things difficult for you and Della, just starting out on your romantic journey together.'

He scoffed at that and said, 'never goin' to happen.'

'What would you give now just to be able to go to the beach, or out for a meal?'

He pulled a face which suggested that he wasn't bothered.

'I'm fine like this.' He rubbed his lips and then said, 'I have had an idea about this woman.' He sounded doubtful but I knew he wanted me to prompt him to say more. There was a time when I would have deliberately not bothered just to wind him up, but on this occasion, I wanted to hear what he had to say. Now more than ever, I needed inspiration.

'Speak.'

'Hypnotist.'

'Hypnotist?' I gave a little nod and pursed my lips.

'Do you remember… oh, I can't remember his name, but we had someone who worked here…'

'Lenny?'

'That's him. Lenny. He did hypnotism. If he did it on this woman, then he might be able to find out if she had really killed someone.' He paused and then said, 'you think that's a shit idea, don't you?'

'No actually, I think it is worth a try. Putting it all into context, it might be the perfect solution. I should have a number for him.'

'She might not agree to being hypnotised of course.'

'I don't think she'll have a problem with it. Why not? We're talking about a pretty extreme set of circumstances here. What is your plan for today?'

'Few more phone calls and checking my emails. I have a few stones in the fire. I just need to see what turns up. You know how this works.'

48

'Not really. Your methods are a complete mystery to me but you keep getting results, so I don't ask.'

Billy grinned. He was a results man, not an in-depth explainer of theory and that was why he was so useful to me.

Chapter Four

When I rang Lenny, I got an answerphone. I kept the message brief and got on with some work while I awaited the call back. Lenny was another larger than life character like Billy, and a Belfast man through and through. He was a stout companion until one day he just decided that enough was enough and he was going to get away from the rain of Belfast to the sun of Spain. He'd be in his late fifties now but he never did make it to Spain. I never knew why.

Lenny was one of those people who was always at the end of the phone and willing to help. He would drop everything to come to your assistance and had done so more than once, but when he had stopped working for me the calls became fewer and fewer until we just drifted apart. He was still there and would still help but, somehow I didn't need the help any longer. That's just life isn't it? By midday he hadn't rung back and Billy had gone home to follow up on some other business unrelated to Stephanie Kuler. I didn't ask.

By 14:00, he still hadn't rung and now I was slightly concerned. For whatever reason, I hate ringing back after I have left a message but on this occasion I did so.

'Hello?'

'Lenny?', I asked. It didn't sound like him.

'No, I am his nephew. My uncle has gone to Spain.'

'Oh. Not on holiday, surely? The flights are cancelled, aren't they?'

'He moved out there four months ago. He moved me into his place until he returns.'

'Oh, I get it. He is returning when this is all over?'

'He's not sure. He might be, or he might stay. I can pass on a message.'

'Do you have a number for him?'

'Well, the thing is, he wrote a list for me with the names of people I am allowed to give the number to.'

I gave the nephew my name and was relieved to hear that it was on the list.

'In fact, your name is top of the list. He talked about you a lot.'

'Nothing complimentary I hope. We had some adventures', I said, feeling gratified that I was the first person he thought about when compiling the collection of suitable acquaintances.

'He told me.'

He provided me with a telephone number and an email address. I didn't keep him on the telephone for long.

I sat there thinking about my options. I was going to get in touch with Lenny for old times' sake if nothing else, but the possibility of him hypnotising someone now seemed remote. In the end I emailed him, feeling resistant to the idea of phoning a foreign country (don't ask why, I don't know the answer) and within a few minutes he had responded.

Yes, he was pleased to hear from me and no he could not hypnotise someone by email. There was more but that was the main bit. I explained my idea about Stephanie Kuler without giving too much away, and in his reply he stated that it was potentially a good idea. He also gave me the name of another hypnotist and expressed his regret that he couldn't help personally. Lenny said the case sounded fascinating and that was based on only knowing a fraction of the details. I wished him well and then rang the person he had recommended. There was no answer and no means for leaving a message. I rang Stephanie Kuler instead.

'How would you feel about being hypnotised, or have you already tried it?', I asked after a few pleasantries had been exchanged. She seemed a little taken aback.

'That's fine. No, I haven't tried it. You know someone who can do it?'

'I have a number to ring on the recommendation of my usual hypnotist, who is unavailable.'

She laughed and said, 'your usual hypnotist?'

'On retainer, you understand.'

'Of course. If you make the arrangements and let me know. I am a bit of a loose end these days, working from home like many other people, so I should be free when you call.'

'Great, I'll get on to it. I don't suppose anything else has come to you?'

'No, sorry.'

'Why did you never want to find out about your family, if you don't mind me asking?'

'I suppose I just never felt any compulsion to do so. My life was okay – as good as anyone else's. My real family never figured in it and I suppose it is a case of not missing what you never had.'

'You weren't just a bit curious?'

'A bit. But not enough to find anything out. Also, I didn't think I would like what I found. I couldn't picture some sort of reconciliation with hugs and tears and time spent getting to know the family I had never met before, like some TV programme. *And this is your sister Courtney and your brother Wayne*, that sort of thing. They didn't want me and don't forget, whoever they were – whoever my mother was – they never tried to find out about me. Is this relevant?'

'It might be. You have come here as something of an enigma. Anything you know might help. It might only be your mother who abandoned you, not the entire family. You might have siblings who would love to meet you and who you might really get along with. And you don't know the reasons why she gave you up. Perhaps she died in childbirth. I don't know for a fact, but you seem to have a low opinion of your mother when perhaps she died giving birth to you, or maybe she is still alive but ashamed of what happened and thinks that you don't want to know her. I have a feeling that a parent isn't allowed to track down a child they gave up, but I could be wrong. I wouldn't ask you about this if it wasn't potentially relevant.'

She seemed to accept that but also to think that it was a step too far, and this juxtaposition made me just slightly suspicious; she wanted me to dig around in her past to find that she had committed murder but wasn't prepared to risk meeting up with her family and siblings if she had any. The two might well be linked. For all anyone knew, it might have been her mother she'd murdered, the trauma of the event

53

blocking it from her mind as suggested by Billy. The latter was going to dig around for skeletons in the family cupboard but now was not the time to tell her this.

Her next words came out of the blue and fairly threw me.

'I am going to a party tonight if you fancy it.'

***

Coronavirus had killed thousands of people in the UK by this point. Parties, like everything else, were out except if you were a moron. And yet here I was getting ready (the work of ten minutes if you're a man, of course) and thinking whether I needed to buy a bottle of wine.

It was ridiculous. *I* was ridiculous. Yet, she had made a very convincing case.

'There will only be a few people there and they will socially distance', she said.

'I don't think so', I said. It was no half-hearted protest either. I meant it. I didn't want to catch the plague and die. I didn't want to dress up. I didn't want to socialise. Even though there was almost nothing on the TV that I wanted to watch, not even on Netflix, I just didn't want to go out with a load of strangers and try to make small talk, that thing at which I am least adept. Don't get me wrong, I liked a party now and then but always with friends, people who didn't expect me to be the life and soul and didn't want me to chat incessantly. I liked the company of people who already knew what there was to know about me and didn't have to bother with the laborious process of getting acquainted.

Now, as I have mentioned, Ms. Kuler was an attractive woman and clearly intelligent, but she was a number of years

54

younger than me and we moved, I suspected, in entirely different circles. Come to think of it, since I didn't move in *any* circles (or in any other geometrical shapes), the situation was probably even more grim than that in terms of a possible match.

There was another consideration too; somewhere in the **Official Handbook of Private Investigation and Sundry Other Jobs that Defy Easy Description** (Parker and Sons, Publishers, 1984, revised 1997) there was a paragraph (page 9, I think) which stated, amongst other things, that you really shouldn't, under any circumstances, socialise with clients. There was a time limit from the end of a case to the beginning of any form of relationship but even then, it was discouraged. It made perfect sense, but she was persuasive too.

'It is just for a bit of a lark. Nothing heavy. You'll enjoy it. I bet you haven't been out for weeks.'

Try *years.*

'My friends will enjoy meeting you.'

'Okay, okay. Not my sort of thing but I will go along.'

That was fine. We arranged a time and she told me where I was going. Then she asked if I could pick her up and it all made sense; she needed a lift. I had fallen into a trap of sorts and I felt stupid at once.

Only morons went to parties during lockdown. I, therefore, was a moron. When I told Billy what I was doing, he agreed with that assessment.

'You're not going, surely?'

'I said I would.'

'Unsay it', he said. But I didn't unsay it.

Since I was driving, I couldn't drink but that was okay because I had bravely climbed on the wagon about ten years previously. The only reason I bring this up, is because she didn't know that (why would she?) and had therefore consigned me to an evening of sobriety in the company of total strangers. So, let me make this clear; I wouldn't have been drinking anyway but I would be the person most in need of a drink simply to make myself sociable. It was my own fault for being easily swayed. Would it have been any different if she had been fat and ugly? Yes. In that case she could fuck off.

The car started first time although it hadn't been used for a week or two. I drove to her house, through the city, following the instructions delivered by an exotic-sounding woman from France who lived in my satnav. Just as an aside, I will mention that satellite navigation in Billy-world became *stalactite navigator*. Anyway, back in the real world, I was surprised by the amount of traffic on the roads during lockdown. It was thinner than before but plenty of drivers were venturing forth in their vans, cars and trucks. There were three particular junctions that I habitually encountered to get to the city centre and each of these proved to be much less of a barrier than was normally the case. Aside from a slight delay brought about by a police check, I got through all three in no time. If there was any benefit to a pandemic than that was it, I suppose, for me at least. It was of little comfort to the family of someone who was suffering, but in the tiny bubble that comprised my world it was enough.

It took a minute or two, but I actually began to find the act of driving pleasurable again and this was down solely to the fact that I wasn't just chugging from one set of lights to the next. Not only that, but the city itself seemed to have changed, as if the plague had helped to clean it of grime and the deposits left by years of hatred. The architecture of Victorian prosperity – Belfast wasn't an ancient city – had been bolstered by buildings of the modern era which added their own lustre to the solidity and subdued grandeur of Northern Ireland's capital. Money was being spent, luring yet more investment and with this tide of new prosperity came an influx of workers and students from other countries, making the city something of a late-blooming melting pot, if that isn't a mixed metaphor.

It was good to see and because I wasn't simply snarled up in traffic and frustrated at the lack of progress in my journey, it was plain to see also. The virus had thinned out the streets of course but someday soon surely the people would venture out again when it was safe. A group of kids had definitely not got the message though, and they were hanging around, smoking, spitting, generally messing and most definitely not observing the two metres distance. Everyone knew that if a youngster caught the virus they would probably survive, but they would inevitably spread it to others who might not. Such worries did not seem to concern them, and you couldn't voice these opinions without sounding prissy. Most people seemed to recognise the danger, but the young, foolish and invincible did not.

Anyway, generally speaking, Belfast was on the up. You could easily forget that blood had frequently run in the streets. The bombings and shootings, the worst of which had occurred in the early seventies, had killed hundreds and for a time filled the world's news outlets with images reminiscent of the Blitz. In 1972, the death rate was well over one per day but there were several spectaculars which had stuck in the mind and gained a mention in some history books, some of which had yet to be written. Into this mayhem the army had been dropped and expected to patrol and protect, the latter an impossible task.

Who was to blame? Both sides. Billy and I shared one tradition and it was part of us like our heart or lungs. But that didn't mean that my particular tradition was perfect or blameless.

Whatever, I loved this city. It was known, if it was known at all, for all the wrong things: The Titanic, which you may have heard, sank, George Best, arguably the world's greatest footballer but wayward child and alcoholic, and similarly Hurricane Higgins, who ploughed the same furrow but in the sport of snooker. Such a spectacular alcoholic was George Best that we named an airport after him.

And then there were the Troubles of course. To describe a long-running and at the time, impossible to conclude, campaign of murder, terror and destruction as 'The Troubles', is a magnificent example of British understatement. Or maybe it is Irish understatement? The Irish called World War Two, 'The Emergency'. Yes, it was a bit of an emergency. Certainly, the Poles and the French, the Belgians, the Greeks, the Russians et al, thought so.

There is a generation for whom the Troubles never really happened but until the unexpected peace came, Belfast and the entire little country was known for bombs and bullets. People could be blown to pieces as they went to work or were picking up the children from school. Bodies found in ditches. Police officers having to gather body parts and put them into bags just to remove the carnage from the streets. Kneecappings, tar and featherings... Images in black and white. Bombs razing some old building to the ground and people running for their lives, sometimes into the path of another bomb. Belfast had earned its place in the history books all right.

In the context of world events, the Troubles were a tiny blip in mankind's inexorable assault of greatness and intellectual superiority over the animals. But those three-thousand, six-hundred deaths in a population of one-and-a-half million were devastating. For context, the population of the USA, great benefactors of the IRA, is two hundred times greater than that of Northern Ireland. If you multiply out the country's casualties by that figure you arrive at the number 720,000. That is how many deaths there would have been had the Troubles arrived in America rather than Ulster.

Those were the bad old days. I remembered them well. I was glad they were gone and yet the memories hung around in my head like shadows of alleys and ill-lit streets. In that way they continued and informed, sub-consciously now, my thoughts and actions. The Troubles were a collective wound that never quite healed.

***

She looked stunning. That worried me a little because we were not on a date exactly. She was a client and I was the hired hand; that was the extent of our relationship, a consideration which was further complicated by the fact that if I was successful, she would end up in prison, which some might say wasn't such a good result at all. I was happy to take the money – I wasn't running a charity – but it was starting to trouble me that success was going to be judged on some fairly warped criteria. What further troubled me was that she was so sanguine about it.

It was a risky strategy, but I offered a compliment and opened the car door for her whilst not implying that she was merely a sex object or, as a female, too weak to open the door for herself.

She accepted the compliment without returning one of her own (fair enough) and smiled as she climbed elegantly into the car. So far so good. I wasn't sure why I cared, but to take that line of thought further, I wasn't sure why I was here. Straightaway we couldn't 'socially distance', unless I insisted that she travel in the boot whilst I drove. Or *vice versa* in which case she couldn't drink, and I had to suffer the indignity of travelling in the boot of my own car like an abductee in a Danish crime drama. At another time I could have been accused of over-thinking the situation, but that virus was killing thousands of people and I did not belong to that group of morons who thought there was no need to adhere to the precautions. I believed in a coronavirus that you could see under a microscope, but not a God that you could not, and I was putting my faith in the science.

She was wearing jeans and boots along with a suede jacket, all of which looked expensive. I would say that it certainly suited her, but she was the sort of woman who probably suited most things. I got a hint of alcohol on her breath; maybe just a quick gin and tonic before leaving the house?

'You know the way? I can put the address in the stalac… satnav.'

'I can find the way. I'll give you directions.'

'Fine. I will trust your sense of direction in that case.'

She was putting her seatbelt on but paused to glare at me.

'Are you saying that because I am a woman, I have no sense of direction?'

'I didn't mean that. It was just a flippant remark.'

'I'm joking. I'm not a raging feminist and my sense of direction is actually bloody awful, but I *do* know the way', she said, archly.

Inwardly, I breathed a sigh of relief as she finished slotting her seatbelt into place.

'Lead on MacDuff.'

'Shakespeare.'

'I never thought about who said it.'

'It should be *'lay on MacDuff'*, but that's not a very useful phrase.'

'In that case *lay on.'*

A short drive took us to a town house in a prosperous part of the city where doctors, solicitors and architects lived and had done so for generations. This was a place which had not been too bothered by terrorism as far as I knew but that wasn't a complaint if it was true. If you are lucky enough to get through The Troubles without being, err, troubled, then so what, and besides that was history.

'Nice round here', I said as I pulled into a space between a Mercedes estate and a Porsche 4x4. 'How are you going to introduce me?'

'As a friend. Is that okay?'

'Fine. You can't easily explain how we came to meet.'

She smiled but said nothing as we made our way up a short path which led to a flight of steps and a grand front door painted black. My stomach began to boil or rumble in protest as I found myself suddenly nervous. I had faced greater challenges in my life, including tours of duty in various unpleasant places with the army but situations like this were different. No doubt she would be great company and equally her friends were sure to display endless charm and dazzling wit, but I wasn't quite ready for that and certainly not when I would be exposed to it at distances of less than the required two metres. The real problem was me.

I wasn't quite anti-social but…

'A penny for your thoughts', said Stephanie, as we waited for the recently knocked door to be answered.

'I was just thinking.'

'I know but about what?'

I sighed and said, 'I'm not sure.'

Thankfully the conversation was cut off at that moment when the door was thrust open by a middle-aged man with a large gut, a blue striped shirt that had come untucked from his chinos and a bald head. Brian, as he was introduced, had a huge smile but oddly piggy eyes. I immediately felt nothing about him, and apathy hit me like a tidal wave. It would be a long night. There were things I would rather have been doing and I ran through these as he ushered us inside, having given my companion a hug which obviously broke the rules of lockdown and made me very wary indeed. A night spent in an OP would be preferable for me. Even a night spent watching a box set of 'Birds of a Feather' would be better.

'This is my friend', she said coyly to Brian.

'Ahhh', said Brian and at once *I knew that he knew* how my path had crossed with that of Stephanie. It annoyed me that she had discussed her strange predicament with someone other than me, but then I realised that she had probably been banging on about it for years. Brian, I am sure, was a *confidante* and no doubt loved the attention given to him by the exotic and charming Stephanie Kuler, with her American name.

From some other part of the house I heard music playing; the tail end of a Rolling Stones song, soon replaced by the Beach Boys. I could imagine the playlist; a bit of Abba, U2 *feat.* Boner, Del Amitri, Brian Adams, Celine Dion and, for a bit of wildness, The Spice Girls. They might even play some Oasis to show that they were still edgy and cool and not just a bunch of fuckwits heading to middle age.

I was to discover that this house was massive: three storeys, a basement and real depth, from street to back garden. But it wasn't so massive that we could all manage to stay two metres apart as promised. The passage through to the kitchen, the hub of many a party including this one, was no more than a few feet wide. Stephanie was behind me but not at the required distance. She and Brian Big-Belly were in a sort of a tight huddle as they laughed and giggled their way through. I have to admit that I felt a stab of jealousy now that I had been so easily supplanted by one of her work colleagues but that was forgotten when I reached the source of the shit music, the kitchen. Two metres between each person? There were about eight people in a space of about three metres by five. You don't need to work the maths out to see that the deadly virus which had already killed hundreds of thousands worldwide was plainly not expected to visit this kitchen, in this house, in well-to-do-ville, Belfast.

'Fucking hell', I said.

Brian, behind me, broke off his conversation with Stephanie to reassure me.

'It is a wee bit cramped but sure, once you've had a drink, you'll be fine.'

'Ya reckon?' I was comforted as I recalled the well understood and documented fact that the virus couldn't get me if I stood in a room full of slightly pissed, middle-class party goers.

Stephanie fired a nervous look at Brian, but the source of her anxiety was not the cramped space filled with people but rather that I might react badly and make a scene. Worse, she might not get her lift home. Worse than worse, she might have to go back now and miss the party. I wasn't surprised by her attitude; here was someone with a seriously fucked-up set of priorities as evidenced by her desire to go to prison for a crime she had so far got away with.

'It'll be fine. I'll introduce you', she said. Brian smiled expansively and I noticed that his teeth were very crooked. Somehow, Stephanie already had a drink in her hand – something coloured blue – even before she had got to the kitchen. It was like an alcoholic ambush. Her drink was waiting on a table, ready for her arrival. There wasn't so much as a can of Coke for me.

From unseen speakers, the Beach Boys were finishing their song. I moved into the kitchen past the buffet (or, if you were Billy, the *buffoon*), which struck me as another great way to spread a contagion, where I was introduced to the other guests. Joel, Ronnie, Stephen (possibly with a 'v', I didn't ask) and Rob were the men. They ranged in age from late twenties to late forties. Brian was late forties in my estimation, but the gut and bald head aged him rather, so he might have been younger. It was interesting to see how middle age spread... er, spread. Joel the youngest, had no gut. His stomach was as flat as a dodo (Billy, again). Ronnie and Rob were in their thirties, and in each you could see a developing layer of blubber beginning to strain just slightly against their leather M&S belts. Stephen had a properly developed gut and fine moobs which looked just about okay under his Next black and white-patterned party shirt, but which would look bad on a beach, especially set against his Ulster tan.

The women had a similar spread in age. Joan was the oldest. She was normally sized on top, with a pretty face and dark hair in a bob, but her bottom half was enormous. Her arse alone made social distancing in this confined space impossible. Karen, Briege (token Catholic), Sue and Georgina formed the remainder of the group. They all welcomed me heartily, with smiles and raised drinks before going back to their conversations.

Otis Redding was singing *Dock of the Bay* and I wished I was there with him. My *party-holding-a-drink-hand* was still empty and I wished I could down a few generous tots of dark rum to get myself in the mood, or get myself *out of* the mood I was in, which was something akin to despair tempered with hostility. I didn't like any of these smug, apparently disease-proof people. I didn't like their music, their clothes, the chit-chat, their trousers, their smug... hair. I wanted out and Stephanie could catch a bloody bus home.

Somewhere along the line she had been relieved of her jacket and now I felt the need to take my own jacket off, for the heat was slightly too much for me in this small, tightly packed space. In the end I draped it over the back of a kitchen chair and hoped that I remembered to take it with me when I left, for I had no plans to return.

Eventually, someone noticed that I did not have a drink and brought me a Diet Coke from a fridge decorated with amusing fridge magnets which held in place a small assortment of domestic crap including a classy little calendar detailing bin collections. A crappy drawing of a fire-breathing dragon indicated a family home, the kids no doubt shipped off to grandparents, another move forbidden under lockdown regulations.

Stephanie – she later suggested that I could call her 'Steph' – disentangled herself from her friends and sidled over to me, her blue eyes somehow brighter than before. She looked happy and I tried to reciprocate.

'You okay?'

'Yeah, fine, you know…'

'It's hard when you can't drink. Mingle a bit. Chat to the fellas.'

'I don't know them, or work in the same sort of fields as them. I am fairly sure we have nothing in common.'

'You don't know until you try', she said, reasonably. Whilst that was generally true, it wasn't true in the manner she so breezily suggested.

'We're not exactly socially distant, either.'

'Oh, we're fine. I know all of these people.'

'You know they're not infected?'

'Do they look infected?'

'I don't know what an infected person looks like. Do they go through a zombie phase before dying?'

I had spoken too loudly, and my words were overheard by Steph's friend, Georgina, who came over for a chat. Maybe I was becoming paranoid, but this felt like a deliberate move to smooth things over before the unwelcome visitor who didn't really fit in – that's me by the way – ruined things for everyone else. This group had decided unilaterally that they were too nice, too posh, too well-connected and too intelligent to catch Covid-19. They didn't need to do anything other than pay lip service to the measures put in place by the government. Had they not been Northern Irish, I had no doubt they'd have voted for the Liberals (or *Liberians*, as Billy called them) at the last election but the Liberians didn't field candidates in this country. Their liberal approach to life would follow them into death. The virus shared their politics and it didn't care who it attacked; everyone was equal.

Georgina was well on her way to becoming pissed.

'Hi. Steph has told me all about you', she said. I exchanged a look with my party companion and she gave a me a little encouraging nod. A slight sheen of perspiration had broken on her brow.

'Really? You know how we know each other?'

'We all know.'

I turned to Steph.

'They all know?', I queried. 'I mean, know as in *know*?'

'They know why I hired you.'

'The whole thing?'

Georgina interrupted at that moment.

'You are going to prove that she killed someone. She's told us all about it.'

Now, let me explain how I felt at this point in the night. Firstly, I still wanted to get out of there. It felt wrong with a capital 'R' as Billy would have it. Secondly, I still harboured grave reservations about my new friends. But (and here is the awkward bit) since I was here, it was better that someone was bothering to talk to me than being ignored. Georgina was pretty and intelligent, in fact exactly the sort of friend I would have imagined Steph having. In another time and place she would have been the sort of company I would have sought. Therefore, chatting to her and Steph was no great hardship had it not been for the threat posed by the virus.

But I still wanted out of there.

'I shouldn't really talk about it', I said with a shrug. 'Client confidentiality.'

'You have that in your profession?'

'Of course. There is no escaping it in any occupation nowadays, but it makes sense too.'

'But since Steph has told us all about it, you can talk about it. I mean she is standing right here.' She pointed to her friend and Steph gave an obliging wave.

'Talk away', she said.

'Well, in that case… The thing is that if I manage to do what she wants, she will go to jail for a long time.'

Steph nodded her agreement. Her eyes seemed to glow or glisten. I wondered if she had taken something.

'But they might find out that it was justifiable homicide', said Georgina, raising one eyebrow.

68

'They might', I said. I wasn't sure about the term she had used, if it was applicable in British law but I knew what she meant. 'Or they might not. Steph herself isn't sure about the exact circumstances. Most murders are just that – murders.

'So why are you doing it, if you are worried about her going to prison?'

'Well, I'm not worried. She has taken me on to do a job and I will try to do it.' I looked at Steph assuming that she would be crestfallen at my forced admission – I didn't care if she went to prison – but she beamed at me as if I had just *rescued* her from there.

'Wow' said Georgina.

'What else can I say? The best that Steph can hope for is that I don't find any evidence of this murder.'

'In which case, you have failed', said Georgina with a chuckle.

'Exactly.'

'Do you think she did it?'

'I couldn't say.' I turned to Steph and jokingly asked if she had done it.

'Of course. Guilty as hell. That's the only thing I know for sure. The rest of it – the details – are gone.'

We chatted for a while before Steph detached herself for a period of minglement. Georgina gallantly stayed with me and we continued to discuss the strange case of Stephanie Kuler.

'How long have you known her?', I asked.

'She only came over in September. We aren't in the same department but we share a staff room. She has more or less admitted from the outset that she killed someone. It isn't the first thing she said or anything, but once we knew each other a little and got onto the subject of the great, important, philosophical arguments of life, she told me all about it.'

'What did you think?', I asked.

'That's a good question. I mean, I would have been within my rights to consider her a complete nutter, wouldn't I, but she told me the whole thing with conviction and complete sincerity. It sounded true. It sounded like she truly believed it.'

She gave a shrug. Somehow, I believed her more than I believed Steph.

'But changing the subject, I am a bit wary about this gathering because we are all too close together.' I said this, in part, because I was enjoying her company and wanted to keep the conversation going. Georgina had, unwittingly, given me a reason to be at the party, someone to talk to.

She sighed and gave a slight, awkward smile, the sort of thing you employ when facing up to bad news with resignation and stoicism.

'I know what you mean. The problem for me, is that this is my house and Rob over there is my husband and this party is his idea.'

'Ahh. Sorry, I didn't mean to pass judgement.'

'It's fine. You're right. What Rob says goes, whether it's a good idea or not. In fact, if you were to ask him, he would say that he only had good ideas.'

'That's blokes for you', I admitted.

'You're the same?'

'Now that you mention it, I usually admit to my bad decisions. I have even been known to apologise.'

'Christ. Where have you been hiding?'

'Yep. I'm a great bloke, alright.'

'Rob has packed the kids off to his mum and dad's place. We're not supposed to do that either.'

'No. I shouldn't be agreeing too heartily here since you are my host', I said with a smattering of genuine regret.

'Agree all you want. You are correct on every count.'

'Well, in that case, I'm not keen on that buffet either. A great way to spread infection.'

'Yep. Yet again you are correct. I told him that too, but he is always correct.' She smiled again but it was a sad smile. I hardly knew this woman but the cracks in her life were already all too apparent.

'You're not married?'

'No. It never quite happened for some reason', I said, wistfully. Suddenly, there was a connection between me and Georgina, but it was one we couldn't exploit. If she had given me a slip of paper with her phone number on it, I wondered how honourably I would have behaved in the coming weeks. She was attractive, intelligent, funny… more or less perfect in the context of someone you are meeting for the first time. We knew nothing of each other's annoying traits. There was nothing for us to fall about yet.

These things always happen at parties. It's the drink. Even though I had consumed no alcohol, it was the drink which had brought us to this point.

'Would you like another delicious diet cola?'

'Well, since you put it like that, it would be...'

'Delicious?'

'Yes, delicious. I always say you can never have too much diet cola.'

Georgina made her way to the fridge to get my drink and when she returned, she said, 'if you don't like this party now, it is only fair to warn you that it is going to get worse.'

***

The night wore on. Georgina and I met up periodically and chatted, each time with new observations to make and each time her slightly more drunk than before. But drunk or not, she was good company. I spent some time talking to the blokes and the subject did not once, if you can believe this, stray onto football. Even more oddly, having not once mentioned football they didn't talk about rugby either, that game so loved by Ulster's middle-classes. Men either liked one game or the other. Or neither.

Or both.

But it was still something of a strain for me. Two of them worked at the university as lecturers, one was a doctor. Well, I had nothing in common with them. I talked in vague terms about my work as an investigator, but I avoided mentioning my background as a soldier for such things brought with them a degree of risk even in this post-terrorist world we now inhabited. They probably knew anyway. The citizens of

Northern Ireland were experts at finding things out through seemingly innocuous conversation. It was part of life there.

Naturally, I spent time with Steph and she too got drunker and drunker, whilst retaining her charm and easy wit. She made no mention of the fact that Georgina and I were getting along well and I didn't know if I should feel a little bit jealous of this omission until I recalled that she had only invited me in order to get a free lift there and perhaps as a secondary consideration to ensure that she wasn't the only single person present.

My suspicion that she had taken something other than alcohol subsided as time passed.

But then the 'worse thing' that Georgina had warned me about happened. I almost didn't notice at first but as the hands of the clock neared 2300, I saw that the kitchen party had fewer people present. I thought we were down to six or seven, but I was sure no one had left unless they had done so and not bothered to tell me. Then I spotted Brian taking a beer from the fridge and sneaking out of the back door to the long garden I had glanced earlier. He was followed by Steph, by now very wobbly on her feet. Only Ronnie, Georgina, and two of the women were left. And me, of course.

Georgina must have spotted my puzzled look for she was next to me a second later.

'The others have decided to social distance after all', I said with great wit.

'Something like that. Another drink?'

'No thanks. If I have another fizzy drink my seams will come undone. It's happened before – messy business. So where have they gone?'

'You remember I said it would get worse?'

'Yeess', I said, hesitantly.

'That's what has happened. They're outside having a puff.'

'Ahhh.'

'Very middle-class. This is what they did at uni. It is their God-given right.'

'What about you?'

'Not my thing. I'd rather swig gin from a bottle that I keep hidden in the airing cupboard.'

'Mother's ruin?'

'We have to get by somehow. Actually, it's not that bad. I take a drag now and again at parties so that I don't get accused of being a bad sport or of ruining the night. But I don't do drugs really.'

'Nor me. It wasn't really a common thing when I was growing up. Glue-sniffing and solvent abuse for me. Great times.'

She looked aghast.

'What? I didn't go to uni. And I am a lot older than most of these comedians. Times have changed.' I shook my head and stared off into the distance of a kitchen cupboard as if recalling the good old days. 'I didn't really by the way. A sheltered life.'

'Hmm. I don't believe that.'

'Maybe not sheltered but very different.' A thought occurred to me then. 'What about Steph? Is she a big drug user?'

'Not so much now but she says she used to do coke.'

'Shit.'

'And she might have taken a couple of funny little pills tonight. Brian usually has something in his pockets. A little pick-me-up, he would say. He's a shit.'

'He doesn't look the type.'

'There is plenty I could tell you about him.'

'Just going back to Steph, I know she's your friend and I don't want to compromise you, but this drug taking… could that be related to this so-called murder? There is absolutely no sign of any murder and yet she insists she's done it. You know all this. The police have paid little attention to her. It just seems like utter crap.'

'You could be right. Not my field of expertise. Rob was a bit of a high flyer in the city years back. Heroin and cocaine were part of the scene, so he told me. He has a really nasty side to him, which I attribute to that. Quite paranoid sometimes and very aggressive, just this side of violent, when he doesn't get his way. I'm not saying that Steph is like that, but it could have changed her.'

'It would explain a lot.'

She gave me a sad smile and I was tempted to take her in my arms. I think she knew that. Instead, I blew air from my cheeks.

'I'm going outside. I want to have a look at this', I said. 'You coming?'

'I'm afraid of what I might see. You go on. I'll still be here when you get back.'

Against my better judgment, I squeezed her arm and was rewarded with another sad smile.

'If I left him, he'd fight me for custody of our daughter.'

I didn't know what to say.

'I'm coming back. I just want to see what they're up to.'

I squeezed past the depleted kitchen party group, including the conjoined entities that were Joan and her arse. A flight of three stairs led past an oddly situated bathroom and into a hallway with a basket full of Wellington boots and a coat rack of scarves and coats. A bobble hat, looking very home-knitted had fallen into the boot basket. I almost picked it up on my way out just to help tidy up.

The door was open and I could smell the weed long before I stepped outside. As soon as I set foot in the garden, I knew that I had committed a *faux pas*, or a 'fox pass' as Billy would have said. But I learned something in the process; it is socially unacceptable for a non-drug user to stray into the demesne of a group of friends happily enjoying a leisure cigarette. It was akin to a fully dressed person turning up at a naturist convention or a naturist turning up at… anything other than that.

As one, they turned, stinking joints in hand and glared at me. I smiled as insincerely as I could.

'Ah, there you are.'

Rob, looking very surly, asked if I wanted one.

I declined. The others looked happy enough but stoned. Steph by contrast was pretty far gone, a fact which she emphasized by falling sideways into the bouncy castle that was Brian.

'Fuck', she said.

I was turning for the door, when Brian, the conciliator, suggested that Steph had had enough and would I mind taking her home.

He was holding her up.

'I don't want to go home', she slurred.

'For fuck's sake', snarled Rob. In my innocence I was ruining his party. For nothing more than a second or two I pictured myself sinking a fist into his educated face. That moment passed quickly.

'Come on Steph, let's get you home.'

She didn't protest, not even when her friend and supplier held her out almost at arm's length in an invitation to take her away. The rest looked on, their cigarette hands down by their sides as I took hold of Steph's arm and guided her away from her friends. She dropped her cigarette on the ground. I wondered if someone would finish it off for her once she had gone.

I had already decided that I was going to ditch her as a client. I would ring her tomorrow with the grave tidings so that she would not protest tonight. I couldn't be bothered with the fight. My mind was made up that her problems stemmed from drug use. The story she had given me was complete lunacy. That's not to say that *she* didn't believe it but even still, it was pure fantasy brought about by the ingestion of strong drugs. I was pretty pissed off by it all.

'I will give you a hand getting her into the car', said Georgina as she took an arm.

'Thanks. She's in a right fucking state', I said. Together we bundled her through the hall, down the steps, down the path, through the gate, along the road and then next to the car by which point she was almost completely inert and floppy like a corpse.

'Bloody hell' said Georgina getting her breath back.

'People are heavier when they're unconscious', I said, which was not true of course. I unlocked the car and between us we practically threw her onto the back seat.

'How are you going to get a seatbelt on her?'

I looked down at the form on the back seat, wondering if she was going to puke on the leather upholstery on the way home. Leather was quite good if someone puked on it – wipe down. She looked terribly uncomfortable and somewhat dead.

'I think I'll leave her like that.' She was much less appealing now, curled up, pale, unconscious. It was as I gazed at her form that I noticed her suede jacket missing. That thought led me to realise that my own jacket was missing.

'Fuckit', I swore.

'What?'

'I left my jacket behind.'

'You get her home. I'll bring it to your office tomorrow. I am going into town anyway.'

It sounded like a lie but the thought of seeing her again had more than a little appeal.

'Do you mind?'

'Not at all. Get her home before she's sick.'

Chapter Five

She wasn't sick in the car but getting her into her house was going to be one hell of a job, not because she struggled against my efforts but because she was incapable of helping me by using her own legs. The one advantage of her totally unresponsive state was that she made no noise or fuss of any kind as I attempted to get her back inside the house without waking the neighbours. I remembered the route back and at this time of night during lockdown I barely saw another vehicle on the road. It was once I pulled up outside that my troubles began. She was a dead weight to drag from the back seat and could barely stand as I tried to find her house keys.

That didn't work.

Whatever she had taken had done a good job of temporarily wiping out her nervous system. She was, in local parlance, wrecked.

Still without her keys, I decided to move her closer to her home. Thankfully, it was a short walk from the car to her front door and once I got her there, I was able to sit her down with her back against the door frame as I searched her bag for a set of keys.

It was a small bag. Inside I found a mobile phone, a purse, a tampon (still wrapped) and a packet of tissues, but no keys. The answer to my newly developing dilemma was galloping towards me at speed. The keys, as you have already figured out, were in her jacket pocket; the suede jacket that Brian had so helpfully taken from her as she came in, the fat bastard.

I stood there for a moment, seized with something just short of despair, and then searched the heavens looking for an answer which was unlikely to appear in bright lights. I quickly ran through the pros and cons of the situation. On the pro side, I had been slightly worried in case she had an alarm which I would be unable to turn off. Now, since I couldn't even get in the bloody house, that worry had been eased off my shoulders. By itself that fact failed to lift my spirits and for that single 'pro' there were several 'cons'. I discounted them all at once since I was left with one course of action only, and there was no point in delaying. Yes, I was going to put her in something similar to the recovery position and leave her outside on the path leading to her front door.

There ends this chapter in the story. Good night.

Chapter Five-A

But I couldn't do that, could I? Which is not to say that it didn't cross my mind. I was heartily pissed off by now, but I enacted the one course of action that was left to me and did so with a vigour and clarity of purpose that can only be summoned in times of severe duress.

'Right, let's get you back into the car. And if you fucking puke, you'll be cleaning it up in the morning'.

There was no response.

Much less delicately than before, I hoisted her to her feet and pulled one arm across my shoulder before more or less dragging her out to the car. Her legs had contributed nothing to this move. She was almost corpse-like.

Back at the car, I propped her against the front passenger door as I retrieved the remote fob from my pocket and opened up. Still holding her in place – I was getting the hang of it now – I pulled open the back door and sort of rolled her round so that she was aligned with the back seat from whence she had come minutes before. It began to rain gently as I did this.

I could have let go of her at this point and she would have fallen into her place like a felled tree but the danger of her hitting her head was too great and the thought of cleaning up all that blood was too much. So now I started to lower her down, ensuring her head just missed the top of the door frame.

I let go and she collapsed the rest of the way after which it was just a matter of twisting her legs so that they would fit in the footwell. She groaned as I did this which was encouraging since it indicated to me that I wasn't manoeuvring a corpse.

It was a thankfully short, traffic-free drive in which I wasn't stopped by the police and forced to explain why I was taking an unconscious woman to my house.

Back home I had to reverse the technique I was getting so good at, and then drag-carry her inside.

I briefly imagined what the neighbours would think if they saw me.

Yes officer, I saw him dragging a drugged woman into his house. Midnight it was. Remember it clear as day.

As I said before, by this point, I was finished with her. There was no way I was looking into this case any further. All that I asked was that she didn't die during the night.

Still holding her up, I surveyed my living room, deciding on a place to dump her – yes, that's how I felt about it – and realised that it was going to have to be the floor. She was going into the recovery position again, but it would be tricky if she was on the sofa, which left only the rug. I lowered her gently, feeling as if my back might break, and then pulled her over until she lay on her side. By trial and error, I rearranged her limbs so that an approximation of the recovery position was achieved and then, in a final token effort aimed at improving her comfort, I removed her boots. When I straightened up to survey my efforts, I was unimpressed. I have to say that it looked as though she had been dumped there or had simply fallen over and knocked herself out. Whatever. The final touch was to drape a blanket over her, leave a glass of water nearby and then to put the main light out. I switched on a table lamp as I made my way upstairs to bed.

***

In the morning, I awoke at about 07:30, tired but clear-headed. The house was cold for I had recently turned the central heating off, and rain, carried on a biting wind, battered the window. The events of the previous night came back to me in tiny segments and I remembered that I was meeting Georgina in the office, ostensibly for the purpose of getting my jacket back. It would have been far simpler for her to run inside and get the bloody thing, but it was fairly clear that she had an ulterior motive; something to do with her husband I was guessing.

'Yeah, what a night', I was thinking when I remembered Steph who I had left downstairs.

'Shit', I said, and quickly dressed.

She wasn't dead, which was good. And she hadn't been sick which was even better. At some point during the night she had crawled onto the sofa and pulled the blanket over her and there she lay now, totally out of it as far as I could tell. I had no intention of disturbing her, so I returned to my bedroom and then went for a quick shower before dressing again.

On a normal day, I wouldn't have bothered with breakfast but this morning I was famished, and I remembered that I hadn't even gone near the contagion-laden *buffoon*. Not so much as a sausage roll had passed my lips. Well, my mind was made up; I was going to make breakfast and if I woke my unwanted guest then so be it.

By now she had turned over, but she was still there and still out for the count. I made my way quietly to the kitchen and closed the door behind me to make coffee and toast. I didn't want to wake her. Firstly, I didn't want the hassle but secondly, I thought she was better off asleep as she recovered from the previous night's excesses.

Weighing on my mind, as I prepared the lavish meal, was the prospect of telling Steph that her custom was no longer wanted. I deemed it unlikely that she would simply accept my decision with a smile and good grace but I hoped that she would understand my reasoning which was that she was a drugged-up lunatic who had imagined the whole thing. I didn't want to be unpleasant about it but the truth was the best option for all concerned.

When she awoke – *came to* might be a better phrase – she would hardly be on top form and might just stumble off into the street with my rejection of her echoing in her brain but without the will for an argument. The fact she was here made it easier to pass the news. I didn't want to tell her by text. This all felt a little bit like breaking up with someone and I had never once in my career dropped a client.

By 09:30 she was still out of it. I didn't try to wake her but I needed to get to the office. A quick survey of my fridge revealed a selection of possible recovery foods: a can of diet cola, a Twix and a bottle of Lucozade Sport. I left these near her, along with a brief note explaining what had happened but not the fact that she was dumped. Lastly, before I abandoned her for the next few hours, I left my spare keys and then locked her in with my own set.

The wind was dying down, the rain easing and the clouds moving on as I drove. There were buses and cars as usual and now people had begun to wear the masks that they had been told were useless in the early stages of the pandemic. I don't know what had changed. I didn't know what the truth was about anything now.

It felt good to be in the car for even that short drive, as if I were snatching back a little bit of normality. I parked in the street (there were plenty of spaces now) and made my way inside distributing the mail as I always did.

Billy joined me as the kettle boiled.

'I miss the big coffee machine', he said, his voice dripping with pathos.

'Yes, these are terrible times. Thousands dying, the economy crumbling, no cappuccino. I don't know how you keep going. You're a marvel.'

'So how was your hot date?'

'Interesting. Put it like this, I have dumped Stephanie Kuler as a client.'

'That's a shame. Tell me what happened.'

Billy sat silently as I relayed the night's events to him. He continued to listen when he rose to make the coffees and stayed quiet until the end.

'Fuck.'

'Arseholes', I said. 'I have never met so many pricks in one place at one time.'

'Not your scene at all that', he commented. 'Mind you, it fits with the few bits and pieces I have found out about her. But that was a waste of time now if she isn't a client.'

'Tell me anyway, since you're here.'

'Okay. In no particular order, she has a drink-driving offence in the US.'

'Not surprised.'

'She and Mr Kuler had a kid. He got custody and she fucked off back to Britain leaving the kid behind.'

'Jesus.'

'Did that slip her mind, by any chance?', asked Billy.

'To be fair to her the subject didn't come up but she certainly never mentioned a kid. What else?'

'A disciplinary procedure against her with her employer in the US. No details but from what I can gather she was given the option of resigning which she took. Not much on her in this country and no details about her family yet. That could be very hard to come by.'

I nodded.

'I was forgetting; we don't need them now', said Billy. 'Shame that, I was just getting going with this. I really thought the hypnotist thing was going to be the key to it. Oh well, *that ship has flown*, as they say.'

'Dead as a pancake?', I ventured.

'Dead as the proverbial pancake', he agreed.

'I'm not looking forward to telling her.'

'Chill yer horses. You could just keep her on. It's no skin off your arse.'

'I *could* do that, but it is just a dead end as far as I am concerned. It sounded like bollocks from the start, but now I know a bit more about her and her habits it makes perfect sense that she harbours this belief about a murder. Christ knows what the drugs have done to her brain over the years. If you spell it out bit by bit, it just comes across as pure fantasy.'

'Okay. You lose money though.'

'Money isn't everything. Sometimes you have to elevate yourself above worldly concerns and seek a path to enlightenment and shit like that.'

'Whatever. What do you want me to do in the meantime?'

'Let me know what else you find out about her – just out of interest. I will be back in touch with any other stuff that comes up.'

'Fine by me, but I think you are making a mistake.'

He left the office singing, 'Stranglers in the Night', his butchered version of the old Sinatra standard. Oddly, he had a good voice although he confined himself to nonsense songs. Another of his was, 'What a *Fiend* we have in Jesus.'

I checked in with my contacts in Hong Kong who were looking into the disappearance of Curt Johnson. Neither had anything else to offer me which wasn't a great surprise. My belief that he had even got close to that place was minimal to start with. This was a bad time to live in, or travel to, the former colony with a great deal of subtle sabre rattling coming from the Communist dictatorship who were threatening to remove its last vestiges of democracy and freedom. Perhaps with the Chinese economy now booming, it was time for them to re-align the cash cow that had been Hong Kong, but whatever the reason, I felt like expressing my concern to my distant associates.

What prevented me from doing so was the belief on my part that their communications were being monitored. Did they know what the Commies had in store for them? In previous months there had been a military build-up on the borders with Hong Kong, but the news had gone quiet on the subject. I picked up my Huawei mobile and looked at it. There seemed little point communicating my fears with them using *that* if the stories of electronic infiltration were to be believed.

I was slightly surprised when the buzzer sounded and remembered that Georgina had arranged to drop by.

'Hi.'

'It's Gina. Georgina', she corrected.

'Come up', I said, pressing the button to release the door mechanism.

I met her at the top of the stairs.

'Hi.'

'Hi. Social distancing, remember.'

'Okay by me. Probably too late for that after last night', she said.

I led her to the uncomfy chairs and reclaimed my jacket and another she had brought with her.

She frowned.

'I was going to take that to Steph afterwards.'

'She's at my place', I explained.

Georgina's frown deepened. I could see she was disappointed and although there was nothing going on between me and Steph, or me and Georgina, I felt the need to explain.

'Her keys are in the jacket pocket', I said retrieving them and dangling them in the air like a not very good magician.

'Oh, I see. I didn't think of that.'

'Nothing happened. She was in a bloody state. I got her to her front door before I realised that I couldn't open it. So I took her to my place and left her on the floor in the recovery position. She was still alive when I left this morning.'

'Good to know.'

'Anyway, thank you for bringing my jacket. How's the head?'

'Not so bad, strangely enough. I've had worse hangovers. It was a shit party.'

'Worse for you. You had to clear up.'

'Hmm. Rob is still out cold. He won't really be up and about 'til three. That suits me fine, really.'

'I avoided the buffet in the end. I know you probably made it and it was very nicely done but I didn't want to risk it.'

She smiled wearily.

'I could do with catching up on my sleep. You don't get properly rested after a heavy night.'

'Well, I can offer you a coffee. As you can see, we have a deluxe chrome kettle with safety features and executive spout.'

'Sounds great. Are you having one?'

I did not want another coffee; two was my normal daily limit which I had already reached.

'I certainly am. I made it sound so appealing that I can't bear to go without now.'

I busied myself with the drinks, my back to her as I asked the next question.

'Did you come here just to drop my jacket off?'

'That and the chance of a coffee from a kettle with extra safety features.'

'Well, this is your lucky day. Milk and sugar?'

'Just milk please.'

When I asked this question of Billy he had always asked if I could stir it with a milky spoon. When I stopped asking, he would request two sugars and one milk.

'You didn't enjoy yourself last night. Maybe if you'd been able to drink... I could have ordered you and Steph a taxi. Are the taxis running still?'

'I have no idea. If the driver has a plastic screen between him and his passengers it should be okay, I suppose. But the problem wasn't the fact that I was driving; it was the fact that I don't drink. So, even if I had come on foot, I wouldn't have been drinking.'

'Oh. I didn't know.'

'You wouldn't know. We hardly know each other. I used to drink but I gave up about ten years ago.'

'I see.'

'You are assuming that I was an alcoholic?'

'Erm. That's very personal to you if you were or weren't…'

'It's fine. I wasn't but I thought it might happen, so I gave up before I had to worry about it.'

The conversation dried up a for a moment and we sipped our coffees in silence.

'Those people last night…', I began.

'I don't much care for them either. Joan is okay. Ronnie is bearable. Brian is a dick. Steph is okay but a bit of a loose cannon. The drugs and everything – it isn't me. I want you to know that.'

'You said as much last night. I wasn't keen on them either – the guests, not the drugs. Not my type of people. I have to admit that I felt a little bit inadequate; their intellectual inferior by some margin.'

'I wouldn't worry about that. They might have brains the size of planets but they're thick in other ways. They spend so much time trying to be clever that simple things in life have passed them by, like not being pricks.'

'Things between you and Ron aren't good?'

'Rob. We get by like lots of other couples. What seemed like him being charming and witty when we met is just irritating now. His humour is just smugness. I can't raise a smile these days.'

'I can't say I understand the problem from first-hand experience. The eternal bachelor. It has its advantages, I suppose.'

We were no longer the regulation two metres apart but as she said it hardly mattered too much after last night. If I was going to be infected then it had already happened.

'So, what happens next with Steph?'

'If she is still alive when I get home, I am going to tell her that she is no longer a client of mine.'

'Simple as that?'

'I don't see any point in carrying on. In my mind it is the drugs that are the problem. I don't think I am over-simplifying things by saying that. Whatever she has taken has fried her brains and left her with this delusion that she has murdered someone. This hasn't cost her a penny by the way. She gets out of it without having spent any money.'

'You don't think there could be a grain of truth in what she says?'

'No. Do you?'

'She really believes it.'

'Doesn't make it true. People believe all sorts of things when they have taken drugs. I am categorically not an expert in this field, but when you look at the context of what she is saying and then factor in her drug use, it is natural to reach the conclusion I have reached. No one, that we know of, has been murdered, and she possesses no details of any sort about this alleged crime. Surely it is more likely that this gets fixed in her brain as a result of drug use than as a result of her actually doing it?'

'I suppose so.'

'But you're not convinced?'

She sighed heavily and looked upset, maybe even on the point of tears.

'Honestly… I was probably just hoping to have a reason to keep in touch with you.'

'You could have run back into your house last night to get my jacket.'

'I could have.'

She looked a little bit embarrassed now.

'I'm sorry', she said.

'You don't need to be. I'm flattered. We can keep in touch if you like. Why not?'

'There is the small matter of my husband.'

'Georgina, if you want to keep in touch, then that's fine. It would be nice. Let's just take it as it comes.'

She nodded.

'Deal?'

'Deal. I'd better get going. Unless you want me to come with you to break the news to Steph?'

'That isn't a bad idea. Would you mind? I haven't exactly been putting it off but I did want her to be *compos mentis* when I mentioned it.'

'It's fine. I can follow you.'

The traffic was light and she had no problem keeping me in view for the short journey to my house. Her car was a brand-new Merc, so there were some advantages to being married to the gruesome Rob. It might have been his car, but I wasn't going to ask.

When we got back, I had the sneaking suspicion that Steph had probably come to and skulked off to recover in her own place, which is what I would have done in the circumstances. However, I was wrong. In the hours that had passed since I left her alone that morning, she had not stirred, a fact evidenced by the untouched soft drinks and chocolate. Steph had changed position on the sofa and nothing more than that.

'Holy mother of… is she alive?'

I shook her by the shoulder and thankfully she stirred.

'I need the toilet', she said as she rose.

'Upstairs, straight ahead of you.'

Steph didn't speak and didn't seem to register the presence of her friend either. She stumbled upstairs, zombified.

I looked at Georgina.

'See what I mean? How could I take her claims seriously now?'

'Fair enough. I don't mind taking her home but maybe you should spare her the bad news until such time as she is more with it.'

'Or this might be precisely the right time to break it to her.'

I heard the toilet flush.

'She might not remember if you tell her now. I can drop her off and tell her if you like. She will probably sleep for the rest of the day and then ring you tomorrow. At least I will have started the process of her understanding what has happened.'

'That sounds like a good plan. I would be grateful.'

The toilet flushed again.

'She is still alive.'

'Yep.'

'How will she take it, do you think?', I asked.

'If and when it finally sinks in, she'll be upset. This is a big deal to her.'

'I'll have to sell it to her as an opportunity to stay out of prison. For most people that would be reward enough.'

'Not for Steph apparently.'

The toilet flushed again.

'Is this some sort of code, she's using? Cistern Morse?'

Georgina laughed.

'It's a laborious way to communicate.'

'Lavorious? I think you're right.'

It was another few minutes before she staggered downstairs looking slightly less dishevelled than before but not in great shape.

'I'm taking you home, Steph', said Georgina, plainly. 'You've had a rough night.' When Steph merely blinked, she spoke again. 'I'm taking you home. Do you understand?'

Steph nodded this time and mumbled an apology although I wasn't sure if she knew what she was apologising for.

Georgina took her friend by the shoulders and began to guide her out of the room and into the hall.

'Make sure you have her keys', I said.

'I've got 'em. I'll try to explain what is happening, with you and the murder and so on.'

'Thanks. Give me a ring when you get back.'

All the time we were nearing the front door and I squeezed past now to open it. The sun had come out and I squinted.

'I'll speak to you soon.'

When they were gone, I straightened up the living room and then slumped, wondering how I had ever hoped to solve a case like this.

Chapter Six

She rang the next day, which was no great surprise.

'I'm sorry.'

'That's fine', I said awkwardly. Her behaviour at the party and afterwards wasn't the real problem here and we both knew it, although she was no doubt mortified at having got into that state.

'Look, I know that you want to ditch me as a client, Georgina told me.'

I said nothing.

'But I would like you to reconsider. I know what you must think of me.'

'The party was a mistake. For all concerned. I should never have agreed to go to it and I only got invited so that you had a lift; that much is apparent to me. But your behaviour that night did at least give me an insight into the paranoid delusion you are having about this so-called murder. Steph, this is just something that your brain has invented as far as I am concerned. You probably need a doctor instead of someone to investigate.'

'That's not true', she protested mildly. She sounded utterly disconsolate, as well she might.

'Which bit? Honestly, my words might sound harsh but I am doing you a favour. This murder never happened. You think it did because your brain is fucked up by drugs. Now, if I didn't possess a few rarely used scruples, I could just string you along and take your money and make a token effort at finding out who you had killed. But the truth is I am never going to find them because you never killed them. I am looking for something that doesn't exist. It isn't fair on you. I am being as honest as I can be here.'

'I did do it. You don't understand what this means to me.'

'Actually, I think I do. If you are willing to risk prison just to have your mind put at ease then it means a lot clearly, but me finding this murder victim isn't the answer. I am foregoing my wage to tell you the truth. You need to lay off the drugs and see a specialist doctor.'

There was a profound silence, but she was still on the line.

'For me personally, the one good thing to come from that party was that it made sense of your state of mind. It wasn't just the booze or the weed was it? Your friend Brian was supplying you with pills too. These things fuck your brain up. How many years have you been doing this sort of thing?'

She answered but avoided the question at the same time.

'The two things aren't connected.'

'That is like an alcoholic denying that they have a problem with drinking.'

'It's not. I do have a problem. Not as big a problem as you think but it is there. I'll admit that. But the murder is real. I know what you are saying, and I understand how you would make the connection, but the two things are not linked at all.

That murder happened. I did it. That feeling of horror is as clear as anything I have ever experienced. I know that all the other details are missing but that feeling is there all the time. It never leaves me. I know that I killed someone.'

'And why can't that be the drugs? Or what I mean is, why can't that be an effect of the drugs? People believe all sorts of things…'

'Because this never goes away. I don't take drugs every day. I'm not really an addict or anything – far from it, in fact. I don't even drink every night, maybe a bottle of wine on a Friday night when the week has finished. The pills are just a party thing for me. I won't go to another party for weeks or months maybe and I won't have any pills until then. In fact, I could go to a party and not take them at all. I am not addicted, no matter what you might think. Taking a few pills or smoking a bit of weed doesn't make you an addict. I don't have anything in the house. I don't crave it. If you wanted me to give it up I could. I could give up right now in fact.

'But what never goes away is the knowledge that I killed someone. I feel myself looking down at the body and the sheer terror and horror and guilt. It's just that I can't see the body itself and I can't tell where I am, or when this happened. But if you could feel it, you would understand that I'm telling the truth about this.

'If you want me to beg, then I will beg but I can't live with this. I know it might not seem like it, but this is eating me up. Even if I go to prison I have to know. This isn't some flash in the pan. I'll double your fee…'

'There is no need…'

'Let me finish. I'll double your fee. I'll totally kick the drugs, whatever. But please just keep me on and try to find out what I did.'

'Steph, I... I don't know what to say.'

'I'll have a lie detector test at my own expense, anything... please'

I pulled a face and scratched the back of my neck. I wasn't about to take double the fee – that wasn't fair – but I didn't really want to know about this case. I blew air from my cheeks and glanced at my phone as though it held the answer, or I could see Steph looking imploringly through the little plastic mouthpiece.

'I will stick with it for another week. I need you to undergo hypnotism. The same fee as before but I add on the costs for anything above and beyond.'

'Agreed. Thank you.'

'This doesn't mean I believe that it happened. I don't actually want to find the person you think you've killed because I don't want you to go to jail.'

'I know.'

'But I don't expect that to happen because I know you didn't kill anyone.'

'But you will try?'

'I will try.' A thought occurred to me then. 'What if we did find someone that you had killed, would we have to tell the police?'

'So, you think there is chance that I did?'

'It is a theoretical situation I am talking about.'

'I am not sure. But thank you. When do you want me to see this hypnotist?'

'I'll be in touch.'

***

On the surface of it, she had made a compelling case – no doubt she thought so and it had done the trick – but I was no more convinced about the sense of carrying on than I had been previously. Maybe the stuff about her drug-taking was true but it didn't alter the basic fact that nobody had ever turned up as verification of her claim. What *had* changed perhaps was the potential 'get-out clause' we now possessed; if we found the body of the person she had murdered, we had the option of informing the police, or pretending that nothing had ever happened. I wouldn't say that it was a neat solution but – bear with me here – if it could be proved that the dead person had deserved their fate, then morally I could perhaps overlook the murder.

That didn't sit easily with me but since I did not expect to find a corpse it wasn't an immediate or even long-term difficulty.

If nothing else, I had cleared the air. If there had been any doubt before, I had now swept it away; I did not believe that Stephanie Kuler was a murderer, and I was continuing with the case at her insistence. That had been my position from the outset but now I felt that it was totally unambiguous, and I suppose there was always a chance that I would uncover something else in the meantime. I might find proof that she had killed someone. Equally, I might find that she had not. That thought cheered me a little even if I couldn't quite picture how that state of affairs would manifest itself.

When the hypnotist rang me back, I knew we were on to the next phase of the operation. Maybe he would get to the heart of the problem. I explained the situation to him.

'That sounds very peculiar indeed.'

'Yep. It's hard to view it any other way really. I have spoken to her at length about the implications of this case.'

'She would obviously go to prison.'

'I have told her that and she accepts the risk. She is determined to put this matter to rest so what I am hoping you can do is to…'

'Well, hopefully if there is anything in her subconscious about having killed someone then I will be able to get to it. It wouldn't be of any use in court, but it might give you a pointer as to whether or not you were wasting your time.'

'Could it give us more than that? For instance, could it tell us who she killed or where the body is?'

'It's hard to say. I would be tapping into an event that is recorded but hidden in her brain. She might replay the event but it won't be a commentary on it, if you see what I mean. I don't envisage her telling me where she is or when it is. She isn't going to state the date. It is more likely that I will uncover the motive behind her actions and she might betray the identity of the victim by using their name, for instance. I will record it and you can pick the bones out of it.'

'I see you what you mean. She isn't going to begin by saying, *'here we are at the house of such and such, that date is third of March 2005''*

'Exactly. You might pick those details up in some other way but it is unlikely. The main thing is it will give you pointers and it might tell you whether or not it happened. However, I should warn you, there might be nothing there at all, or there might seem to be nothing there. If that is the case you can't take that as definitive proof that the events you want to know about *didn't* occur. Nothing in the process is proof of anything. That is my disclaimer if you like.'

'I understand. She is a willing subject if that helps.'

'It makes it easier to get her under certainly. Once I have done that, she can't particularly resist.'

We made the arrangements for the following day and I rang Steph to confirm. She seemed pleased and viewed this as a positive step. I wondered what she would think if no evidence of the murder showed up. I didn't imagine that she'd give up just because a hypnotist couldn't find anything, and he had also made the point that nothing he did was proof of innocence or guilt. We'd see.

Chapter Seven

They both turned up at 0930 the following day and exchanged socially distanced greetings. It was all very cordial, like orange squash. I led them down to a small interview room at the far end of the office.

'You'll be slightly less than two metres apart', I explained. 'I am sure you can manage.'

The hypnotist, whose name was Graham Balfour, said that he didn't mind. He was tall, bearded in the fashion of the day and maybe a few years younger than me.

They both refused the offer of a hot drink and I said, 'I'll let you get on with it. I will be in the office, but this room is sound-proofed.'

And that was it. They went inside and Graham unpacked the few props he had brought with him including a recording device of some sort. There was nothing to do but wait. Had it been a séance or an exorcism, a certain amount of entertainment value would presumably have been added – flying chairs or screams maybe – but for me at least, the event was entirely without spectacle.

I checked my emails and there was one from my friend in Hong Kong stating that he was certain that Curt Johnson had never reached the former colony. It was easy to get lost there, yes, but getting there from abroad undetected was another thing altogether. It seemed like one more dead end but that's how it went sometimes; I didn't promise happy endings. It was only to be expected since I specialised in other people's leftovers, the cases they didn't want. There were a few more things to check but I was certain that Curt Johnson was not in Hong Kong. Where he was now was another matter of course. There was no apparent reason for him to disappear, apart from the seeming difficulties in his marriage.

I had a photo of him on the computer and I brought it up now, lest an examination of his face gave me some sort of clue about the man or his whereabouts. He was in uniform with the rank badges of a corporal. His hair was crew-cut. Johnson was not smiling. Something about him made me think, 'knob' and an image of his body being found in a skip flashed through my mind.

Stephanie and Graham spent about forty minutes together and when they emerged, she looked happy, if a little care-worn, and he looked satisfied.

'Maybe we could do with that coffee now', he suggested.

'Of course. Productive?'

'I would have said so. Obviously, Stephanie hasn't heard any of it and it is for you to decide what it means, if anything, but there was plenty to come out of it.'

I made three coffees and opened a packet of Nice biscuits. I have never known if they were *Nice* as in the Mediterranean city on the south coast of France or the rather more prosaic *nice*, meaning the word with which to describe their adequacy in biscuit terms. Billy, naturally enough, called them *Niece* biscuits because he insisted that his brother's daughter liked them.

In general, I never talked about the biscuits, but some people probably did.

We chatted for a minute or two just to be sociable.

'What is your main line of work?'

'I do some shows. Not the big time but it's okay in the clubs. I help people with addictions or phobias. That's my bread and butter.'

'Never anything like this?'

'Not quite like this but a few bits and pieces which have turned up interesting facts about people. Past lives, for instance, is a big thing.'

'Is it genuine?', asked Steph. 'When people start talking about a past life, is it really their own past life they're talking about?'

'It's very hard to know. Often, they come to me suspecting that they have lived before. Sometimes, something they say substantiates that claim – at least of the surface – but sometimes there is nothing. It doesn't prove anything either way.'

'What do you think?'

'I don't know. Honestly, after all these years I am open-minded about it. Obviously, if I closed my mind to the possibility of reincarnation and so on, then I would be potentially cutting off one line of income but nothing I have seen has made me take a definite view one way or the other.'

'Do you think people try to trick you?'

'Trick *me*?'

'Say things when they are hypnotised which are just made up?'

'Oh, I see. No. They can't. If they're hypnotised then they can only speak the truth, or a version of it anyway. I could trick them of course, but I don't.'

'But how do you know they're really under?', I asked.

'I know. Listen to the recording and you'll understand what I mean.'

He passed across a little SD card and said, 'it's all on there.'

'You aren't staying? To interpret?'

'There's nothing to interpret. It's all there for you. What you make of it is another matter, but it's all there.'

Steph held up the card and said, with some wit, 'the entire contents of my brain has been downloaded onto this tiny piece of plastic?'

Balfour smiled.

'A small part of it, yes.'

***

I checked that the card played on my laptop before he left, clutching the cheque which was his agreed fee.

When I was alone with Steph, I looked at her and raised my eyebrows.

'You ready for this?'

'I reckon.'

'You have no idea what you said?'

'No idea. I don't remember a thing about it.'

'Does it feel as if someone has been poking around in your brain?'

'It doesn't feel like anything at all.'

I pressed play and we listened intently. He had warned that the first few minutes would seem fairly inane as they chatted seemingly without purpose. But this preamble was part of the process he had explained. Gradually the tone of the conversation had changed, and Steph had answered his questions with an increasing detachment.

'How do you feel right now?', he asked.

'Relaxed. Tired.'

'Happy?'

'Not sure. Content.'

'Where were you born?'

'Oxford.'

'Lovely place.'

Steph made no reply at this point, so he prompted her.

'You don't think it is lovely?'

'I dunno. Full of students.'

'I suppose it is. Are you a student?'

On the recording she made a scoffing sound.

'You aren't a student?'

'Nope.'

'Would you like to be one?'

She repeated the scoffing sound yet again but this time slightly louder.

'What do you want to be?'

'I dunno.'

Steph reached over and paused the recording.

'What's up?'

'Does that sound like me?', she asked.

'Well, it isn't him, so it must be.'

'That's probably how I talked when I was young. I've never heard my young self talk before.'

'That's the hypnotism for you. You didn't seem to suddenly go under, it was just gradual.'

'We were just talking – then nothing – and then we were talking again. All of this stuff happened in the 'nothing' bit.'

'Shall we listen to a bit more?'

She nodded and I pressed play once again

'Do you think you'd like to be a nurse or a teacher?'

'Not a teacher.'

'A nurse then?'

'Maybe.'

'What do you think your mum and dad would like you to be?'

A silence followed but then she spoke again.

'I don't have a mum and dad.'

'Everyone has a mum and dad.'

'I don't.'

'Who looks after you?'

'Malcolm and Susan.'

'They're not your mum and dad though?'

'No. They try to be but they're not my mum and dad.'

'Do you like them?'

'They're alright.'

'Do they buy you nice things?'

'Well, I suppose so. Sometimes. They have to buy me clothes and I get stuff for birthdays and all.'

'What age are you, Stephanie?'

'I am nine years old', she replied with a certain defiance in her voice as if the question of her age should not have been raised.

For a minute or two Balfour seemed to lose his grip on the young Stephanie's focus and it was possible to ascertain a tiny degree of frustration in his voice. He remained patient as they discussed several TV programmes which she liked, a favourite dress, a man named Uncle Keith....'

I paused this time.

'Uncle Keith?'

'Yeah, I'd forgotten about him. He was a friend of Malcolm and Susan. Not really an uncle.'

'Was he okay?'

'You mean, did I kill him? I don't think so.'

'Could we get in touch with Malcolm or Susan?'

'I think he is dead. Susan is still alive, or she was about five years ago. Malcolm died of bowel cancer in case you were wondering.'

'Keith?'

'No idea. He seemed old then, so he could be dead too. He was okay if I remember. Quite kind.'

She intercepted my suspicious look.

'No, genuinely kind, not creepy or anything.'

'Okay. Just checking.'

We returned to the tape.

'Who is your favourite teacher at school?'

'Mr Campbell. He's the only one who is nice.'

'Do you have a boyfriend at school?'

'Eugh. No way.'

I caught Stephanie smiling at her innocent repugnance. She paused the recording.

'It's hard to believe this is me.'

'It's you alright.'

'I couldn't have killed someone at that age, surely?'

'I don't think you killed anyone at all. Shall we listen to some more of this?'

'How long have you lived with Malcolm and Susan?'

'I dunno. I think I moved there last summer.'

'Where did you live before that?'

'In a home – Duxbury House.'

'Did you like it there?'

'No, I hated it. I hated all the people there.'

I paused the recording. Steph pre-empted my query.

'I remember it. I didn't think I'd hated it quite so much as I claim there.'

'Kids can exaggerate. I always said I hated school for instance but when I left, I realised that it hadn't been as bad as I made out.'

'Are you wondering if I hated it enough to kill someone there?'

'We could check if anyone went missing around that time.'

'Okay. Good idea.'

'You seem nervous', I said.

'I think it is because we are getting to situations where we might find out who I killed. It is becoming real now with great rapidity.'

I doubted if she was correct since I still had no belief in her claim. I pressed play.

'Do you mean the staff or the other boys and girls?'

'All of 'em.'

'There must be some that you like?'

'Nope. I hate them all. They're horrible. They're horrible to me and they're horrible to each other.'

'You mean the other children? They're horrible to each other?'

'Everybody is horrible to everybody.'

'But some of the staff must be nice?'

'Miss Cotton. She's okay.'

'No one else is nice?'

'Nope. Just Miss Cotton.'

'In what way aren't they nice?'

'The food is horrible. They call me names. There is a man who calls round to talk to us and he is horrible and creepy.'

Without stopping the tape, I glanced at Steph but she just gave an urgent shrug as if to say, let it run.

'What do you mean?'

'He takes the people away one at a time to speak to them. He smells and he touches them.'

Steph was frowning heavily now.

'Has he touched you?'

'No. He only touches the boys.'

'Have you been in a room alone with him?'

114

'Yes.'

'Has he done anything?'

'No. Not really.'

'What do you mean by not really? What sort of things does he do that you don't like?'

'I just don't like being in a room alone with him.'

'What do you think should happen to this man?'

'Dunno. He shouldn't be allowed to come and see us.'

'What's his job?'

'He talks to us about things.'

'What things? What sort of things does he talk about?'

'If we're okay at school and how we're feeling. Just stuff.'

'Does he ever ask you things you don't want to talk about?'

'Spose.'

'Like what?'

'Dunno. School, that sort of thing. If I feel sad.'

'Anything else?'

'No. Just that stuff.'

'Would you like to have a mum and dad instead?'

'Spose.'

'Would you like to find your mum and dad?'

'I... dunno. They might not be very nice.'

'Why do you say that?'

'Well, they didn't want me.'

'Why do you think they didn't want you?'

'Dunno. I must have been bad.'

'Do you remember your mum or your dad?'

At this point there was a long pause. The room was almost silent. Stephanie sniffed.

'Stephanie. Do you remember anything about them?'

I glanced at Steph as we listened, hoping for a reply. Her face was still. She was utterly transfixed by the recording, staring at the start/pause button as if willing it to force the sequence along. She didn't look at me and the silence continued.

'Stephanie. Do you remember something about your dad? Is it something bad? Can you tell me about it? Maybe I would be able to help.'

Stephanie – the young one in the recording – made a sound which became a sob and then crying. This continued for maybe twenty seconds before Balfour intervened.

'Did something happen? Is there something you want to talk about?'

The crying eased off and then she said didn't want to talk about it.

The two chatted generally for a minute or two and her mood seemed to lift and soon the problem of talking about her father had disappeared. She was happy again. He tried to take her further back into her childhood, but she seemed stuck where she was at nine years old. He brought her forwards in time with greater ease and she talked a little bit about her teenage years which were fine, with only the usual boyfriend troubles and teachers who, she claimed, didn't like her. By this point it was clear that the breakthrough moment had passed. Her tears at the mention of her dad were the most obvious clue as to the problems of her past. We listened to the end by which point Graham and the adult Stephanie were talking about normal things and generally wrapping up the session.

The recording stopped.

'So, what do you think?'

I asked the question already knowing what conclusion she would have reached but, naturally enough, I didn't think it was quite so simple.

'I think I killed my father.'

'What you listened to there doesn't prove that.'

'I know but it points in that direction, doesn't it? I know that I killed *someone*, so he seems the most likely victim. It's a start. That's where you should be looking. You have all the details of my life.'

'You did miss a few out, Steph. Your husband, your child, your disciplinary at work...'

She blushed slightly and said, 'you have been busy.'

'This is what you hired me to do. These are details which I found out, but you could have given them to me.'

'Maybe I was embarrassed. Besides I gave you what is relevant.'

'Okay. It was quite an omission.'

'Well you already know that I didn't kill my ex-husband or my child presumably, and the disciplinary didn't relate to having murdered the office cleaner or the lady who worked in the canteen.' She was defensive now, which was understandable. These had not been good times in her life.

'What was it for?'

'Is that relevant?'

'It might be.'

'Christ. I will tell you but you will automatically jump to the wrong conclusions about it.'

'So, my judgement is that bad?'

'No, I'm not saying that, but I know how it will look.'

'Worse than having killed someone? Worse than that?'

She sighed and swore. Her reluctance made me think that she had a store of embarrassing revelations she didn't want to share.

'It was lateness.'

'Lateness at work?'

'Obviously.'

'You got sacked for that?'

'I resigned.'

'Your lateness was such an issue that you had to resign? How late were you, a year? This must have put a strain on your marriage.'

'My marriage was under strain right from the start.'

'Can we just get this out in the open so that we can move on? Was it drugs and booze that made you late? I am actually trying to help you if you remember. Based on the other night, I think I have already seen you at nearly your lowest ebb, so you can't make things much worse by being honest with me.'

'It was booze. And some drugs. Mainly booze, okay? I don't want you thinking that it was drugs and that's why I think I killed someone. I really did kill someone. Whatever I might have done, whatever I might have taken… I really did kill someone.'

She paused but when I made no reply, she started up again, defensive once more.

'The drugs weren't a big thing. You think that they have affected my brain, or given me delusions, or false memories, or something but it has nothing to do with the drugs. But that's why I didn't mention it.'

'This is stuff you didn't mention before we went anywhere near that party, remember?'

'Even so. Even if I hadn't got myself so fucked up at the party, you'd have put two and two together and got four.'

I frowned.

'That *is* what you get', I said.

'What?'

'Four. That is what you get if you put two and two together.'

'I meant five!', she exclaimed with embarrassed frustration. But that's what you would have thought. In fact, that's what you're thinking now, isn't it?'

'Yes.'

'Jesus.'

'I will still look into this. I said I would take you on again as a client. I can't help having my suspicions though.'

'Fine. What about the hypnotist? Plenty to go on there.'

'That is definitely the next line of enquiry.'

'I'll leave you to it then.'

Steph, it has to be said, looked utterly bewildered and almost distraught at this point and I did feel more than a little bit sorry for her. Whatever chemical abuse she had put her body through – and I was sure it was to a greater extent than she admitted – had taken its toll in my inexpert view. She had her reasons and now she had to battle demons which would have tested the resolve of anyone. However this had come about, she was totally convinced that she had committed murder and that was a difficult thing to live with if you weren't the murderous kind, I supposed.

'If anything else occurs to you...'

'Yes, I'll be in touch. I'll see myself out.'

'Are you okay?'

She stood, ashen faced.

'I'm fine. I'll let you get on with your job.'

I stood too but I didn't make any attempt to follow her out. I heard her go down the stairs and then the communal door opened and shut behind her.

Chapter Eight

Billy turned up with cakes in one of those white cardboard boxes that afternoon. I would have said it was an untypical Billy thing to do but there were no *typical* actions that you could easily attribute to him.

'Cakes? Where did you get those from?'

'I had them delivered to my house. Online ordering, pay by card, delivered to your door. They put 'em on the doorstep, ring the bell and then fuck off. No human interaction required. It's great.'

'Yeah, it, er, sounds good. Just surprised at you. It's more of a lady type thing to do.'

'Racist.'

'If we had a lady working in the office then she might do something kind like this but with blokes its beer and insults, things like that. Not cakes. I do appreciate the gesture.'

'I didn't say that any of the cakes were for you.'

'Well, fuck off then and take your shitty cakes with you. They look horrible anyway.'

'I didn't say it… but one of them *is* for you. That shoe bun', he said pointing.

'In which case I would like to retract my previous criticism of the confectionary/bakery items you have brought to the office.'

'Thank you.'

'And it's choux bun.'

'That's what I said.'

'No, you said shoe bun, like a shoe that you put on your foot.'

'How do you know I meant that type of shoe?'

'Because it's you Billy, that's how.'

He shook his head and I made my way to the kettle. I was going to put myself over my two cups a day limit, but it wasn't every afternoon you had buns (you might call them cakes) delivered in a white cardboard box.

'So, what's the latest with the mad axe murderer?'

As the kettle boiled, I explained what had happened with the hypnotist. Billy listened attentively.

'What made you change your mind about keeping her on?'

'She offered to double the fee.'

'Fuckin' hell. Result, or what?'

'I'm not going to take double the fee. But she is desperate. I still don't think she did it but maybe there is something in her past that is causing this whatever it is – delusion.'

'What about all the stuff with the drugs and so on?'

'She says that is nothing to do with it. In fact, she has said she'll knock off the drugs just to prove a point.'

'A lion can't change its spots', Billy replied, both pointedly and erroneously.

We were socially distant as we drank and ate. Billy had been socially distant his entire life.

'So, what do you want me to do?'

'I think you should look into her childhood. She mentioned a care home called Duxbury House. It would be interesting to know if there is any scandal there, or if any children – or staff I suppose – went missing. I want to know what age she was when she was taken into care and what the reasons were. Like I said, I don't think she killed her dad or anyone else but there could be some sort of trauma in there buried deep.'

Billy nodded. He had cream from his bun around his mouth like a four-year-old eating birthday cake. His table manners were perfect, so I knew he was trying to make me laugh. So, I didn't laugh, just to annoy him.

'You think you can do that?'

'I reckon so. We could be barking up the wrong horse', he warned.

I smiled despite myself.

'We could, but we have to look into everything. I am going to look into her visits to the police. I want to know what she said to them and what they said back.'

'Bugger off, probably', ventured Billy.

'Probably.'

'This is probably before she came over here', he advised me.

'It is. She has already told me where she went, so I just need a way to find out what was said.'

We got to work after the coffee and cakes had made the short journey to our stomachs. Billy was surprisingly expert on the computing machine as he called it.

For my part I emailed an old friend who worked for the police in London and told him my problem. He was a desk-bound sort these days, Monday to Friday, nine to five, and he replied almost straight away asking me to give him an hour.

I caught up on a few other bits and pieces and then he emailed back asking if he could talk to me on the phone.

I agreed and the phone rang a few seconds later.

'I'm outside in the rain having a fag and talking to you on my mobile. I don't want anyone listening in.'

'I didn't know you smoked.'

'It's an e-cig. Bloody stupid thing. More of a prop really – gives me a reason to get out of the office. Anyway, I have a name and a home telephone number for someone who dealt with this woman.'

'Good work.'

'Yeah, it is sort of. He's not supposed to discuss it with anyone as you know, so he wants some cash.'

'Oh. How much?'

'Two hundred. It's a lot.'

'Two hundred! I'd want details of Pablo Escobar's current whereabouts for that money.'

'I know but that's the deal. Take it or leave it really. He wants the money up front too. I have his bank details. If you do a bank transfer on your computer, he should get it more or less at once. When he sees it, you can ring him. He's at home now. By the way, you realise that Pablo Escobar is dead?'

'How much do I owe you for that?'

'Free.'

My contact passed me the details and I thanked him. I opened up the company account on the computer but paused before I went any further. There were a number of risks to be considered, not least of which was that I might hand over this cash only to discover that the information he had was rubbish. That was the least of the risks. I had also to consider that the money transfer could easily be traced straight back to the company in the event of an investigation into this officer's conduct. My crime was less severe than his, I supposed, but I was essentially offering a bribe.

Still, it seemed as if I had no option if I wanted to learn what had gone on between Steph and the cops.

With some trepidation, I made the transaction and then waited for ten minutes. I had no idea if that was even necessary.

When I rang, he answered immediately.

'Hello.'

'Did you get the money?'

'Oh. Let me just check.'

I waited. I presumed he was on his smartphone or his laptop but within a few seconds he came back to me.

'Got it. Thanks. What do you want to know?'

'Just about your interview with Stephanie Kuler.'

'She came in and asked to speak to a detective. I was free at that time and she was brought to me. She wouldn't discuss it with the desk sergeant or anyone else. I explained to her that whatever she said couldn't remain confidential between me and her and she accepted that.'

'She told you what she did?'

'She said that she'd killed someone, so obviously I began with the usual questions, who, where, why, that sort of thing. She didn't have an answer to any of those basic things. I asked her what made her think she had killed someone, and she said it was a feeling.

'It sounded pretty stupid. What is your interest in this, if you don't mind me asking?'

'She wants me to look into it for her.'

'Christ. Good luck. She was a lovely lady, and we aren't going to charge her with wasting police time. Not a chance… but by her own admission she had no evidence. If she killed someone, then nobody noticed.'

'Okay, but did you investigate? Did you investigate any aspect of it?'

'With what? Where could we have started?'

'Missing people, maybe from years ago.'

'Cards on the table here… I had a quick check of the database we have but there was practically nothing that could possibly have been anything to do with her. Detectives have a mountain of stuff to deal with. We prioritise. Some things are more important than others and the truth is if we just worked our way through every crime, in order, until we reached a certain conclusion, and couldn't go any further, then we'd never get anywhere. A huge number of crimes don't really get investigated properly because we just don't have the people or the time to do it.

'Our bosses know it and they expect us to check out the most important things and basically ignore the rest of it. That's just how it goes. Even though this was a so-called murder, without a body or any evidence of any sort it just becomes… nothing.'

'So, it wasn't a murder?'

'Without sounding glib, who was killed? If no one was killed, then it isn't a murder. It isn't even a crime. Wasting police time is all it was but she wasn't doing it out of spite. If you ask me, there was just something wrong with her.'

'How did she seem?'

'Fine. She wasn't agitated or particularly upset, it that's what you mean. She was calm and rational. If she'd even given us a name, we could have looked into it but there was nothing to go on. There was nowhere to start.'

'What about murders in other parts of the country?'

'Good point. I did ask her if she'd been anywhere else and could have done it there. You know, like Scotland or somewhere but she said not. Obviously, people have been murdered and in some cases the killer hasn't been found but I guarantee you that she couldn't have been linked to any of them. Even if she had decided to confess, if I had just handed her a murder on plate and asked her to claim responsibility, the forensics wouldn't have matched up. We have to be careful these days. Our evidence has to match the crime, which is fair enough.'

'Right, okay. Is there anything more you can tell me?'

'Sorry. That's about it. In my opinion she needs medical help. A psychiatrist or something.'

'One last thing then. Is there any record of crimes she has committed? Anything?'

'I didn't check but I can do when I go into work next. You can ring me next Thursday if you want. Same number.'

'I might. If I need you again?'

'Fees apply', he said.

We left it there.

***

I sighed and looked over at Billy who was staring intently at the monitor on his computer. He had been listening of course.

'A dead end', I said.

'Worse than a dead beginning. With a dead beginning you don't have to waste any time.'

'I had never thought of that. Yet more wisdom from the great seer, Billy.'

'That's what you pay me for.'

'Yes. What about you?'

'Duxbury House – Wikipedia. Always start with the basics.'

I left him to it but he came back to me with a few *basics* quite quickly.

'Obviously I am going to verify these facts and dig around a little, but just to be getting on with, Duxbury House near Oxford was a county council run care home with up to thirty children. It was closed in 2013 and the site was razed.'

'I can guess what is coming next. When there is bad news these councils, after they have been found out of course, not only jump through every hoop there is but destroy the place where the bad things happened.'

'Correct. Bolting the stable door after the horse has closed. No blame was attached to the council, but it was found that over a period of twenty years there had been systematic child abuse. They always say 'systematic'. Do they even know what it means?'

'It's just the way these morons talk. They don't introduce new measures – they introduce *a raft of new measures*. Once one dick starts talking that way, they all do it. Practically no one ever used the word *furlough* before this pandemic, now everyone is using it. You don't have libraries anymore but *learning resource centres*. There is even somewhere that has a *knowledge park*. What the fuck is a knowledge park? *Healthcare facilities* instead of clinics. *Hubs* instead of... whatever hubs used to be called. Carry on with the grisly details.'

'I'm glad you got that off your chest by the way. It was all carried out on boys. There were three staff involved and all were jailed on about fifty sample cases. There were accusations of activity by Muslim grooming gangs which had been facilitated by staff within the home but none of these could be proven. It was easier to pull the place down and start again in the end.'

'Any disappearances?'

'Yep, but it's going back a bit – 1972 – Rosalind Martin, eight years old, disappeared one night and was never seen again.'

'Stephanie Kuler wasn't born until 1988.'

'Rosalind Martin was the only one and all the sexual abuse stuff was against boys. These bastards get themselves into jobs where they can abuse children. Fuckin' warped.'

'From the hypnotism session there is no mention of abuse at the home.'

'Maybe that isn't where the crime happened. Or…' He held up a single finger for emphasis, 'maybe that is precisely where the crime *didn't* happen.'

'Please explain the difference, Billy', I said with a tiny degree of exasperation.

'Well, what I am saying is, if she didn't murder someone but there is a traumatic event in her past which has made her believe that she did…'

'Yes?'

'Maybe it happened there. The stimulus for whatever has gone wrong in her mind could well have been at the home. She is abused, or maybe she sees someone else being abused and it puts the idea of murder in her mind where it sort of takes root and becomes, to her, a real event.'

'Does that happen?'

'It could do. I mean, the mind plays tricks. Add all the drug use in subsequent years and it could be a right load of scrambled egg in there.'

'And the drug use could be a result of whatever she witnessed or experienced. But it only made matters worse after the short-term relief she felt from getting stoned', I said, half to myself and half to Billy.

'You see', said Billy triumphantly. 'Now we're onto something. She did mention the boys being abused. Maybe she imagined herself killing that man who used to come to visit. Let's face it, this is much more likely than anything else we have got.'

'It does seem to fit.'

'Damn right it does. Even people who don't take drugs can get events from their past mixed up. I can remember things that I think I did when I was a wee boy and yet I know I didn't actually do them. One of them is where I am on the Malone Road and coming up to a corner. Instead of just going round the corner I cut through someone's house. I actually go through the front door, down the hall, down a little flight of steps, through the kitchen, out the back door, down another short flight of steps into the back garden and out through the gate. No one sees me. I can even remember that I'm absolutely brickin' it.'

'But you never did it?'

'Not on the Malone Road!', he said aghast. It was one of the most prestigious areas in the city and hardly a haunt for the likes of Billy and me.

'We have to keep an open mind. What about you try to track down some of the other kids at that home; mid-nineties to when it closed. If there are any that remember Steph, that would be even better.'

'Sounds good. I have a few other bits I want to check out too.'

'That's fine. Maybe my new and very expensive contact in the cops can come up with something. Ultimately Steph is paying for it, although I can't very easily put it down as expenses.'

'Aye. An entry entitled; 'Bribes to police', would look suspect, right enough. Better call it 'sundries'. That covers everything.'

'The good thing about this is that, if we are right, she doesn't have to go to jail. That aspect of it has always troubled me.'

'It has never troubled her. Weird.'

Chapter Nine

Billy was tight-lipped for the rest of the day but that didn't mean he wasn't making progress. On previous occasions, he'd stored up every snippet he possessed until he could finally fit them together as one cohesive piece of... I suppose you would call it... detection. Generally, he liked to present me with the finished product, and it was a technique that suited us both fine for he could get on with what he was doing unhindered and, basically, so could I.

At 16:30 he announced that he had finished.

'I'm going home. I need to think.'

'You have bits that don't fit yet?'

'Aye. She's a funny one, isn't she?'

'Without a doubt.'

'I have a feeling that this is just the camel that sank the tip of the iceberg.'

I nodded at his cod wisdom. Strange to say that I had known him so long I actually understood what that meant.

I finished soon afterwards and closed up, switching off the lights which had been on despite the bright sunlight outside. I paused before leaving the confines of the hall we shared. It was difficult to think that the tiny virus which was causing such mayhem was outside in the air, looking for another victim who could easily be me. Someone said at the time, and I wholeheartedly agreed, that had we been under siege from tigers we would have accepted the need for caution more readily. The fact that the virus was essentially invisible in an everyday context made our precautions seem a little over the top. I think at this stage in proceedings we were getting to the point where the novelty (for some) of the lockdown had well and truly worn off and a return to normality was practically a demand, a right even.

Funny to think we had seen it coming though. We had watched in increasing horror how the virus had started out in China, come under control (seemingly) and then taken hold of much of Europe, marching through country after country like invading troops. Italy seemed to be the worst affected for a time and the pundits, expert and inexpert alike, were predicting that within weeks our own epidemic would be following a similar trajectory. But even knowing what was in store for us we seemed to watch and wait, as if maybe it would pass us by if we didn't make a fuss and kept hidden behind the metaphorical sofa. Looking back, I don't know why we thought that.

In many ways I was reminded of the old double album I had possessed as a kid; Jeff Wayne's War of the Worlds, which began with Richard Burton warning us about Martians watching us from outer space and making plans for the conquest of our planet. As they did so, mankind carried on, blithely unaware that agents of doom had already finalised their plans and would soon be on their way. For me, Coronavirus represented the Martians, but this was real and known and expected and terrifying. Phlegmatic to the last, we waited and then sprang into action. Behind the scenes there must have been preparations being made and the idea of herd immunity was being bandied about. I just accepted it and did what I was told. I'd never had a particular problem with doing as I was told…

Of course, I didn't stand there all night. I took a deep breath and stepped out into the virus-laden air of the city, locked up, and began my walk home. We were told that the air was cleaner because the traffic which usually made it otherwise was now so sparse. I wouldn't have noticed but I was certainly sleeping better at night, getting off much more quickly and not having to get up fifteen times to go to the toilet. If that was lockdown for you, then I personally was thankful for it.

I passed very few fellow voyagers through life on my walk: two Chinese students with face masks (which they often wore anyway), a drunk man in a shiny grey business suit, two uniformed cops in their PSNI garb, which to my eyes just looked wrong (white shirt?), and a skateboarder with a woolly hat and a mass of dreadlocks spilling down his back. He was the only one who made no attempt to keep two metres from me and an image of him falling under a bus came to me unbidden.

Contentment gave way to a feeling of rueful deliberation, the sort of thing that makes you want to listen to sad old ballads when you didn't actually want to be cheered up but rather needed to embrace your mood and work through it, maybe with a glass of Bushmills, or in Steph's case, a line of coke. I suppose I felt lonely. I could have rung Georgina but that would have been the wrong thing to do. You might be thinking that, despite knowing that I did it anyway, but I did not. That didn't stop me wishing that she'd make the call instead but that didn't happen either.

I could easily have listed life's disappointments at that time. There were plenty.

When I got in, I cracked open a can of Coke, slumped in a chair and checked my mobile in case she had rung.

She hadn't, but you already knew that.

***

The sun was bright enough to wake me and that was a good way to enter the new day in my opinion since we associate the sun with hope, and life, and the happy carefree days of our distant youth. Isn't it the case that we had long hot summers? We only believe it because the wet, miserable times when we were stuck indoors watching the *Double Deckers* and *The Aeronauts*, or *Belle and Sebastien* have been blotted out. Maybe our brains are programmed to remember sunlight.

As was my habit, I lay there thinking about the day ahead. There was no great pressure on me with this case simply because I was never going to find that thing that she sought – a dead body. I would seek but I would not find, to paraphrase the Bible. Steph would have to content herself – or come to terms with – something less than murder, although I was far from convinced that she'd accept anything other than a blood-soaked mess of her doing.

The events at Duxbury House seemed to be the most likely source of the illusion of murder. It struck me then as odd that her brain had not, in the years between the present day and the day on which that seed had been planted, turned her story into something more elaborate, even if that extra detail was just as erroneous as the original material. Literally nothing new had come to her. She felt that she had killed someone – she knew, was how she put it – and yet no extra chapters had been added to that basic premise. The who, what, why, where, when remained notable for their total absence. There was as much

136

evidence to associate anything with this murder as there was for the existence of God.

I shook my head. At least I was getting paid to look into this, whereas no benefit could be attached to belief in God. Well, no *financial* benefit.

My mind switched to Georgina. I wondered if she was lying in bed now, staring at the ceiling as I was and wondering how to escape the trap which was her marriage. Perhaps it wasn't as bad as she made out. She and Rod/Ron/Rob almost certainly had good days too, when things seemed okay and life was a bright wonderful experience and not simply a grind to work through until the blessed relief of death. As things stood there wasn't too much I could do to change her situation, especially since they had a child together.

No matter how bad it was, she couldn't easily up sticks and walk out, for she already feared the ensuing custody battle which she somehow felt he was going to win. I didn't know if that was true or not and I also didn't know either of them well enough to really understand who was at fault as their legal and holy bond to each other began to disintegrate. My natural sympathy lay with her; I liked her and didn't like him. He was rich, boorish, loud, cocky. He liked his wealth and the trappings including the trophy wife, the clichéd BMW, the big detached house in the most prestigious part of the city. Rob was a sneering high-flyer, a smug moneyman.

In the garden on that night, I had spotted the ridiculous Gaelic tattoo that had extended down his right arm, stopping just short of his wrist. This was his way of showing that, despite the wealth, the good suits, the fancy car, he was a rebel at heart, a free-spirit who lived the high life, embraced danger and controversy, lived on the edge, one day at a time and to hell with the consequences. He was a wild man really. Or, as it was also known, he was a pretentious knob.

In contrast to Rob the Knob, I did not possess the knack of making money. Did that make me jealous of him? He would certainly think so. He'd be disappointed if he thought there existed people who weren't at least a little bit envious of him, yet I could see his future and it was not good. His waistline would get larger, his cheeks redder, his hair thinner, his liver more knackered until it silently began to give up. He would still try to be the wild man as the years progressed, but it would be harder and harder to maintain and more and more ridiculous to behold.

I had met this man only once but managed to map out his entire life, giving it an inglorious, perhaps painful ending. Materially I had much less than him but what I did have was my modest collection of campaign medals from my years in the army, the years which had moulded me but about which I rarely spoke. Even Billy and I barely spoke about the army, which was probably the one thing we had in common. So, genuinely, I wasn't envious of him for reasons of my own, which possibly only make sense to me.

How would Georgina fare as those same years passed? Would she stay with him, would she leave and take the child so that they might start again? She looked after herself without being overly obsessed with her appearance. I suppose you would say that she was a natural beauty, someone who would age well. Maybe one day her shitty husband would catch himself on and become a better person, not just the garrulous, office-based daredevil of today.

I cut him out of my thoughts and imagined her for a minute. How could we meet again, innocently, and spend time together just being alive? Nothing complicated. That would suit us both for now.

I rubbed my eyes and climbed out of bed.

I was going to work from home today. It was no great hardship going to the office, but I didn't have to be there. After breakfast I switched on the computer and took the unusual step of watching the TV news as I waited. I had given up on the BBC by this point, a once great institution over-run with smug socialists who knew better than the people who dutifully paid their licence fee. Honestly, I didn't know where to get the truth from these days, not just the doctored version of it they wanted me to have. A few more hundred people had died from the virus but there was no talk of hospitals being overwhelmed or of government ill-preparedness. I didn't know if the government had got it right or not, but events seemed to be under control.

I switched off when they began interviewing some no-mark political activist who began ranting about the so-called Nightingale hospitals which had opened but which were apparently underused. In a rare moment of clarity and even-handedness, the BBC presenter did try to make the point that it was better to have these hospitals ready but empty than not there at all with the consequent overcrowding of conventional hospitals. The 'activist' – who pays these lunatics? – was having none of it. I had seen him before, his little bum-fluff cheeks suffused with righteous anger demanding a national government with Tony Blair and Gordon Brown brought back to take the helm. I couldn't have done his job – that level of relentless anger and indignation would have worn me out.

I put these thoughts out of my mind now.

Now I would check out my other cases, one of which had gone rather cold. Freezing. It concerned a railway employee who had gone missing and was thought to be in New Zealand. I had one contact over on the other side of the planet, someone I had never met, but they had come up with a total blank. Again, I suppose that New Zealand was a great place to lose yourself but in parallel with the supposed Hong Kong disappearance of Curt Johnson, there was no single piece of evidence pointing to their arrival in the new country of their choice.

That was the thing about the cases I took on – they weren't bloody easy. I've alluded to it previously, but these were things that the police had already investigated and then put on file when no further headway could be made. The cops had already been in touch with their counterparts in NZ and had come up with nothing. The airlines had no record of this man, likewise immigration.

He had disappeared. So why New Zealand? I had nothing more to go on than his wife's insistence that was where he would go if this ever happened. It was difficult for me to imagine the conversation which might have brought this tiny gem of information to the fore. That in itself was suspicious.

'Hello wife.'

'Hello husband.'

'How are you?'

'I am very well. Did you know that if I ever decided to leave you and seemingly disappear without trace, that I would go to live in New Zealand?'

'No husband, I did not know that.'

It was all a bit convenient. A cynic might have thought it was a red herring to get us all looking in the wrong place.

I had asked her why he would go there, and the answer revolved around their honeymoon in which they took a hired campervan around both islands, exploring the cities, the mountains, the beaches and the wildlife. I have to admit it sounded idyllic, but my natural suspicion made me think that things had subsequently been less so, to the point where she had decided to bump him off.

Naturally enough she wasn't paying me to come to that conclusion, that just happened to be where my mind led me each time. I felt the same way about Curt Johnson and his wife, the latter who was paying me to find her husband. I sensed, without having met their (missing) partners, unhappy marriages in both cases but it was too much of a stretch to think that I was investigating nothing more than elaborate double bluffs. For an unhappy spouse to disappear was not typical but the cases I took on were not typical. A simple divorce would have been easier to achieve and ultimately less painful.

In the case of the railwayman – his name was Mark Collins – I really felt convinced that I should be looking closer to home, but she wasn't paying me to do that; the contract didn't stipulate that I could dig up her patio, for instance.

My NZ contact was coming to the conclusion that Collins had not come back to the country of his dreams. He had checked out the locations that his wife had stated as their favourites on the honeymoon and had asked around, done everything he should have done. There was nothing. Not so much as a hair on Mr Collins's head had made its way back to New Zealand. I would have to tell his wife this and offer to bring the search closer to home, but I was fairly sure that she would refuse. I was not trying to make money from the poor woman, but it was only natural that I shouldn't give up just because he hadn't been where she expected him to be.

How would she have felt had he turned up on the other side of the world? It wasn't my concern, but I couldn't avoid a certain curiosity about it. A photograph of him enjoying a swim in some secluded cove, hand in hand with another woman, was not going to be a sure-fire indicator of a happy and enduring marriage to his wife back in Northern Ireland. She would have to know but it was going to be a bitter blow if she was hoping for some sort of reconciliation.

I frowned.

My life was so much simpler. It wasn't perfect and I was likely to die alone but there were so many complications that just didn't crop up in my life.

I had to ring her but something other than apathy stopped me from doing so. I felt as if I needed to prepare for the conversation I was going to have, to get my excuses for not carrying on lined up, written down in a logical sequence that I could simply repeat as she pleaded with me to keep searching for him. Chief amongst the difficulties I had in dealing with her was a certain evasiveness when it came to giving me a reason why he might abscond. In her view, or the one she shared with me, their life together had been good. They had good jobs, a nice house, good holidays and were planning to have a family. For some people this would have represented the ultimate Stepford Wives nightmare but not apparently for Mark Collins; he was *totally up for it*, she had claimed.

At the time it had seemed like an odd phrase to use, slightly too flippant in relation to years of future bliss and the subsequent disappearance. Maybe my suspicions were firmly rooted in the belief that this perfect, shared life sounded too good, as if it had been created in her mind whilst leafing through a lifestyle magazine. If this was her dream and his nightmare, I doubted that their marriage was worth saving. It was understandable that she had to know what had happened to him of course. If he was living the high life as a surf bum in Plymouth, smoking pot and catching waves, then that was very nice for him; he at least knew what the outcome of his disappearance was. The same could not be said for Mrs Collins who quite understandably sought – and I hate this word, but it fits – closure.

I rang her from my mobile without compiling a list of questions, mainly opting for this to precipitate action because I despise delay and indecision in myself and in others. Billy and I got along well because we were not haverers. We got on with things without arsing about.

She answered and we got down to business after minimal pleasantries had been exchanged.

'I'm sorry Mrs Collins, but there is nothing to indicate that your husband has gone to New Zealand. My personal view is that he is much closer to home. Travel is difficult at the minute, but he could have got to Europe without much problem before the pandemic struck.'

'I'm not sure. I had it in my head that he had gone there. It was our happiest time.'

I wanted to point out that if it was, as she claimed, their happiest time, then why wouldn't he want her there with him when he reprised this period in his life? To say so would not help my situation or hers.

'There is no trace. Both the police and my investigator have drawn a blank. Nothing apart from your own feeling

143

suggests that he has gone there. I think we should be looking closer to home. And another point– you might not like what you find out. If he has left you thinking that the marriage is over…'

'It isn't like that. We were happy. I know exactly what you are thinking and why you are thinking it, but we were happy together and had lots of plans.'

'Maybe he has run away from those plans.'

'We talked about things. He had every opportunity to tell me if things weren't right.'

'Maybe that is how *you* saw it but not how *he* saw it. He might have felt hemmed in or trapped.'

'You are making a lot of assumptions.'

'I know and I am sorry. You didn't hire me to make assumptions about your marriage but in my experience, this is the sort of thing that makes a person disappear. I wouldn't be doing my job if I didn't look at the possible circumstances behind the case. To understand why someone has acted in a certain way might be the biggest indicator of where they have gone or even if there is any point getting them back. I would imagine that you could have your marriage annulled or whatever if he isn't coming back.'

She began crying and I wasn't too surprised. You could say that I had exceeded my brief rather by suggesting that her marriage was over. Presumably, despite what he might have done, she still loved him; it wasn't an emotion which could be turned on or off. Had I been in her situation I think it would have been the uncertainty that would have brought me closest to cracking. Had his body been found, hope would have been removed in an instant, but at least it would have been a starting

144

point for another phase of her life. Potentially. What did I know?

'I'm sorry. I can keep looking but I think he is in Britain somewhere, or maybe Ireland. He could have gone south without showing his passport.'

She stifled a sob and then said, 'maybe I should go to New Zealand.'

'No. No, you shouldn't. For one thing you probably can't get a flight out there at the minute and for another you would simply be following in the footsteps of someone who has already looked in the places you intend to look. You have the advantage of knowing what he looks like but is that enough if he isn't there?'

'I don't know what to do.'

'Look closer to home. With all the information you have given me that is all I can suggest.' I let her hang on the line in silence before I spoke again. 'Is there anything else you can add? Something that you didn't want to consider, or you were embarrassed about?'

Silence.

'Well, I am sorry that we didn't get a result. If there is anything else I can…'

'Wait. There is something else.'

I bloody knew it.

'What?', I asked, keeping the exasperation from my voice.

'I think he was in trouble.'

'With who?'

'I'm not sure', she said.

'Okay. Why do you think he was in trouble? How could you tell?'

'I found a gun in a drawer one time.'

'A gun?'

'A small gun.'

'A pistol?'

'I suppose so.'

'Is it there now?'

'It's gone. I already checked.'

'Did it go when he disappeared?'

'I suppose so. It might have gone before that but when I checked it wasn't there.'

'And what did the police say when you told them this?'

Silence. I broke the silence for her.

'You didn't tell them, did you? You didn't want him to get into trouble. And now he might be in much bigger trouble than you could have imagined.' I shook my head, although she couldn't see me do that down the 'phone. 'You have to tell the police at once. If you don't, then I will. I will be sending you a bill.'

Chapter Ten

Whether you would call that a successful conclusion or not, I couldn't say, but for me it was case closed. I paid my NZ investigator and updated him on the latest development. It would be a few hours before a response was forthcoming unless they happened to be awake right now.

That cleared the decks for me to concentrate on Curt Johnson and Stephanie Kuler. Curt, well, I didn't know how to proceed with him. It looked very much as if his wife was going to be in receipt of a phone call from me telling her that the end of the road had been reached unless she wanted to look closer to home. I wondered what she hadn't been telling me. Was there a pivotal secret, conveniently overlooked, that would seem irrelevant against my brilliance as a detective? Who knew?

My reverie was interrupted by a phone call from Bill.

'Lone Ranger's office, Tonto speaking.'

'Tonto, been ringin' the orifice', he said.

'I'm not there.'

'No shit, Clouseau. Anyway, I have news on Duxbury House.'

'I'm listening.'

'Remember all the stuff I told you about yesterday?'

'Yep.'

'Well I got in touch with someone who worked there and remembers Stephanie Kuler. Remembers quite a lot in fact.'

'That's good. Can the details be shared on the phone?'

'Yep. Stephanie went there when she was about three. Before that she had been with some other sort of facility for younger kids, infants and the like. She won't remember much about this.'

'Okay.'

'Stephanie was in and out of that place over the years. She was a nice kid but troubled as you might expect, so she would get fostered and it wouldn't work out so she'd come back and so it went on and on in a cycle according to this woman.'

'Did she sound reliable? With it, I mean?'

'Yeah, she did. She was a bit taken aback with my accent at first but we had a decent chat about yer woman. Now, the rest of it may or may not have some bearing on what happened to her, but he says that the child abuse was an open secret in the place. Anyone who spoke about it or raised any doubts was ignored or bullied into keeping quiet, their job at risk, all the usual stuff. So, for someone like this lady – single parent, two kids, needs the job – the easy option was to keep quiet and keep her head down.'

'Fair enough. We've had our own scandals over here too. Kincora and Bangor Grammar School; paedophiles operating almost in plain sight. Everyone knows but no one dares to speak out.'

'Jimmy Savile.'

'He probably wasn't even the worst, just the most famous. Go on with your story.'

'So, it was an open secret that there were paedophiles being invited there in the guise of counsellors. There were threats and recriminations if anyone spoke out. She said that several people lost their jobs because they dared to speak out. One friend of hers was dismissed on trumped up charges of physical abuse because she asked her manager about it. Once she'd done that, she underwent a disciplinary on charges of having hit a child, which she lost in short order, was dismissed and then no one would listen to her accusations because it seemed like sour grapes. This all happened dead quickly. The woman wasn't in a union, couldn't afford a solicitor, so had no one to help. One day she was in work, the next she wasn't. Gardening leave.

'Now, about the grooming gang thing. This woman, let's call her Theresa...'

'What's her actual name?'

'Theresa. Anyway, she says that there were some Muslim men who came and went now and again. They were young and suspicious. Those are her words. Immediately it sounds more than a bit racist. They were suspicious because they were Pakistani. You can see how these things – the veracity of someone's claim – fall apart. She says that they came and met with some of the older girls. She went on to say that she thought they were sometimes taken away in cars. She was much less certain on all of this stuff. She was sure about the boys and the counsellors who came to see them but not sure about the grooming gangs. If there was a germ of truth in there

149

then it was almost overshadowed by what would look like plain, old racism.'

'So, God knows what the truth is', I said.

'Yes, but it does paint a picture of an unhappy place. Like Tracy Beaker with menace.'

'Like what?'

'Tracy Beaker. It's a TV programme with… anyway, its set in a children's home. I have watched it with my niece.'

'I'll take your word for it. Carry on.'

'Okay. Duxbury House was not a nice place and it sounds like everyone knew what was going on, but no one knew how to speak out. Now here is where it gets interesting. Are you sitting?'

'Seated', I confirmed.

'Well, get your ears around this. One lady, who had worked there from probably the mid-seventies, decided to become a whistle blower the day after she retired, figuring that no one could get to her once her employment had ceased. She only told this lady.'

'Theresa?'

'Theresa. She only told Theresa and no one else what she planned to do.'

'Okay.'

'She made the complaint and within a week she was dead.'

'No way', I said, genuinely shocked.

'Way.'

'Fuckinell.'

'Exactly. This lady really put the cat amongst the chickens and then she turns up dead from a heart attack. Found dead in her favourite chair with a boxset of El Dorado videos next to her. Just come through the post.'

'El Dorado, that shit BBC programme?'

'The same one. I don't think that's an important detail unless you think that the BBC killed her.'

'You were the one that mentioned it.'

'Yeah, okay. Anyway. The lady in question was sixty-five and a heavy smoker, a bit overweight and so on.'

'So, let me guess. She was a prime candidate for a heart attack and nothing more was ever heard of her complaint against Duxbury House?'

'That is correct.'

'That could be coincidence', I said in my role of devil's advocate. Bill always said devil's *Advocaat*, like the drink.

'But that only helps make the case that it isn't a coincidence. What I mean is they could silence her easily and make it look like a totally innocent, natural death that wouldn't even be thought of in any other light. And what do they do with a complaint made by someone who has just died and can't therefore be called as a witness to any subsequent hearing or procedure?'

'I assume that they should still investigate but when she dies, they have a get out clause just handed to them on a plate.'

'Correct again. Put it like this. If someone came to you asking you to investigate something and then that person died, would you carry on? I mean in the case of natural causes, not an obvious murder.'

'No. Slightly different because I would expect not to get paid in that case, but the basic principle is correct. Do we have any way to link this to Stephanie Kuler?'

'Not from my point of view but this is something we could bring up with her. I'm not saying that she killed this old lady by the way, but it does all add up to something traumatic, I suppose.'

'What about we all get together tomorrow in the office?'

'Socially distant?'

'Always.'

'Fine, give me a bell when you have the details; my diary is free for tomorrow.'

'Do you have a diary?'

'In my head. And it is nearly always free, before you ask.'

I was going to ask him if he had invited Della on a date, but the line was dead.

Was Duxbury House the scene for the trauma that triggered this chain of events, the ones leading to a murder which had only happened in the damaged mind of Stephanie Kuler? It made more sense than anything else I had to work with. I felt encouraged, and even more so when I checked the caller ID on my next call.

***

'Can you talk?'

'Yeah, of course I can. I am at home.'

'I just thought your wife might be there.'

'I have a wife? No one told me. No one told her, come to that.'

'I just thought that a man of your age must be married. Oh God. this isn't going well. I didn't mean to say...'

'Georgina, it's fine. I know what you mean but I am not married. I have been left on the shelf like an unwanted... sock.'

I should have thought of something better than 'sock' but she laughed as if my wording had been a deliberate and conspicuously successful attempt at humour.

'I just wanted to chat', she explained.

'Well that's fine with me. Just finished for the day.'

'Where are you? At the office?'

'I didn't go in today. That's the big advantage of being the boss, that and being able to fiddle tax returns.'

She laughed again. You couldn't blame her with such razor-sharp wit on display.

'Are you alone?', she asked again.

'Yep. Just me. You still think I am married.'

'No, not that. You might live with someone.'

'It is just me alone in this big house, unless I am being burgled and I don't realise it, in which case there are at least two of us. Where are you?'

'On the bus.'

'Oh. The signal is good. Have you been at work?'

'I go in one day a week just to answer telephone calls and that sort of thing. The rest of the time I am just milling about and looking after Jess.'

'Jess? Jess is your daughter, I take it.'

'That's right. She is at nursery today, so I get in and then walk round the corner to pick her up.'

'And what time does Rod get in?'

'Rob.'

'And what times does *Ron* get in?'

'Ha. Funny. About half six. Usually he stops off at the Washington on the way home with his workmates and comes back half-cut but I don't even have that respite available now. Me and Jess – Jess and I – would have a bit of time to ourselves to watch CBeebies without him blundering about and telling me all about work in his loud voice. Like I give a shit. He never stops talking.'

'People who talk a lot are generally talking about themselves, I have noticed.'

'That's him. Anyway, I get less of that time these days. I have to make his tea now, which I can't be bothered with. Usually he would stop off at KFC on his way home.'

'He is still enjoying the bachelor life by the sound of it.'

'That's exactly what he's doing.'

'I don't know what to say.'

'I know. I just wanted to hear your voice.'

I laughed but in truth I wasn't sure how to proceed.

'Well, I am in the office tomorrow afternoon if you were at a loose end.'

***

I was too old to be excited about something like a telephone call from someone of the opposite sex. I'll let you decide if that is true or not. Anyway, I felt quite content and thought that it might be nice to have a drink. Drinking when under great strain is never a good idea and I had never done it. Really. I had always saved my drinking experiences for the good times but even then it had started to slip in the wrong direction. Was it the case that I was having too many good times? I wouldn't have said so but anyway, here I was, times were good, I wanted a drink and I couldn't have one because I had pledged to myself that not another drop would pass my lips.

I had none in the house. That wasn't a measure taken to spare me from temptation but genuinely because I had no need of it. Nor had I so many visitors that I was required to entertain at a moment's notice, or at all. But now, right now, I would have liked a drink. A whiskey. It wasn't the peaty flavour of the drink or any of that old marketing horse crap, I just wanted to feel slightly inebriated. Luckily the feeling passed and I spent the night sober and watching Inspector Montalbano on DVD. It put me in mind not so much of solving crime but of going on holiday, although the

Inspector's beat on Sicily looked a bit dusty and dry. I think it was the perpetually blazing sun that made me think that way.

After it had finished, I made a coffee and then sat on the sofa thinking about just whatever came into my head, which inevitably consisted of Steph and Georgina for two entirely dissimilar reasons. I didn't really know what to do about either of them.

Chapter Eleven

They turned up on time. On the phone Stephanie had sounded almost enthusiastic about the meeting as though a breakthrough was imminent, but here, sitting in the office with some potential revelations to deal with, she looked much more unsure. The reality of her situation was the same, but I guessed that her perception of it had altered. What had been an almost theoretical event was being acted upon and made real with facts being added to the foundation, building, bolstering, filling out, strengthening. A flimsy premise was being turned into a screenplay which would one day be acted out much to her detriment for she was the principle character: murderer and then jailbird. They do say be careful what you wish for. Billy might have said that some *pigeons were coming home to roost.* But he didn't, I just thought it on his muddled behalf.

Ever the gent, Billy stood as Stephanie Kuler entered the room.

'You haven't met Billy. Stephanie this is Billy and Billy this is Steph. I will get the deluxe coffee pot stoked up if you would like a drink.' Both of them looked adequately pleased about this suggestion. There was little in the way of small talk as I made the drinks; Steph could be chatty but Billy was much less so until he got to know, like and trust someone, which didn't always happen at once and in many cases never.

157

Steph was pensive when I returned and sat with them. I had moved the uncomfy chairs slightly further apart for the sake of social distancing, subconsciously prompted no doubt by a slight rise in deaths from the plague reported the previous day. It wasn't going away quickly.

'The main thing for today is to talk about Duxbury House. Billy has been doing a bit of research on the place and I thought if he passed on what he had learned it might spark something, or give you ideas about possible events.'

She nodded and Billy got to work relating the details he had unearthed. Every now and again he looked at Steph for reaction, but that did not particularly interrupt his flow and in a few minutes he had finished. I studied her throughout this process. A frown remained fixed on her face and she certainly appeared to listen with interest, if not enthusiasm. If there was any spark of recognition then it was not obvious to me but perhaps she was a good actress, or perhaps too apprehensive for anything of the sort to show.

Billy spoke of the older lady who had died, and it seemed clear to me that she was hearing this tale for the first time.

When he had finished, she gave a little nod and then lifted her coffee cup to her mouth. There was no tremor in her hand, no sign of increased anxiety, nothing.

'Does any of that ring a bell, Steph? Does it make you remember something you had forgotten?'

'Not really. I am hearing about that place from a different perspective. Before I had my own memories of it but I didn't know anything about that lady who died or anything.'

'We're not suggesting that you killed her by the way', interjected Billy. 'It wouldn't have made any sense for you to do that in the circumstances.'

She nodded but somewhat distantly as if her mind was taking her on a journey of its own volition.

'I remember Theresa.'

'What was she like?'

'Yeah, she was nice if I recall. Someone you could talk to, but I'd forgotten about her.'

'Is there anything there that you had forgotten about?'

'Not really, but it all came out in the hypnotism didn't it?'

'I think from my point of view, this could be where the idea that you killed someone came from. Billy and I are thinking along the lines of a traumatic event which prompted some type of false memory to plant itself in your brain so that you now think you killed someone when maybe you just thought about doing so. Just imagine that you are lying in bed one night, thinking about the day you've had and something bad that someone did to you or that you heard about. Maybe you had a dream and when you woke you had forgotten about it, but it was tucked away in your mind. Maybe it had got stored in the wrong part of your brain, filed away in memories instead of dreams.'

'But is that a thing which even happens?'

I looked at Billy.

'We don't know but this is a place where bad things happened generally and may have happened to you', he explained. 'If what we are saying is correct then it seems likely

159

that it happened here. Unless there are some other terrible events in your life which you haven't mentioned?'

'I don't think so. So, what you are saying is that my memory of this event is false? Maybe it is some derivative of PTSD?'

I said, 'maybe, it is. There is nothing to suggest that you actually killed someone, don't forget.'

'Look, we are not experts at this but maybe we could take you to someone who is.'

'A psychiatrist?', she offered.

'Someone like that, or maybe a counsellor of some sort. I am sure there are such people. I *Gongled* this last night...'

'*Gongled?*'

'He means *Googled*, I said, glaring at Billy. 'He's an idiot. He didn't go to school.'

Thankfully, she saw the funny side of it and smiled, her good mood returning. Perhaps it was the thought that there was a legitimate reason for her belief in having committed murder that stopped far short of having actually done so.

'Well, what I was saying is that there are such things as false memories. There is even something called *false memory syndrome* which is more serious. It could be that you are affected by it which would explain everything you have been going through. Because this false memory is such an extreme event it makes sense that it was triggered by a place such as Duxbury House where so many bad things happened. Some of this is supposition at the minute', admitted Billy.

'I imagine it would be a relief to find out that this was the source of your concerns?', I said.

'Of course.' She hesitated. 'But I think I would have to really *feel* that it had happened that way. It wouldn't be enough just to find out that it might have been that way. Do you know what I mean?'

'I do actually. It has to change your brain chemistry perhaps. You have to fully accept it or it will linger in your mind.' From the corner of my eye, I saw Billy nodding and it was apparent that the three of us were reaching an accord. 'So, the next thing is to make that happen. We need to find someone who can make it official if you like. You need a person to explain it and give you ways to cope with it or to work it out of your system.'

'What do you suggest?', she asked, hopefully.

'A doctor, or more specifically a psychiatrist. If we go to the NHS, you'll be lucky to get so much as a telephone consultation with them at the minute, but if we go private I think we can go to the top of the queue and just cut out all the bullshit referrals and waiting times. Obviously, it comes at a cost.'

'That doesn't matter, I'll pay', she said urgently.

'In that case, you can either do it yourself or we can arrange it for you. The thing is, if we are right about this then you don't really need us any longer.'

As I said these words, a tiny pang of regret rose in my stomach and then subsided again. I could see that she was doubtful about being cut free at this point.

'I would rather you made the arrangements. I don't know…', she sighed before continuing. 'I think I would feel reassured keeping you on until this is sorted. If this doesn't work out, then I might need you again.'

'Right leave it with us. We'll be in touch.'

It was a happier Stephanie Kuler who departed a few minutes later. When I looked out of the window into the far distance, I could see the giant shipyard cranes picked out by brilliant sunlight, their yellow frames combined to spell out a capital letter 'M'. If it was a sign, I didn't know what of.

'What do you think?'

'On the surface of it our work is done', said Billy, contemplatively.

'But you are doubtful?'

'No, it's not that. This false memory thing has got to be it, and if anything the difficulty will be in selling it to her. Like she said, it's going to have to change how she feels, not just give her another possible way of considering it. It's like when a relationship ends and you're trying to convince someone that it is for the better and that she wasn't worth it and all that bollocks, well it just does no good if you can't make them feel it, if you can't make them stop loving that person.'

'This sounds like the voice of experience.'

'Let's be honest here, we've all had our hearts broken.'

'Okay. This all makes sense. Let's make the arrangements for her and see how we go.'

***

Billy made a phone call to a private hospital called Cedar Woods which sounded expensive and possibly even foreign; California or Israel perhaps.

'Dunmurry', he explained.

'Okay. They can take her?'

'They want her to see a doctor for a first referral but it shouldn't be a problem, from what they have said, to make the move to a psychiatrist. After that its *hey bongo* and off we go. Next Friday if we can confirm that she is available.'

'Let's do it.'

***

After they had both gone, I made a short trip out of the office to the Spar shop for some socially-distanced shopping. I had just missed the lunchtime rush which had probably consisted of about five people at most and had made my modest purchases and exited within two minutes. The till person was protected by a screen, but I noticed two bottles of hand sanitizer nearby for their personal use. She was about eighteen and lived her life in the full glow of teenage lethargy. The transaction was carried out without eye contact being made and only a mumbled thanks.

One of my purchases was a packet of cookies, the ones that come in a bulky plastic tray and a loose-fitting outer cover which disguise the actual size of the biscuits within. So, for just less than £2 I had eight biscuits which were much smaller than those illustrated on the packaging. When you worked out that each small, disappointing confection had a unit cost to the consumer of twenty-five pence, it was a rather dispiriting moment.

But Georgina, when she *just happened to drop by*, didn't think so, largely because she didn't eat one. I just couldn't bear the thought of having nothing to eat other than some now-stale 'Nice' biscuits, which didn't exactly scream, *corporate hospitality*.

'We meet again', I said.

'At your centre of operations.'

'I call it the 'Nerve Centre'. Notice how we have got two computers not just one and we have the use of the photocopier upstairs in the solicitor's office.'

'Amazing.'

'This is just the tip of the…', I tried to think of a suitable Billy-ism, 'iceberg.' And failed. 'I even got some new biscuits in. We have *an arrangement* with the Spar shop.'

'What is that arrangement?'

'Anything I want, I go in there, pick it up and then pay for it.'

Georgina laughed.

'That arrangement is more common than you think', she said.

'How was Roy last night?'

'Rob. He wasn't too bad. He ordered in pizza, bought wine, doing the whole wonderful husband thing. The three of us watched some bloody awful cartoon film on Netflix. He was on his phone the whole time and asleep shortly after that.'

'Sounds idyllic.'

'Better than normal perhaps. The bit where he fell asleep was the highlight for me. The problem was that it was late by then. I put Jess to bed and polished off the wine.' She smiled sadly. 'The whole time I was thinking about you.'

'About what a great investigator I am?'

'That sort of thing.'

'Is there something you'd like me to help you with?' It was a genuine enquiry but she gave me a raised eyebrow look in return.

'Where do I start?'

'I mean in a professional capacity. Perhaps I could dish some dirt on him.'

The minute I had said that I felt like a total shit. I didn't like the bloke but that didn't give me the right to help destroy his marriage. I was actually feeling a bit lost with the whole situation. What was I supposed to be doing? Why had I invited her to the office?

'That isn't exactly what I want.'

'I guessed that. The problem is that I don't really know what I should do or how I should behave. What we are doing is wrong.'

'We haven't done anything wrong. Not yet anyway.'

'No, but it is on our minds. Or put it like this, it is on *my* mind.'

'I just like being here', she said.

'Is it the kettle?'

'You know what I mean. I like being with you. You're so different from him.'

'That's what you think now. Maybe I am *exactly* like him.'

'Are you?'

'No, but you don't know that for a fact do you? I am a fair bit older than you for one thing. How do you know that I am not a big drinker, worse than him and violent too? How do you know that I don't spend my free time watching re-runs of epic FA Cup finals? I might have a shrine to Kylie Minogue in my living room. I seem better than Rog now but that could all pass with time.'

'I would take the risk. Besides I don't believe any of that. Re-runs of FA Cup matches? Not really you. The shrine?'

'Madonna.'

'That's worse.'

'The thing is I don't know what we should be doing. You don't want to leave him because he will fight you for custody of Jess. I totally understand that but what are you suggesting we do, have an affair?'

'It sounds terrible when you use that word.'

'I could use a different word but it would be the same thing. I don't like Rolf either, even though I hardly know him, but I am not sure what we should do.'

'Just enjoy being together and take our time and see what happens.'

'You might get tired of me quickly.'

'Probably, in which case I will ditch you.'

'That's the point really. I know you are saying that as joke but that is what will happen.'

'You don't know that. You're not the one doing anything wrong. It's me who is in the wrong. If he was a better person, a better father and husband, things might be different, but he doesn't even try these days.'

I didn't say anything but listened instead. She ran a hand through her long hair and then smiled her perfect smile.

'It's all very tempting. I have to admit you feel the spark straightaway when it's there. It's like the old notion of love at first sight.'

'Maybe that's what it is.'

'Are you ready for one of those biscuits yet?'

'You're changing the subject.'

'In every relationship the subject of biscuits eventually comes up.'

'If we weren't socially distancing, I'd punch you in the ribs.'

'Playfully?'

'Probably not.'

'Fine. Let's take it as it comes, day by day, that sort of thing.'

'Okay.'

'Okay.'

'Do we still have to socially distance?'

'Yes.'

She had been leaning against the edge of a desk but now she straightened and came towards me.

'Our first kiss', she promised.

***

Well, there you had it. We had officially crossed a line. I didn't think it would last but what the hell? If old Rock couldn't treat her right then...

But it still didn't feel right to be honest. It felt good, but not right. I would just see what happened.

'How are you getting on with Steph?'

'Professionally speaking?'

'Is there another interpretation of my question?'

'What I mean is that she invited me to that party, and I wondered if she had hoped that something more would come of it.'

'Did anything more come of it?'

'Obviously, but not with her. You and me. To answer your question, I think we might be making headway.'

'Good.' She didn't press me for details, and I didn't offer any specifics.

'She said she'd stay off the drugs and there is a programme of treatment we are going to try.'

'So, you don't think she killed anyone?'

'I never did. You know how deeply she believes in all of this, but we might have a way through it. She seems encouraged.'

'I haven't seen her since the party so I have no idea about the drug-taking stuff. I think she was quite taken with you but she must realise that her behaviour put you off.'

'There was never anything there. I am not blind to her good looks but even before I got to her house to pick her up, I knew she had only invited me to get a lift. It's not a great start.'

'I suppose she can be selfish. Most people are. She's okay though. Nice enough. The whole thing about the murder wasn't the only thing she ever spoke about or anything. She was obsessed by it but didn't bore the arse of everyone with it.'

I was listening but there are times when I think I lapse into a profound silence. This was one of those times.

'What's up?', she asked.

'I was just thinking, but don't ask me what about. Whatever it was has gone now. How many years age difference do you think there is between us?'

'Does it matter?'

'Not now. It might later.'

'Ten.'

'You seem certain.'

'It was a figure I clutched from the air. It doesn't matter to me.'

'Next question then. What is your dream?', I asked.

'You sure about this?'

'Yes. I asked the question after all.'

'The dream is to live somewhere nice with a simple job, simple house, the sun in the sky, eating freshly-made food every night. Just me, you and Jess.'

'Italy in that case.'

'I love Italy. Not Rome or Naples but maybe just somewhere in the mountains. The simple life. I'd like to write a book too. A hundred words a day on an old typewriter. Just me in a little attic room with an old-fashioned record player and a few oddments. The window open and the smell of fresh olives.'

'Do olives have a smell?'

'No idea and they taste bloody horrible too, but I am just painting an image for you. At night we could take a walk down to the beach and have a swim and watch the sun sinking on the Med in a dazzling shower of orange and yellow rippling on the water's surface.'

'That's a fair bit of detail there.'

'This is what I dream about every night. I get it all organised in my head as I am getting ready and then start dreaming it once my head is on the pillow. I have built it up over the years but that is always the same basic thing. Sometimes in my dream I move out there by myself and find the man of my dreams and sometimes I have already found him and we go out there together exploring and looking for the perfect place to settle down, with mountains, the sea, beaches, a little town with a market, a café and a bar.'

'A Spar shop?'

'Naturally', she said shaking her head. 'We find our perfect house and make our plans for how we are going to do it up. We get the whole thing re-wired, new floors and roof, new windows and doors, new plumbing and electrics. While that is being done, we *sort of* camp out in one room and then we fix it up from scratch, buying stuff from flea markets and auctions and doing it up.'

'And when that is done you write your book?'

'I reckon.'

'Sounds good. You wouldn't miss Belfast?'

She looked out the window, across the city to the harbour, the shipyard and the coast beyond.

'Maybe', she said with a sigh. 'But it will always be here. I can come back and visit but I don't think I would. I lived here all my life apart from about two years when my parents moved to Newtownards of all places. There isn't much to keep me here perhaps. Ron will never move, I know that.'

'He's called Rob', I reminded her.

'Not anymore, not in my head at least. The only thing the name Rob had going for it is that it rhymes with knob.'

I laughed.

'Will I be in this dream tonight?'

'You have been since I met you. Before that it was just some random bloke. It's much better that I actually know the person I want to have this new life with.'

I was going to point out that it was never going to happen. This was all just pie in the sky and that we all got crushed in the end and lived our second best life if we were lucky but somehow, looking at her face, suffused with hope and optimism, I couldn't utter the words. I didn't want to ruin her dreams. They were all she had, and in that respect, she was doing better than some.

'What about you?'

'I dunno. A whippet farm in Comber.'

'Seriously. What is your dream?'

'I am too old.'

'That's rubbish.'

'My dreams have changed over the years. I always wanted to be in the army and to win a medal for bravery. That sounds completely stupid now that I say it.'

'I don't think it does.'

'But then I did my time in the army, didn't get any bravery medals, left and my dreams changed. Recently I have thought I should have been a professional boxer – I was a decent amateur – but my dreams change. In some ways I am happy enough with my life as it is. This thing with you, whatever it is, is just a bonus.'

'So, if I asked you to come to Italy with me for this fresh start, would you come?'

She needed me for her dreams until someone else came along so I said yes. It wasn't necessarily a lie, but I knew that it would never happen.

'Italy has its downsides too.'

'Not in my dreams', she replied.

Chapter Twelve

Cedar Wood was set in a small wood – I suppose you'd have to say it was a wood, but whether it was composed of cedars or not I couldn't say – set well back from the road, on a hill leading out of the city. A curved driveway led through beautifully tended lawns and flower beds, the effect being, whether intentional or not, of approaching the grand house of the wealthy businessman who had perhaps built the city. Where there might have been a Bentley parked there was merely an Audi Q7, and where the stately home should have dominated, there was in fact a modern redbrick hospital with chrome features, yards of glass and a stone portico. It was still impressive.

I glanced over at Steph and smiled but she looked nervous, worse than I had seen before, her face fixed in a near grimace. She had insisted that I go with her and I could hardly refuse since she was paying me, but I would have expected that a friend would have been more appropriate for her and a greater source of comfort.

'This is it. There is nothing to worry about.'

'It's not the place, it's what I might find out.'

I parked between a metallic grey minibus and a Lexus 4x4, but we didn't leave the car immediately. It was early but the sky was cloudless, the purest blue expanse I had ever seen. The temperature was already in the twenties (*centipede* in Billy-talk).

We had spoken about her doubts, but it was time to reiterate them, lest she refuse to get out of the car.

'The doctor just wants to hear about the problem. They're not going to diagnose you and they certainly aren't going to ring the cops. This is just the first stage they go through to make sure that you get the right treatment.'

'That sounds like you're reading it from a glossy brochure.'

'It probably does say that in a brochure somewhere but essentially that is the case. Come on. Let's just get in there and get started.'

She was wearing jeans and white trainers today along with a lightweight jumper that hung loosely on her shoulders. It was a movie star look and she carried it off well, especially in the grounds of Cedar Wood, which, now that I looked at it, could have been someone's Beverly Hills mansion. Steph wore her hair pulled back in a ponytail accentuating her great features. I could see why she and Georgina were friends; beauty attracted beauty.

We both climbed out of the car and I locked it before asking her if she was ready. Her confidence seemed to have returned in some measure as she answered.

'Come on', she said. 'What are we waiting for?'

The Beverley Hills effect was reinforced by the receptionist who was young, pretty and wore a white uniform as if she was a member of the clinical staff. Everything inside was spotless, modern, efficient, laden with chrome like our work kettle. We signed in and sat for a short time waiting to be called through to the surgery.

'It's very chrome-y', said Steph, conspiratorially.

'I don't think that's a word but I know what you mean. It is part of the whole Cedar Woods experience. They don't want you sitting in a wipe-down plastic-seat waiting room with a load a coughing school children, a fat woman in leggings and flip flops with breathing problems, an old man with a gammy leg and a drug addict who just sits in the corner singing and doesn't have an appointment.'

'You paint a picture with words', she said, laughing.

My witty retort was prevented by the sudden appearance of another receptionist in white who called us through with a Hollywood smile and a diluted version of a Belfast accent, almost American sounding.

We stood but I had to ask her one more time.

'Are you sure you want me there. I might look like your father.'

She raised an eyebrow and said, 'big brother maybe.'

The doctor was a woman in her late forties, well-dressed but managing to seem relaxed and friendly. This, I thought, is where your money goes. She was only as good as any other doctor, so you're paying to get to the top of the queue and to be treated like a celebrity. She had a bottle of hand sanitizer on her desk and nearby a mask, both of which spoke of an awareness of the need for Covid-caution, the intent rather than the act. The wall behind her held the expected certificates declaring her to be a doctor, I imagine. The University of Larne or somewhere. There was a photograph obviously taken by a professional photographer showing her beaming in the company of a well-dressed man in middle age and two very pretty young women in their early twenties. If my detective skills were any good at all, it seemed to me that she probably knew these people. Just a hunch as they say.

'I only know a tiny bit about you, Ms Kuler', said the doctor after we had sat and the basic introductions had been made. I was, according to Steph, her friend. Well fine, if that's what she wanted. The truth as I didn't need to be there in any capacity.

She began with the usual shocking admission; she had killed someone. From there the story developed along now familiar lines – familiar to me, that is. I watched Steph as she spoke about her situation with total conviction and occasionally fired a surreptitious glance at the doctor to see how she was taking the news. Of course, she didn't allow shock or disbelief to register and took the whole thing in her professional stride. In twenty-odd years she'd heard it all.

When Steph had finished, she sat back in her chair. She had told the whole story, which in truth was a series of blanks held together with some sort of invisible narrative tape, and had done so in a rational-seeming and eloquent manner.

'Okay. Well, my first thought is that this is a false memory. Have you heard of that?'

'We have talked about it', said Steph.

'If you witness an event, you generally get a certain picture of it recorded in your mind. The picture will have some level of detail but often not very much, especially if the event is not important to you. The example that is often used is of passing someone on the street. You might register that they wore a green jumper for instance but nothing else because you didn't know this person, didn't stop to talk to them and there was no major event or even minor event attached to their presence. In most cases you pass someone and don't register anything about them but let's continue with this person in the green jumper.'

Steph nodded. I nodded too although I didn't have to. I just liked the story.

'You notice this person because the green jumper is very brightly coloured or has a pattern on it. Now someone asks you about another detail of their appearance. What colour was their bag? The person in the green jumper is long gone so you can't check but it is only natural that you think you have noticed their bag. You notice the jumper, so why not the bag?

'So what colour was the bag? First of all, you think it was green – you have that colour in your mind. Then you decide that they would not have two green things on, so you think it was yellow. Then you get asked about the pattern on their jumper. There was a simple motif; what colour was that? Well, it can't have been green because that wouldn't show up very well, so you pick another colour. Eventually you have created an entire look for this person and most of it is completely wrong because you didn't actually take much notice.

'If you hadn't been asked for any of this extra detail, you would almost certainly have forgotten all about this person, their jumper and what colour it was. Now, however, you have a false memory of an event. That is just one example of how it can happen. Sometimes you merge events together into one event. When the police interview witnesses, they take into account that the descriptions of events can be very inaccurate. Witnesses can inadvertently add in detail which wasn't there but which they think fits the events they saw. They might want to be a good witness out of a sense of duty, so they tell the police what they think might be most helpful to them. Later, even though much of what they say has been wrong, they themselves accept it as the truth because the police officer wrote it all down and thanked them. They have been validated if you like, and in the process the information they gave over has also been validated. From now on it is the truth but in reality, it never was.

'Several witnesses to the same event might give several versions of what they saw. Sometimes only the detail varies but often much bigger details are conflicting. Things that happen during periods of great stress are often recalled inaccurately simply because there is so much going on that the brain is unable to retain an accurate record of the event. The passage of time doesn't help. Having dreams doesn't help. Taking certain types of drug certainly doesn't help.'

I nodded and made an effort not to look across at Steph.

'Now when we get to the stage where these false memories are impacting upon your daily life we call that False Memory Syndrome, and my first thought as a GP is that that is the problem here. You are struggling to come to terms with an event which never happened. A murder is a very extreme false memory to have but there is no doubt in my mind that this is a false memory.'

Steph sighed and frowned.

'Everything you have said makes sense but to me it still feels like it happened', she said.

'Which is why we need to refer you on. Initially I would like you to see a psychiatrist and then take it from there. I am sure we can help you, Stephanie.'

'So, you think it is a false memory?'

'Based on what you have told me, I don't think it could be anything else. These happen to everyone, but your case is more extreme than most. I once took two things back to a shop because I realised that I didn't actually need them as I had supposed. The shop was fine about giving me a refund because the stuff was unused and still in the packaging. They set about doing the refund on the till and then told me that I had only purchased one of the items at the shop. I argued with them but when they showed me their copy of the credit card receipt only one of the things was on it. They had the proof so I just had to accept they were correct. I got my refund and took the other item back home, completely perplexed.

'It sort of played on my mind all day until, as I was trying to get to sleep, I remembered that I had bought the other thing in a different shop because it hadn't been in stock in the first one. This was a false memory because both things should have come from one shop – so that is what I had remembered. The fact that I had to go to a second shop wasn't important, so my mind just forgot about that detail. If I had had to go to court for some obscure reason, I would have sworn on a bible that I had bought both items at that shop. But I would have been wrong.

'False memories. They happen all the time but in most cases they're not important.'

I looked across at Steph, pleased for her that we were edging ever closer to a resolution. Her face seemed to express relief. Her expression seemed to say, *'we're not there yet but I have hope'*. And when we parted company with the doctor, she was grateful and pleased that she had come. Maybe it was a small step for her, I don't know, but it was an important first move in the mission to eradicate this murder from her mind.

In the car I said to her, 'that went well.'

She was clicking her seatbelt into place.

'It did. I do feel quite encouraged. Not out of the woods yet but it's a good start.'

I nodded, pretty pleased with the whole situation. I started the engine and then said, 'so are you coming around to the view that you didn't kill anyone, now?'

She thought about this for a couple of seconds and said, 'no'.

Chapter Thirteen

She rang me when her appointment came through and asked if I would go with her once again. It was a week away which gave me time to try to clear up the Curt Johnson case, so I agreed. She then asked if I wanted to go out for a drink.

'I don't drink', I stated, plainly.

'You can have a coke or something.'

'Also, I don't normally socialise with clients.'

'The investigator's code?'

'Something like that.'

'You actually just don't want to go out with me', she said.

'I suppose not. There is a big age gap, we have nothing in common, you're a client and I can't help remembering the party we went to and what a disaster that was. It's nothing personal.'

'If you change your mind...'

'I've got your number.' I wasn't going to change my mind. 'I'll pick you up next week for the hospital.'

Her response sounded sulky as if my refusal to meet her was of more importance than the success of her treatment.

'Right. See you then.'

She was gone. I sighed as I made a note of the date and time in my diary and then I just sat, taking time to order my thoughts. The need to do so coincided with my mind going blank and I found myself just staring, suffering from a transitory case of investigator's block. It's not a serious condition.

A hundred other things whirled around in my brain but eventually I came onto the topic of false memories, which at least related to what I was trying to do. In particular I recalled Billy's strange dream or memory, of cutting through someone's house to get to the next street, and I found myself smiling. It wasn't the act which raised his doubts but rather the location; the Malone Road was much too posh for him. It was only natural that I try to sort out some false memories of my own. The trouble was, how did you know which were false and which were real? That was the whole point about them; they seemed real, fiction masquerading as fact.

There were a few things which raised my suspicions but only now did I have a name to give them or the possibility of explaining to myself that they might not have occurred, or occurred as I remember them. These were things which had troubled me slightly, although they hadn't brought my life to a standstill. One related to an incident in which a truck had gone out of control and almost swiped me from the pavement.

Twenty years or more had passed and yet I could still picture the artic trailer as it careered down the road almost seeming to catch up with the cab. In my perfect recollection it was probably at forty-five degrees out of alignment which, since it was ostensibly travelling in a straight line meant it was at one hundred and thirty-five degrees to the cab. I don't remember the sound of screeching rubber but it must certainly have made a din, and I don't remember the smell either, just that image of the trailer coming towards me as I walked on the pavement on my way home from work. Needless to say, I jumped clear, the trailer passed me by and, as I surveyed the area to see who else had witnessed the event and had also seen me jump away to save my life, I noticed that the rig was now turning left, taking a road onto a small industrial estate.

However, this came to be, the truck and trailer had corrected themselves. As I stood there, shaken by this event, I noticed that there was no one else around. Not one single person. It was early afternoon and I was heading home. I hadn't been drinking or injecting myself with magic mushroom residue and yet the entire population of that busy street had been vacuumed up, leaving me isolated, shocked and bewildered. At the very least I needed someone to whom I could say, *'did you see that?'*.

So, did it even happen, or happen as I recalled, and was there really no one else there? Has my mind doctored the image as time has worn on? I've recounted this event several times over the years and you might assume that I have elaborated the story on each occasion, but on reading the account I have written you can see that it isn't particularly detailed, and with each retelling the story has been as you see it now. I have not added in the presence of a UFO, or claimed that driver had crossed eyes, or wore a blue shirt, but the very fact that I bother to recall the story at all must mean that something out of the ordinary occurred, otherwise all that happened was a lorry drove past me and then turned left to go to an industrial estate, which isn't that thrilling or memorable.

But is that precisely what happened? If so, my false memory was built upon that brief moment when I perceived the trailer to be coming at me and now that I know about the

184

phenomenon of false memories, it seems the most logical explanation. Yet, like the murder supposedly committed by Steph, it seems real to me.

Another false memory to mention isn't even mine; essentially, I am borrowing it from a friend. This friend once told me about a patrol he had taken part in during the Troubles in Northern Ireland. I think he was in south Down, maybe Newry or around that area – *Bandit Country* anyway. He swears blind that this happened; he was walking past either a streetlight or an illuminated road sign – something with a ground-level compartment for maintenance access – when the object in question exploded. It was a small explosion, one which he always thought had been a partially failed detonation of a larger bomb. This is feasible by the way. The bit which he could never comprehend or come to terms with concerned the fact the no one else on the patrol, and there would have been at least three others, noticed it.

Despite his certainty and the respect in which he was held by his fellow soldiers, none of them had heard, seen or smelled anything. I hadn't been there but I believed him for a number of reasons, not least of which was the fact that he had nothing to gain by making it up. Now, having been with Steph when she had spoken to the doctor, I put it down to a false memory. But in this case, in Newry, I didn't doubt that something had happened, but the question was did it happen in reality or just in his brain?

The third thing was something which had troubled me more than anything else in my life. During my illustrious army career, I had had the honour of defending the Saudi Arabians from the Iraqis and of liberating the Kuwaitis from the same bad people. I was very brave but I don't like to talk about it...

Except for this one thing.

One night, not long after the war had officially started, we were warned by a well-placed source to expect a missile attack on our base. Well, not precisely on our base but on the town in which our base was located. The missile in question was a Scud, made by the Russians using WW2 German technology. It had a short range and was very inaccurate necessitating a large target like our town. That night we awoke to the sound of two explosions, one straight after the other. This was our attack. It had to be. We carried out our drills, which involved putting on extra kit which protected us from whatever nasty potions might have been loaded into the missile and then waited.

There was nothing to do but wait. Collectively we went back to sleep and then, upon receipt of the 'all clear', we removed our NBC gear and relaxed. These events all happened as I described, and I can say that with certainty because many years later I watched a documentary in which these things were described. However, the reason why I am mentioning this now in relation to false memory is that the following morning we had a short parade, in which far from being top of the agenda, any mention of the missile attack had been utterly removed.

I was astonished; open-mouthed style, actual, full-blown, over-acting astonished…

As we were dismissed, I turned to my fellow soldiers, or some of them at least and said, 'what about the missile? What about the missile attack?' I was met with bemused smiles or shrugs. No one knew anything. No one had heard anything.

And yet the lights had snapped on after hearing those bangs – bangs which we were practically waiting for, remember – and we donned our kit and masks and everything. One of our NCOs almost had a breakdown such was the shock of the event. We had checked each other out, ensuring the seals on the hoods fitted tightly around our respirators. This was the whole shebang... and now, as I stood there... it wasn't.

It took me days to come to terms with it. I never got to the point where I thought that it hadn't happened, but I certainly got to the point where I realised that it wasn't worth mentioning.

You see – and I didn't think of it this way at the time – the false memory wasn't mine, it was everyone else's. Later, it made sense to me. The army didn't want its soldiers to think that they had been gassed even though those same soldiers had been told that such an event was a virtual certainty given the previous conduct of our enemy. So, to get around this inconvenient event, it simply erased the attack from the official record if you like. It was far more subtle and far more effective than telling us that it hadn't happened. Simply failing to recognise that a missile had exploded in our midst meant that for the majority of soldiers that night, it never happened.

I could go into all sorts of philosophical arguments here; if a tree falls in a wood and there is no one around to hear it, did it make a noise? Personally, I think that it didn't if there is no biological or man-made apparatus around to pick up the consequent vibrations in the air, which are what we consider sound to be. But that's not the point. The point is this: if you interview x-number of soldiers about the missile attack on their town and none of them remember anything about it, did it happen? What if only one in a thousand states that it did happen? What if ten soldiers say it happened, but forty thousand say it didn't? What then? Who is right? Did the missile fall or not?

It doesn't make sense and yet it makes perfect sense. Our perceptions were so easily twisted, precisely when our brains should have rebelled. I never stopped knowing that the missile had fallen on us and I felt like punching the air and telling someone, 'I bloody told you so!', when I watched that documentary years later.

But you know what I am going to say: there was no one to tell.

What of those who had been there on that fateful night but who didn't watch the programme? Their false memories are intact. Even some of those who were there probably watched it but had no recollection of any bangs in the night sky. They might not have recognised the event as something which involved them. This was the attack that we were warned about, the one which we heard, the one which we reacted to, the one which resulted in an all clear being issued, the one which never happened.

False memories. We've all got 'em.

Chapter Fourteen

Curt Johnson. What do we do with a problem like Curt Johnson? Well, for starters I would ring Billy and see if any of his contacts could shine any light on what was happening there. Curt had disappeared off the face of the Earth leaving only some electronic evidence that he had booked tickets for Hong Kong. The police had turned up nothing but she – Mrs Johnson – was certain he had made the intended plane journey and wanted to know what had become of him. That was fair enough, especially considering she was pregnant with his kid, but it did not bode well for a happy ending. Had some information slipped her mind? I thought it likely. No one wanted to admit that their relationship was in serious decline, or that the blame for that might come their way. The fact that she was pregnant made things more complicated.

Billy arrived at 09:30.

'I don't know what I'd do without Netflix', he said. 'Some of the stuff is crap but in amongst it there's some brilliant stuff. Have you watched *Narcos*?'

'Every series.'

'Emilio Escobar. What a dude. Makes the IRA look like nuns.'

'Pablo', I corrected. 'Emilio Estevez and *Pablo* Escobar.'

'Emilio Estevez was a drug lord too? The bastard.'

'I'm sure there were a few nuns in the IRA. Definitely some priests. I meant to ask about the zombies around your area. Still a problem?'

'Not so much. Things have quietened down on the zombie front. Either I am just getting used to them or they are getting used to be being out and about with still-living people. It's a bit of give and take, I think. Tolerance is my watchword. We have learned from past mistakes. Once things have calmed down with the plague, we will have to make sure that zombie children are educated alongside living ones or we'll just end up with the old Protestant-Catholic thing all over again.'

'Or worse we'll end up with Protestant zombies and Catholic zombies.'

'Correct. It's time to start anew. This could be part of a bright new future for Northern Ireland. We should look to a future in which everyone, black and white, rich and poor, Protestant and Catholic, Muslim and Jew, zombie and living...'

'... and all other combinations of the above...'

'... can exist in harmony and peaceful co-existence with a common purpose and...'

'... all that shit...'

'That was a beautiful moment. We should be a double act at the United Nations. Like the Chuckle Brothers but for world unity.'

'Okay, well moving on, I need you to do a bit of digging around. Curt Johnson. Have I mentioned him?'

'The soldier missing in Hong Kong?'

'That's him.'

'No, you haven't.'

'Good. Well, he almost certainly isn't there, so what I want to know on behalf of my client is, where has he gone to? There is a very thin file on him on the computer along with details of his wife.'

I waited as Billy brought the file up.

'Okay, got it'. he said.

He began reading at once. Billy had the knack of being able to grasp a new situation with great speed.

'First thing that jumps out is the fact that this is a civilian address not a military one.'

'I think that since most of the army is based in Britain now, they can buy their own houses without much difficulty.'

'Or it could be that they have separated.'

'She hasn't said so but that doesn't mean anything.'

Billy was still skimming the file.

'Royal Engineers, sergeant, she's pregnant, Hong Kong plane tickets.' He pulled a face. 'I have a theory.'

'Already?'

'It will take a bit of time this one, but I bet I am right.'

'I know you don't like to do this but give me the outline.'

'Okay, my theory then. They're separated. The kid isn't his…'

'So far, so totally plausible.'

'He has been sent off somewhere by the army in a sort of secret-stylee way and she hasn't been told because she doesn't need to know.'

'SAS?'

'Could be. That's why it could be tricky to get to the truth, but I have contacts and ways and means. It's all to do with what people *don't* tell you, if I am right. The problem is, if I work this out, I don't know what you are going to tell her.'

'I'll cross that bridge when I come to it. Get to it, Robin.'

'Robin?'

'Batman and Robin.'

'Yeah, I understood the reference. But I'm Batman.'

'No, I am Batman. I pay you.'

'Batman doesn't pay Robin.'

'He must do. Why does Robin turn up for work and what does he live on?'

'Does Robin have his own house?'

Eventually we got to work but I took a break that afternoon to go to the park, where I would happen to bump into Georgina who had gone shopping. The government had begun to ease the lockdown restrictions, although the two-metre rule still applied. The park benches were all occupied, some by a single person next to whom no one would dare sit.

A few foreign students, presumably trapped in Belfast when the calamity fell, hung around in tiny groups smoking and chatting about philosophy, how to save the planet and how much they hated Boris Johnson, Donald Trump and everyone else who had deprived them of their future. I could picture their squalid student houses, with posters of Greta Thunberg transposed into a heroic Che Guevara type pose and piles of dishes mouldering in the sink next to the wash basket which overflowed with stale hockey kit and a bin filled to the top with rotting lentil burger carcasses and the remains of fat joints.

A generalisation maybe but tell me I'm wrong. It wasn't a complaint. If it wasn't for these young geniuses, where would the next generation of call-centre psychologist/media studies/sociology scholars come from?

There were other people there too, some of whom, for all I know, served a useful function in society, with jobs and who paid taxes and kept the economy going. This was shorts and T-shirts weather. The office girls kicked off their shoes, the men rolled up their sleeves and everyone stayed two metres apart. In the air, unseen, that tiny virus, fragile and barely alive, circled like a microbial vulture looking for a host that would give it life and enable it to reproduce.

Viruses, when you think about it, only want the same things as you and me, the difference is that because we think and reason, we believe that we need more from life than the air we breathe and the food we eat. Viruses live an ascetic life, like monks but smaller. I am not claiming any great affection for them here but what did animal rights protestors think about viruses being killed in their billions? They weren't animals, I know, but they were living things. Didn't viruses have rights too?

'Hello stranger.'

I had only just found a place to sit as I had run through all the deep thinking I have just passed on to you, and now I stood again to greet Georgina. Sunglasses, hair tied back, shorts and white blouse, all she needed was a head scarf and a convertible to complete the movie star look. Somehow, she contrived to look this good without it ever seeming as if any facet of her appearance *was* contrived. It was a knack that naturally beautiful women had, I supposed.

'Fancy meeting you here and other associated clichés', I said. 'I have reserved a patch of grass in the shade two metres north of my location.'

'I love it when you speak with such animal... precision.'

'You're looking devastatingly good today, if you don't mind me saying.'

'I don't mind you saying that. Do I have to give you a compliment now?'

'It's only fair.'

'You look adequate.'

'Adequacy is exactly the look I was going for! You might not think it, but I plan what I am going to wear for maximum effect and to hide my gut.'

'You haven't got a gut.'

'I know. I just wanted someone to acknowledge that fact. So how have you been keeping? How's your husband?'

'No insulting name for him?'

'I think, I've run out. Ron, Rod, Rog, Rock… I can't remember the rest.'

'Well to answer your question, he is fine. I think he is trying to be a bit nicer to me.'

A stiletto blade of pure jealousy was thrust into my stomach as she said the words.

'Well, that's good', I said through gritted teeth.

'Not really. It's too late. He said he thought he was getting a bit fat last night. It was like a confession. I told him that wasn't the case but actually he's been a bit fat for years now. He was going to sign up to a gym when it was all over, cut down on the booze, all that sort of thing. Tried to shag me last night.'

I was a little taken aback.

'Don't worry I told him it was the wrong time.'

'Ah.'

'I couldn't tell him the truth, could I?'

'Which is?'

'That I want to shag you.'

I don't think I blushed, and obviously I was very flattered, but her forthrightness did take me by surprise.

'Well, I don't think we should. Too many people about in this park.'

'But the general idea is a good one?'

'Yeah I would say so. Tricky with social distancing, though.'

'I am sure there are ways and means to get around these problems safely.'

'Yes. We'll find a way.'

We watched a woman pass by less than the required distance from our patch of grass. She was pushing a buggy but it was unclear if there was a child in it or not. She looked completely gone, vacant, as she shuffled along in her flip-flops and sun dress.

When she had passed, I mentioned the zombies that were plaguing Billy and suggested that she was one of them.

'It's becoming a real problem. The worst thing is the mess they leave behind', agreed Georgina. 'Rubbish all over the place, slime trails.'

'They're in danger of becoming outcasts like travellers but... dead.'

Georgina didn't say anything but gave me a little Mona Lisa smile. She stretched and stifled a yawn, exposing a band of flat, tanned midriff as she did so. The sky, as ever, was relentlessly blue, not so much as a vapour trail to break the sapphire sea over our heads. A slight breeze twisted through the trees; the rustling leaves offered up a soporific background din.

'Right now, I'd like to be in a cool room with a double bed, crisp white sheets, a view of the sea, a bottle of wine. Not even the bottle of wine really. I could lie and enjoy the peace. Maybe the only sound would be the water lapping on the beach.'

'Do I feature in this scenario at all?'

'You are next to me. You have just fucked me to within an inch of my life.'

A man in a jumper, sitting nearby looked over as if he had heard.

'Sounds perfect. For now, we have this park in Belfast. No sea but it's fairly quiet I suppose.'

'How do we make this happen?', she asked. 'I need to know that we can be together in that place I have just described. Somehow a dirty weekend in a caravan in Portavogie doesn't quite do it for me.'

'Portavogie is nice, but I know what you mean. We will sort something out. When this is over.'

'It won't be easy. I have a husband and child.'

I really didn't like to think about Rolf in this equation. This thing with Georgina had taken hold quickly. Short of getting Billy to kill him, I wasn't too sure what could be done to negate his influence. Perhaps it was unfair on him but it was too late to go back now, for me at least.

'How is Stephanie?'

'Fine. We have an appointment booked for some therapy type stuff. She seems happy about it although her moods tend to be up and down a bit. Next time I see her she'll be sceptical again. She is still convinced that she killed someone.'

'Hence the therapy.'

'Aye. At least this way she has a chance of staying out of jail. That was the bit that always made me wary. It was never going to be a good result.' I paused, surveyed the sky and was thankful for my modest blessings as they stood at this precise moment. 'She asked me out', I said, matter-of-factly.

Georgina sat up.

'On a date?'

'I suppose so. She suggested a drink. Obviously, I turned her down.'

'Did you?'

'Of course, I did.'

'She's a gorgeous young woman.'

'Granted but so are you and you have the additional benefit of not being a total lunatic.'

'Kind words. People have always liked that about me.'

'In these difficult times, sanity is a great asset, worth treasuring. Maybe in a few weeks Steph will also have some of that particular commodity.'

'What would she think if she saw us now?'

'I'm slightly more concerned with what your husband would think.'

'You could beat him in a fight.'

'Not from two metres distant. Besides it would unseemly to have a fight with him in the park.'

'It would have to be a duel', said Georgina chuckling. 'I can see that making a comeback, you know. Two men armed with bananas, take ten paces each, turn, fire.'

'Boris would approve of the distancing aspect. I suppose some people would still find fault. They'd probably say that you'd broken the law or something. You can't bloody win. Commie bastards.'

'Would you win a duel with Rog?', she asked. She was sitting on her side now, her blouse gaping slightly open, a sliver of bra visible.

'I don't know', I said blowing air from my cheeks. 'I'm just trying not to look down your top.'

Instead of covering up she tugged at her collar to expose more flesh.

'How's that?'

'Much better, thank you.'

The breeze died down and the heat built up. I could feel a thin layer of perspiration build up on my forehead and neck. We didn't speak and somehow there was no need. We had reached that easy-going stage in our relationship very quickly.

'I could stay like this forever', she said wistfully. 'Sometimes you realise just how little you really need in life. Good company, the sun, fresh air.'

'None of which are guaranteed in Belfast but today is an exception. Close your eyes and pretend we're on a beach in Italy.'

'We could go to the beach one day, now that there is a little bit more freedom to go about the place.'

'Where do you fancy? It can only be an hour from your house, remember.'

'That could take you virtually anywhere in Northern Ireland.'

'Bangor?', I suggested.

'It'll be too crowded. Someone we know might see us?'

'On down the peninsula. Plenty of beaches there. Stop off for chips or ice cream.'

'Chips *or* ice cream? I have to choose?'

'Maybe both, then but I can't make promises.'

'If there was no one else around I think I would move closer to you.'

'If there was no one else around, I'd let you. Things will get back to normal and then we can have that trip to the beach.'

'I'll hold you to that.'

'Please do.'

When we parted company, I was fully convinced that someday soon we would be driving out into the countryside and spending that time we had promised each other alone on the beach with the sun, the breeze and the sound of the waves. Strangely, it didn't quite happen like that.

Chapter Fifteen

It was Tuesday when she rang, two days before her first psychiatrist's appointment.

'Oh my God, you have to help me.'

'Of course. But what's happened, Steph?'

'They've found the body. They've found the person I killed.'

It felt like a punch in the guts.

So, there you had it. Everything that had gone before wasn't worth a damn because in fact she *had* killed someone and now that person's mortal remains had turned up. Oddly, I didn't shout *'result!'* for that is what she had been hoping for if you recall. It didn't occur to me to shout that or anything else. Be careful what you wish for. The apparent denouement, the end of her torment, wasn't quite what she'd hoped for. I don't know how she thought it would end but not like this obviously.

'Okay. Where are you?'

'The police station.' There was a pause as she asked which one, she was at. 'Grove Street.'

I knew the place, opposite the old flour mill that had been converted into flats for hipster business types, drawn to the city to make their fortune.

'They're allowing you to visit me.'

'Shouldn't you have a solicitor?'

'I don't want one. I want you. I want someone who can explain the whole thing.'

'I'm on my way.' This didn't seem like the time to point out that there was almost nothing I could do to help her and, as for explaining the situation, well what was I supposed to say? She claimed to have killed someone and now they could prove it. It seemed straightforward. Forget about false memories; events had moved way past that consideration.

It was a short drive, managed quickly in the thinner than usual traffic and I parked in the Dick Turpin *pay and display* car park, run by Robbing Bastards PLC. Or was it a parking hub?

In the bad old days, entering an RUC station had been like stepping into the outer perimeter of Fort Knox. Huge blast walls surrounded the stations and manned guard boxes oversaw all visitors. Antennae reached into the sky, maintaining communications with the cars and officers out on the ground. The police had been heavily armed, their stations like Wild West forts. Things had changed but the security remained and the police themselves were called the Police Service of Northern Ireland as a sop to those who got offended by the word 'Royal' from Royal Ulster Constabulary.

A sergeant looked up from his paperwork smiled and asked how I was. He was in his early fifties and gave the impression of being ready to retire.

'I have come to see Stephanie Kuler. You brought her in a wee while ago.'

'Ah yes. You're not her solicitor I take it.'

'Just a friend really. Well, I was working for her.'

'We did suggest that a solicitor was of more use – no disrespect.'

'No, I agree, but I understand why she has asked for me. Is it okay?'

'Fine, yes. I'll get someone to take you through.'

I had only just sat when a young man in plain clothes came out. He stood between the front desk and the corridor behind him as he spoke.

'You've come to see Stephanie Kuler?'

'Yep.'

'Come through.'

I followed him and the door swung shut behind us.

'You're a friend?', he asked as we walked.

'Something like that. I know that she should have a solicitor but I sort of know what is going on.'

He stopped and looked at me intently. We stood to one side as two uniformed officers moved in the opposite direction as if about set out on patrol. One spoke into his radio, performing a last check before hitting the streets.

'You *know* what is going on?'

'Ha. Well as much as anyone does. I take it she has explained all about her…'

'Feeling?'

'Aye, her feeling. I thought we had got to the bottom of it really but now this.'

'You can have time alone with her and she is being cooperative. She's not even denying it. I wouldn't mind if we could all sit in together and straighten out just what exactly has gone on. I'm Detective Inspector Wilson by the way. I won't shake your hand – the old virus thing. There's hand sanitizer in the room.'

'I don't have a problem with you being there. Believe it or not this is sort of what she wanted', I said.

In the event she was happy to talk with the detective present.

Relief visibly flooded through her as I entered the room.

'Thank God.'

'You okay?'

'Fine. They have been very nice actually. Right do you want me to explain what has been going on?'

'Fine.' I looked at the Inspector and he smiled and indicated that Steph had the floor.

'They found a body in a place called Barton. The police there knew about my claims and found out that I had lived there as a baby. The body is decomposed but they are going to do tests on it and see if it is the person I killed.'

I glanced at the inspector and he nodded.

'The local police force got onto us to make the arrest and we are holding Ms Kuler until they give us further instructions. Ms Kuler has told us that she has always thought she killed someone but didn't know any of the details.'

'That's right. That is why I got hired, to find the body or some evidence.'

'Since we are all working for the same thing, can you tell me how you got on?'

I looked at Steph this time for permission to discuss the case. It would have been hard to refuse but I wanted to maintain the pretence that we had a choice in the matter.

'Tell him. I have nothing to hide. After all this time, I'm not trying to wriggle out of it.'

'For obvious reasons, I was sceptical about the whole thing, but Steph was convinced so I took on the case. The thing is that we thought we had it all figured out. Bearing in mind that until now, not one single shred of evidence existed that she had killed anyone, we had worked out that this was a false memory, which is pretty much exactly what it sounds like; some event or combination of events which creates a memory which doesn't represent actual events as they occurred.

'Steph was due at the clinic this Thursday to take this a bit further and to see if there was treatment or counselling to help her with it. Now events have taken a different turn so that won't be happening I imagine. Unless the doctor can come here?'

'I would have to check.' He rubbed his eyes and then spoke again. 'It is very likely – almost certain – that you will have to go to England', he said to her.

'I know. That's fine.'

'I suppose the question is, does any of this sound familiar? You have been feeling like this for years you say and now we have a body – does it feel like this is the person you killed?'

'I don't know. The truth is I don't feel any different but I have always known I had done it. Maybe I need to see the body or the site or something. It has to be the person I killed, though. It has to be.'

'Funny enough, I don't agree', said Wilson. 'There will be tests done to see if there is any link between you and this dead person. Lots of people have been killed over the years and at the minute the only connection to you and this corpse is that you lived in Barton for a short time when you were a kid and there is a dead body. You wouldn't go to jail for that alone.'

'Of course' she said, flatly.

'I can see all sorts of problems. If you were only there as a baby – this is before you went into care – then it seems unlikely that you killed someone. If you did for some reason manage to kill someone when you were still in your pram you wouldn't be tried for murder anyway.'

Detective Inspector Wilson was obviously amused by his thought that a baby might have killed an adult, perhaps with a particularly vicious blow from a rattle.

I turned to Steph now and said, 'I still think the false memory thing is more likely than actual murder.'

'I agree that I didn't murder someone when I was a baby but there is nothing to stop me going there as an adult and killing someone.'

'The body is old', said Wilson.

'I would have been capable of murder twenty years ago.'

'Well, another thing to establish is motive. You say yourself that you have no motive for killing anyone. The link between you and this deceased person is very tenuous at the minute.'

The discussion went back and forth for another few minutes and it became clear that Wilson, who seemed like a reasonable man and not a miserable bastard like some of his kind, was struggling with the idea that mild-mannered, well dressed, well-spoken Stephanie Kuler could actually have murdered someone. I asked if I was allowed to bring her anything and when she was expected to go to England. The first answer was a *'yes'* and the second was an *'unknown at present'*.

I bade her farewell and left feeling that she was in safe hands. They were not going to mistreat her.

Outside the interview room Wilson and I chatted for another few minutes.

'She'll go before a magistrate and they will decide if she stays in custody or not. The police in Oxfordshire will make a decision about taking her over there.'

'Can I go with her or meet her there say?'

'I'll ask. It's unusual for that to happen but this is a bloody unusual case. I have to say she isn't your common or garden killer type.'

'Nope. Personally, I would have grave doubts about her guilt. I'm still a bit confused about how they made an association between this corpse and Steph.'

'They were demolishing some houses in this place, Barton, and found the body. She had lived there for a short time but then she went into care, is that right?'

'Care and foster homes. In and out of each. Not much of a childhood.'

'Anyway, one of the detectives had been looking at your friend's claims recently and made the link.' I instantly thought of the copper who had done the expensive research for me. Naturally I said nothing. 'He worked out that she was over here and rang us to make the arrest. He was quick off the mark. She'd been in to see him about it sometime last year. They didn't investigate. We wouldn't have either with so little to go on.'

'The timing is odd. She comes to me to help her and then a body turns up.'

'These things happen. Listen. I have your mobile number and I have made a note of the hospital thing. I'll ask about that – it could help us too – and I will let you know if she is to be released on bail but this is a serious charge, no matter how decent and helpful she is being.'

'I understand.'

'She understands too.'

'I'll be in touch.'

He showed me back out of the station and then said, 'you must be ex-police, being in this game'

'Ex-army, funny enough. I more or less got into it by accident. Something of a gifted amateur.'

'Like Belfast's version of Sherlock Holmes?'

'I wouldn't flatter myself with that comparison but perhaps.'

'Well if you ever need a Doctor Watson, let me know.'

'You fed up with it?'

'Politics. Politics in every job.'

'I have a Doctor Watson already – more of a Robin, as in Batman and Robin – but there might be a vacancy one of these days. I'll keep you in mind.'

***

I rang Billy and Georgina in that order and for entirely different reasons.

'Holy shit', he said when I passed him the news. 'I bet she wasn't quite as pleased as she might have anticipated. It's a lot different when it actually happens.'

'My thoughts exactly. They're bound to remand her in custody too for a crime like that. She's been charged and all the rest of it.'

'How does she seem?'

'She brightened a little as we discussed the case; me, her and the detective. It was weird because she obviously isn't a typical murderer and wasn't trying to wriggle out of it. She just seemed bemused throughout as if we were talking about someone else. He's not convinced it was her.'

'What about you?', asked Billy. 'You still think it is one of these false memories?'

'Funny enough, yeah, I do. It still makes the most sense to me. For a while there, I was thinking if they had the body that was it, done. But not now. The copper says that they aren't just going to assume she's guilty either. They still need evidence to convict her which is what we've said all along. They would need a motive too.'

'You know I thought that was it with the old false memory thing and now this. I'm quite shocked.'

'Me too, Billy. Me too.'

When I spoke to Georgina, she was equally shocked.

'Oh my God. I can't talk for long; dickhead is due back any minute. So, she *did* kill someone! All this time and I just thought she was a bit potty and actually she was telling the truth.'

'We don't know that she is guilty of course, but a body has turned up near where she lived as a kid.'

'She didn't kill someone when she was a kid.'

'I would say not. She could have gone back to that place to kill someone, but it still doesn't make much sense.'

'How is she bearing up?'

'Fine. I don't know how she imagined things panning out, but surely not like this. She was shocked to find herself being arrested I think but she is being treated okay. As for the police, they have never had someone so compliant for an alleged murderer.'

'Steph might have pictured it differently, that somehow she and you would locate the body and then inform the cops. Gentler than being hauled out of bed or whatever they did. Listen, I hear him coming back. I'll speak soon.'

The conversation ended that quickly and I was left with just my thoughts. If Steph's predicament was now resolved then it might only have been because I phoned that copper in Oxfordshire about her arrest. I was sure he was the one who had then, so brilliantly everyone thought, strung the case together.

'My work here is done', I said to the shadows.

It was an untidy conclusion, or that is how it felt to me, especially since we had been edging towards a solution which kept her out of jail and hopefully removed the guilt and uncertainty forever.

I was in a contemplative mood that night, a sort of subdued lighting, Pink Floyd, glass of whiskey mood. I could manage two of those only, for the last was the one which I actively resisted. It is also worth noting that we were supposed to shop for essentials only in these plague days and for me, spirits did not constitute anything of the sort. Classifying alcohol as a vital addition to the kitchen larder was dependent on your level of addiction, I supposed; mine was somewhere between non-existent and mild. I wanted to keep it that way.

Lots of the clichés about this time didn't apply to me – for all I knew they didn't apply to anyone – but as an example, I wasn't growing out of my clothes or cultivating a huge *wild man of the mountains* beard. I was keeping myself fit and eating the same amount as I had ever eaten. I cut my own hair, went to work, barely used social media and didn't miss being in company that much. The only thing I saw which did resonate with me slightly was a meme showing a veteran who stated that his life hadn't changed since lockdown, the implication being that he didn't much care for company anyway. In some small part that perhaps did apply to me.

But sitting here in the semi-dark with one of my favourite albums on the CD playing device (thanks Billy), I felt a sort of detached contentment. The world outside was going wrong (or going brilliantly, depending on your perspective) but I could sit here with the door locked, food in the fridge and the cupboards, and keep completely safe. I could even work from home up to a point thanks to the wonders of modern technology. I was safe from the zombie hordes outside.

I would look back on this time with a mixture of bemusement and happiness. Meeting Georgina was part of that, but I had my doubts about how long that could last. When I let my mind drift, it washed up on some shore, the sun high overhead and behind me the cool beach shack where I could relax with Georgina after my morning swim. She would write her book and I would paint.

There was a flaw; I couldn't paint and knew nothing about painting beyond a few crap attempts made at school many years since. But I had to do something to make time pass in this idyll my mind had just conjured from nothing. What better than painting? You sat there, brush in hand, picking out the detail of the scene and turning it into a daub that, from a greater distance than you were currently able to apply, would look like a tree with low-hanging branches, or a zebra on the plains of Africa. Or whatever. The alternative was to do nothing. There was only so much reading and drinking of pineapple juice you could do before your life became meaningless and dull.

Georgina and I swinging listlessly in his'n'her hammocks as the sea breeze cooled us was just a dream, a hope for some better time. Maybe we could have these moments someday, but they could never represent the entirety of our lives. I frowned. The problem with the image I had created from nothing and without really meaning to, was that it was too hot. What I mean is that the beach was too exposed, the air too dry, the breeze insufficient to really cool me down. I had been to a few hot places with the army but a life spent in Northern Ireland was poor preparation for tropical conditions.

My thoughts drifted away to almost nothing as I listened to the words of the next song. When my imaginings had regrouped, we had a villa overlooking the sea in Italy. It had air conditioning. That was better. But none of this mattered. All of these things existed only in my head.

My phone buzzed and when I checked, Georgina, as if she could read my mind, had sent me a picture of a villa in Italy with a view of the sea.

I replied with a text to that effect – that she had read my mind. Maybe our private, shared dream would happen one day. There were complications to overcome but it was worth having a dream to pursue.

That night, I set my mind to dreaming about this holiday, a modest enough aspiration really. I ran through a list of possible bases and even gave consideration to the type of car we'd hire, settling on a Fiat 124 Spyder, the closest we could ever come to a Maserati but perfect for a top-down drive up into the mountains on winding roads. I thought too about the villa, the air con, the pool, the view, the presence of a Spar shop (you've got to eat), but in truth none of these ideas became fully formed because I fell asleep within minutes. If I dreamed my intended dreams, then all record of having done so was gone when I awoke.

Chapter Sixteen

I opened the office window a crack that morning, something I rarely did since the weather tended to mitigate against such rashness. It was fine if you wanted high velocity rain driven by Atlantic winds spraying across the office, lifting papers and gluing them wetly to the walls and that good kettle we had, but in a normal day it was something to avoid.

The traffic outside didn't manage even a muted hum. The birds sang and that was just about it. As I waited for my computing machine to 'boot up', whatever the hell that meant, I heard Billy coming through the door from the street. He was singing as he came up the stairs:

Birds gotta swim,

Fish gotta fly,

I've got a sausage,

I don't know why.

I smiled at his controlled idiocy.

'Morning great leader', he said effusively as he entered.

'Yo.'

'What is on the agenda today?'

'You're going to tell me what you have found out about Curt Johnson', I said.

'But what about the mysterious Stephanie Kuler?'

'Still mysterious.'

'Wouldn't you say she was more mysterious now?'

'Possibly. Or less mysterious. Depends on how you look at it. She told us she was a murderer and now it has been confirmed.'

'But not really.'

'No, not really. Just need to see what the psychiatrist says and then she might be going to England to be interviewed properly. They might need to hire a plane if all the flights are cancelled.'

'Good point. Would it be cheaper if they came over here?'

'She needs to see the crime scene. Or maybe she doesn't, strictly speaking. In my view, she has to be able to look at where the body was found but that's just what I think.'

'Weird. I never saw it pan out like this.'

'Or me. Anyway, Curt Johnson.'

'Okay. Early days, but he and his missus are separated and most likely going to get divorced. He is back living in barracks, not the sergeant's mess but I will get back to that point, and she has a rented flat. She is a primary teacher, actually a deputy head or something, so she's okay for money. The baby is not his…'

'Aha', I said.

'Exactly. The immaculate conception strikes again', he said in reference to a pregnancy created when the husband was away on operations. Frequently the returning husband and his straying wife just pretended that neither knew the truth. In part this was because *he* might also have strayed while he was away from home just as she had done whilst keeping the home fires burning. Many legends had grown up around this grubby facet of army life, including the story that having a packet of OMO washing powder in the kitchen window of your married quarter signalled that you were open to others. OMO, you see, stood for Old-Man-Out. I doubted if you could get a packet of OMO these days but that was the myth.

'Now here is where is gets interesting but a bit vague. The army doesn't acknowledge Mrs Johnson now since they are splitting up and he has seemingly disappeared from his unit. He was troop sergeant but one of the corporals has been promoted in his place and there is no official word of where he has gone. But everyone knows it is either SAS or SRR.'

'Special Reconnaissance Regiment?'

'Precisely. Formed out of 14 Int. as far as I know.'

'After my time.'

'Well, it looks as if he is with them now. And that, in the shell of a nut, is the mostly likely explanation for his disappearance. From the army's point of view, why would they bother to complicate matters by giving this information to a soon-to-be ex-wife? Therefore, as far as she is concerned, he has disappeared.'

'She must have pestered them about it', I said.

'Undoubtedly. And they have just fucked her off. She is no longer part of that big family and that is that.'

'Which leaves a problem.'

'What do we tell her? I have given that some thought.'

'And?'

'Nothing.'

'Hmm. She's going to love getting a bill for this.'

'She wasn't completely honest with us.'

'No, but it all added up to a fair bit of expense. Those investigators in Hong Kong cost a fortune. I've paid them. She needs to pay up. I've never even met the woman.'

Billy looked at me expectantly.

'That's it. I have run out of cases, Billy.'

'Alright. I have a few more snippets to come in possibly about Curt Johnson if you want to hold off for a couple of days, but essentially that is the score with him.'

'So, what about you and Della then?'

'You're obsessed.'

'No, I just think you'd make a good couple. She likes you. Invite her to the cinema. Not right now obviously but just ask her out. You have nothing to lose.'

'Except my self-respect. If she says no, where am I going to go for my coffee and bagel?'

'It won't make the slightest difference. She'll still take your money and just pretend that nothing happened.'

'Well anyway, not that it is your effing business, but I rang her last night', he said smugly.

'And?'

'Answerphone.'

***

Inspector Wilson rang me to say that the psychiatrist was permitted to visit Steph at the station if I was able to organise it, and that it would have to be that morning because she was flying to England on a chartered flight that afternoon from George Best.

'You can come along if you are registered as her representative. This has been a hell of a thing to organise, but the circumstances have been recorded as exceptional. You have to socially distance still, but there is a cheap hotel nearby that will take internet bookings. This is at your expense but the flights are free, courtesy of HM Government.'

'Thanks for doing that. I'll get onto the clinic and see about getting the doc down to you. I'll let you know if there is a problem.'

Suddenly it was all systems go and more importantly I had something to occupy me. Because I was ringing a private clinic, I got through immediately and the receptionist in turn transferred me straight through to the doctor in question. Try doing that with your doctors' surgery.

'Hi. You were due to see Stephanie Kuler on Thursday morning but there has been a change in her circumstances since then and I wondered if you were able to visit her instead of her coming to you? I realise that this would be reflected in the bill.'

'You are her friend?', asked the doctor. She sounded Indian.

'Yes. I came with her to the first appointment.'

'I can't really alter the appointment on your say so, that's the problem.'

'I understand. The change in her circumstances is that she has been arrested. She is at Grove Street station now. It's linked to the reason you were seeing her.'

I heard the doctor typing on a keyboard.

'Oh', she said. 'Are you saying that she *has* killed someone?'

'They have found a body. I know what you are thinking. Or I can guess, but I don't actually think she has. The idea of a false memory is much more convincing than this. The fact that a body has turned up is...'

'Inconvenient?'

'I was going to say, *not necessarily proof of anything*. I still think you should talk to her. This dead body is unconnected. That's just my view but I am sure they won't link her to it.'

'Well...'

'I really think she needs to see you. It will make a big difference to her.'

My entreaty only sounded as ridiculous as everything else that had happened recently and I could picture the doctor thinking through the ramifications of attending to this patient, or of not attending to her. Perhaps it all came down to good old pounds, shillings and pence, for after another short moment had elapsed, she said she'd be there tomorrow.

'Thank you. I will tell the detective in charge to be expecting you.'

I rang the station straight after. It was a brief conversation but I got to speak to Wilson in person, which removed the strong chance that a message would fail to get to him.

With that done, I booked myself in at the hotel and then thought about how I was going to break the news to Mrs Johnson that her husband had not disappeared but was... Was what? If Billy was correct, and I had no reason to think he wasn't, then it was not my place to share military secrets with a civilian. These were secrets that I had no right to know, so if she made a fuss then I could be dragged into a court with Billy close on my heels. There was a good reason why special forces soldiers trained (in some cases) and deployed in secret; to do otherwise cost lives. My guess was that he was in training at the minute but that was none of her business. If anything, the army should have told her something to put her off the scent.

The only option open to me was to say that we had simply failed to locate him. I wasn't happy with that but it would have to do.

So, as far as she would know we had failed but we still required payment. It was a bit shit.

I texted Georgina to say that I would be out of the country for a day or two and she agreed to message me the following night lest I get bored with her and found someone else. She was joking of course.

I spent the remainder of the day browsing the internet for holidays in Italy. It wasn't a huge surprise to discover that everything seemed to be geared up for 2021 when it was to be assumed that the pandemic had ended. Having said that, there was a plethora of vacation experiences (Billy again – he had decided never to use the word *holiday*) available, too many perhaps to make an easy choice. Cruises, villas, coach tours, fly and drive, you name it, it was there. Northern Italy? The great cities? Southern Italy? Coast? Mountains? Lakes? Did I want the hottest weather, or something a little bit out of season, if indeed, such a thing existed?

I couldn't book anything, for I certainly did not intend to go by myself and who knew if and when Georgina would be free to go with me. As I searched, it was clear enough that this might never happen. She was not a free agent. I could do as I pleased, more or less, but she could not. Gently bombarded with images, I could see the attraction of the place and the variety on offer. You could lie on a crowded beach getting skin cancer and drinking shit beer along with thousands of others, or you could tour the mountains in your open-topped sports car, stopping off for pizza or ice cream. You could go snorkelling in the sea or the lakes, take in the grandeur of Rome or Venice, visit the vineyards, trek though Tuscan hills. After half an hour I just had no idea what I wanted to do if we ever got there.

Chapter Seventeen

'Hello again. The doctor has gone ahead of us. We've set aside our biggest interview room so that you can socially distance.'

'Thanks. Did she say she wanted me in there with her?'

'As far as I know. I am leaving the three of you to it. A female officer has been round to her house to collect some clothes and things for the trip. She says she lives alone?'

'Yeah, that's right.'

'And you're packed for a few days?'

'Yep. I have the hotel booked and so on.'

'In that case, I'll take you through.'

The doctor looked up and smiled as I came in and Steph gave me a rueful little wave as if feeling guilty for dragging me out to the station. The door closed behind me and we began at once. I had the feeling of *déjà vu*, except in many respects I really had been here before. This story was no less extraordinary I suppose, but it had been related to me so many times that it just seemed commonplace that someone could believe they had killed another person. The twist was that the body had eventually turned up, which was very nice of it. Nice of it to make the effort after all these years. Other than that, however, it was the same basic story.

Doctor Patel took it all in her stride and smiled politely as the details unfolded but she had surely been briefed about what to expect. For my part, my mind wandered as if the truth was too much to bear, which was not the case. Rather, I felt that my presence was just not required.

'How long have you felt this way?', asked the doctor. It was a good question since she practically claimed to have been born with this feeling which meant that it existed before the murder. It was another argument in favour of the false memory theory.

'It's hard to say. I can't clearly remember *not* feeling this way. Maybe the feeling intensified over the years until I was sure that I had killed someone.'

'Do any details of the murder ever come to you? Even those you subsequently discount?'

'No. Nothing.'

I knew all this.

'So, how do you know it is a murder and not some other event?'

'It's hard to explain. It just feels like a murder. It always has.'

'Always?'

'Since I can remember.'

'If I asked you to think back to when you were ten say, would you have the feeling then? Or if I said fifteen, twenty, anything like that?'

'I'm not sure.'

'If I said thirty?'

'Yes, definitely when I was thirty.'

'Okay, so that is only a couple of years ago?'

Steph nodded.

'I'm interested in when you first felt this way, so maybe we could pin this feeling down to around the time in which a particular event occurred, or a period in your life.'

'You mean when I think it happened?'

'No, when you first had the feeling, or the first time you remember it feeling like a murder. So, if I say when you did your school exams?'

'Which ones?'

'Your GCSEs. Did you feel at the time like you were a murderer? It sounds so peculiar when you say it out loud.'

'No. Maybe.'

'Did you go to college for 'A' levels?'

'Yes. I don't know if I felt it then.'

'University?'

'Yes, but I can't say if I definitely felt it then.'

'So, you left uni at twenty-one? Is that right?'

'Yes.'

'And you are thirty-two now?'

'Yes.'

'Then the feeling really came to you between those two ages, a period of eleven years. Before that it was just something ill-defined like a feeling of guilt that you couldn't connect to any particular event?'

'I suppose that is so.'

I looked at the doctor with admiration.

'Okay then. Unless I have missed something, or there is another part to this which you haven't shared, if you have committed murder which has then given rise to this feeling you carry around with you, it happened in the last eleven years.'

'I suppose so.'

'The question is, have you committed murder?'

'What do you mean?'

'At any point in those last eleven years did you kill someone? We are discounting your youth and your childhood, so if this event ever did happen then it was as an adult. You could look back at the places you worked and the people you met in that time. Is it possible that you killed anyone?'

'I lived in America.'

'Did you kill anyone while you were there?

'I don't think so?'

'Can you think of a reason why you might have killed someone?'

'I don't know.'

The doctor stopped and let a silence fall over proceedings. She was a skilled interrogator for sure.

'I don't think you have killed anyone.'

'It still feels like I have.'

'I don't doubt that. Unfortunately, nothing I have said will make a difference in a court, unless I am called as an expert witness, which is unlikely. What we need to do is to find out why you feel as you do. We need to look back at stressful periods in your life and see if one of these was the catalyst for this feeling. This will take time. It is not enough for anyone just to state plainly that you are innocent. We have to get to the root cause and then pull it out like a weed before you can move on. I am happy to do this if you are?'

'Of course, but there is a problem.'

'I know. You're going to England tomorrow as part of the investigation into what might be a genuine murder.'

'In which case?'

'We just have to see how things work out Stephanie, but you *can* be helped.'

I had contributed nothing but maybe Steph had felt reassured by my presence. If that was the case, and I had given her the confidence to open up to a stranger, then that was fine. We thanked Doctor Patel and she was shown out of the room. A minute later, Wilson entered.

'That's it. We'd better catch our flight.'

***

After a few weeks of the so-called lockdown, the doubters were making themselves heard, protesting that the government hadn't been prepared, hadn't taken action soon enough, weren't explaining things simply enough. Others were saying that lockdown was simply a means to impose draconian laws that restricted the freedom of the individual and made us all powerless slaves. The problem was that the modern world had provided every nut with a platform on which to expound and spread their bizarre conspiracy theories. It was one thing that the parliamentary opposition whinged and whined – that was their dreary job in a sense – but quite another that every unhinged vegan, climate-protesting remainer/rejoiner could share their views on the internet alongside people who actually knew what they were talking about.

It was hard to get to the truth admittedly but easier to dismiss the spoilt-child bias of the vocal minority who just couldn't compromise and accept a world which could never meet their own high standards. However, social distancing *was* a total pain in the arse and I am not pretending that it was anything else. Two metres doesn't sound much until you try to maintain that distance from people who are coming at you from all directions, some of whom have difficulty walking in a straight line even in ideal conditions.

Luckily, we had little difficulty getting onto the Smithair flight and once on board we were seated at the correct distance apart. They had asked that we avoid using the toilet and explained that there would be no refreshments for us. We would be airborne for an hour only and a minibus would meet us at the other side. Our transport held about thirty passengers in its normal configuration and that gave us plenty of room to spread out even if it was a fairly antisocial arrangement. I didn't care. I just wanted to get there and get started, for some reason eager to see the scene of the crime which I hadn't believed existed.

Steph and I didn't speak much, mainly because we couldn't be close enough to make communication easy, but also I think my gentle rejection of her still stung a little. It shouldn't have mattered, not now that she was in danger of going to prison; that single consideration should have provided a preoccupation to put every other into the shade. I was sure she'd find someone else, that is, if she didn't end up in jail, a location which might be off-putting for potential suitors. Blind dates might be tricky too.

The minibus laid on for us looked like the type of thing that normally took the riot squad to football matches or wherever it was they spent their time. This was not executive travel but it did allow us to keep apart. The driver was a civilian working for the police, and he wore a mask. A screen had been bolted to the floor behind his seat so that he was protected from his passengers.

We drove in silence for about forty minutes until we turned off the main road for the village of Barton. I didn't know how busy or quiet this area normally was but there seemed to be plenty of traffic on the roads, the usual mix of private cars and commercial vehicles and only one bus which had so few passengers it was hard to imagine it making a profit.

We had only driven for a few minutes before we were in the countryside, the sort of thing that makes it onto the lid of an old-fashioned biscuit tin and quite unlike anything in Northern Ireland. Much of the latter's housing was rather functional in aspect and for the middle classes living in the country, a sprawling white bungalow was expected really. This looked like the sort of thing Constable might have painted to my inexpert eye.

Barton however, didn't exactly fit with the rest of it, and turning from the main road, lined with trees which screened endless fields replete with crops, it was a stark contrast. A village centre contained the usual establishments; chippy, Spar shop, newsagent, with the slightly off-kilter additions of laundrette and bookkeepers. A snob would say that this indicated a rather low-class area, and they would be correct in that regard. Summoning up my entire knowledge of architecture, it seemed to me that the houses were a mix of council and some older housing trust, maybe put there by a Victorian philanthropist (or *philanderer*, if you were Billy) for the good of their workers in the manner of Joseph Rowntree in York. The council houses were ugly and plain, the others which had been arranged on a grid, were plain but much more solid-looking and homely.

Every avenue was tree-lined, and we drove past a number of parks sparsely populated now with kids escaping the confines of their homes for a time. The day was just getting hotter and hotter as the afternoon wore on and the heat built up in the vehicle until the driver belatedly switched the air con on. I suppose his instructions might have been to keep it off to prevent the spread of the virus, but whatever the reason I was glad when he relented.

We stopped at a set of temporary lights placed near a deserted road improvement scheme and from my safe vantage point I was able to observe two shaven headed boys performing stunts on their BMX bikes, one of which had neither a saddle or a place to put one. A quip related to this discovery formed in my head and then evaporated again for want of someone to share it with. There were four of us in the bus, but we were disconnected souls without a common bond worthy of the name.

I felt a pain in my hip and was reminded that time marched on. No longer did I need a reason to ache, such as a sports injury, just the fact of being alive was enough to generate pains that sprang up unexpectedly and sometimes toured my body like restless spirits. Billy and I shared this problem although he put his recurring aches down to his years in the army and the forced marches he had endured. He was probably correct in that assumption but getting older didn't help.

We moved off again without having any vehicle pass us coming from the opposite direction and soon passed an NHS sign proclaiming us to be in the vicinity of *Barton Healthcare Park*, which may or may not have been a hospital. How would you know? If I'd had my way it would have been a *wellbeing hub*. Through the tangle of hedge and tree I spotted a low red-brick building with an ambulance parked outside. Further on, I glimpsed a distant huddle of smokers in dressing gowns and some with drip stands, defiantly ruining their health on the site of a building put there to improve it. Not for the first time I wondered at the lack of sense shown by our species. It was like flying a Spitfire in 1940 and trying to shoot yourself down.

Beyond that we came to an open green space with a duck pond and an ice cream van with a partly socially-distanced queue. The rules were still in force, but they were becoming unravelled despite government warnings that we risked a second wave of infections.

Just moments after that we came to a building site with high wooden panels all around as if the builders had attempted to build a fort. A weary looking man with Slavic features, hard hat and high-vis jacket raised a barrier to let us inside. The driver stopped after twenty yards and we debussed.

Immediately he began wiping down everything we might have touched with a pack of antibacterial wipes in a move that had become commonplace but which until quite recently might have been deemed rather insulting.

We stood two metres apart.

Wilson said, 'this is it.' He surveyed the site as did we all, taking in the half-demolished houses, the excavation equipment and the foundations for the new houses before commenting. 'Pulling down houses to build houses. It must make sense to someone.'

Steph was silent. Her back was to me and she was staring fixedly at the last remaining house of the old type still standing. A police car and a forensic van were parked outside. A tent had been erected in the garden. Such was the seeming intensity of her stare I assumed that something had clicked, something related to murder but when I asked her, she just shook her head.

'I am trying to soak it up or something to see if it makes sense to me or I remember anything.'

'But it isn't familiar?'

'No, not yet.'

A man in civilian clothes came from the house and removed the overshoes from his feet before making his approach.

'You must be Inspector Wilson', he said before making the oft-used quip, 'I won't shake your hand.'

Wilson introduced Steph and me. Inspector Sturridge seemed markedly unimpressed but that didn't bother me, especially when you take into account the nature of our visit and the fact that one of us was the suspect. Everything had been so genteel up to this point that you could forget that Steph was the person currently under investigation.

Sturridge ran through the procedure in his midlands accent, looking at each of us in turn as though we might be too thick to understand what he was saying.

'The body was that of a forty-year-old man, we estimate. He was found face down under a section of lino in the under-stair space. Concrete had been poured over the body – actually something more like self-levelling compound.'

'How long was he in there?'

'Years. But we don't know how many yet. His skull has been cracked which is looking like the cause of death. Not a very sophisticated murder.'

'But he went undetected for all these years', said Wilson.

'A bit puzzling that. As you can see, they are demolishing the rest of the houses here. The only reason he was found at this point was because some kids broke in to wreck the place before the demolition team got to work. They got a bit more than they expected.'

'Horrific for them', I said. Sturridge glared at me as if *I* had killed the deceased. By association, I was clearly as guilty as Steph in his eyes, which might have been an unjustified but natural way to view matters for him.

'Obviously we are going to be questioning you in relation to this', he said addressing Steph. 'You will have to stay in a cell tonight, but you will be well looked after. You have more or less confessed, haven't you?'

It was Wilson who spoke in her defence.

'Well, not quite. Ms Kuler thinks she might have killed someone, but we don't know if it was this person. She has been totally cooperative with us so far.'

Sturridge looked mildly chastened, if degrees of that emotion can be awarded. I was rapidly forming the impression of a man who liked to get results by any means, regardless of quality and reliability. He was happy for Steph to take the blame if that could be arranged; and why not if she was actively seeking a murder conviction? He was young, perhaps late thirties, but he seemed to have learned his policing technique from watching re-runs of The Sweeney. I didn't like him and nor, it seemed, did Wilson who looked on with distaste.

'So, we're going to show you the crime scene and see if it jogs your memory.'

'Yes. I understand', said Steph, quietly.

'Right then, follow me. You'll have to put on gloves and over boots before you go in.' We walked behind him observing the correct distance. Over his shoulder he asked Wilson a question. 'Is that the same in Ireland? Over boots and gloves?'

'Northern Ireland. Yes. We've had one or two murders to deal with over there.' His voice dripped with sarcasm, but I didn't think that Sturridge would even notice.

We donned our simple gear. When we took it off we would have *doffed* it. Donned and doffed; words creeping into our common lexicon along with furlough, PPE and anti-bac.

'Right, follow me', he said. The door was propped open and I was struck by the fact that it was in good nick like the rest of the house. At first glance this appeared to be a perfectly good dwelling place being pulled down for no reason and this feeling was not dispelled by anything I saw inside. I was sure that plenty of people lived in houses much less well-put together than this, in fact I doubted that those put up in their place would be as sturdy. The windows were broken and I could see that the elderly kitchen had been smashed up by vandals, but much of the décor remained and just needed a bit of cosmetic help. A couple of days work would have made the place habitable but instead of that its fate was to be razed to the ground.

Mind you, who would have bought a house whose last remaining resident was a dead man in his forties? As selling points go it was something for a niche market only; mystery freaks and fans of Midsomer Murders. For no good reason I was reminded of a friend of a friend who had taken a trip to Germany and, upon leaving the airport, had immediately made for the first public phone box to check for the surname Hitler in the listings. So good was the story that I never got around to enquiring if he had had found the name, but I assumed not. I believe that Hitler and his name had gone out of fashion in Germany for some reason.

The hall was bare concrete and tiny bits of rubble cracked under our feet as we slowly made our way inside as if entering the tomb of some lost Egyptian king whose mortal remains had once been guarded by the Sphinx (or *sphincter* as Billy would have it). All we were missing were those burning torches that explorers in films always manage to find for such purposes.

Sturridge indicated the under-stair cupboard and kept on going until he was in the kitchen and out of our way. Behind him I spotted a white-suited technician with a camera, almost a cliché. Wilson followed the other policeman into the kitchen and Steph made her way along until she was parallel with the

234

cupboard whose cracked wooden door gaped open. A light had been placed to shine inside. Steph looked.

We all watched her as she surveyed the crime scene. She stared and stared until I thought something had finally become real to her, some extra detail that had detached itself from the site of the murder and joined with the single fragment of that experience that she carried around in her head. When she turned to me, she spoke.

'Nothing', she said.

Wilson pursed his lips and Sturridge rolled his eyes. He was a sceptic of course and this did not come as a surprise. He would assume that he had wasted his time.

'Nothing at all?', I asked for confirmation.

'Nothing at all. I thought that maybe something would be familiar to me, but I don't recognise any of this.'

I took a deep breath, picking up the pungent tang of urine for the first time.

'Can she have a look through the house?', I suggested. Wilson gave a shrug, but Sturridge gave a grudging nod of the head.

I made my way outside and stood for a moment under the burning sun before being joined by the two police officers.

'Load of shit, if you ask me', said Sturridge.

'It was worth a shot. If you get your lab results sorted then you can check her DNA with that of the body. You might get something from this', said Wilson.

'It's being rushed through. She's just a time waster though. I can feel it in my water.'

'She's not your usual suspect', acknowledged Wilson but not unkindly.

We waited for a few minutes, letting Steph tour the house in her own time. She couldn't run off without us spotting her and besides that was never likely to be her intention.

'Presumably you are checking to see if she has any connection to this place', asked Wilson.

'It hasn't come through yet. We've only just got records on Kuler recently. She isn't as sweet and innocent as she makes out, you know.'

Wilson raised his eyebrows but didn't ask for elucidation. I was thinking how stupid Sturridge was; Stephanie Kuler was not pleading innocence. If anything, the exact opposite was true; she was pleading guilty but just needed a crime to be guilty of. His comments must have related to her drug use in the past. The two things were separate matters surely but not to Sturridge.

When a few minutes had elapsed, I strolled back inside and had a look at the cupboard. I had expected to be called back but when that didn't happen, I took that as tacit permission to take my own tour of the place. The cupboard's floor has been torn up to reveal a space which had neatly contained the body in a curled-up attitude. I guessed the gap had been eighteen inches deep and three feet by three feet or maybe slightly less on one side. A rough imprint had been left at the edges around the body by the hardened concrete, but you would not have recognised it as body-shaped unless you knew what had made it. I wasn't looking for anything in particular; this was just nosiness. I was distracted by the flash of the technician's camera and withdrew from the hallway until I was at the foot of the stairs. Here the wall had been covered with woodchip paper and painted a sickly magnolia derivative colour and possibly discoloured by years of cigarette smoke until a yellow lustre hung about like glaze. Oblongs of paler colour indicated that picture frames had once been suspended in a sequence of four.

A thought occurred to me. Supposing those four oblongs had been created by a set of photographs and taking that idea further, in one or maybe all of those, a younger Stephanie Kuler could be found. I toyed with this idea for a while, weighing up the pros and cons of me possibly finding evidence that linked her to the crime of murder. On one hand that would bring some kind of resolution a bit closer, but on the other, I didn't actually want to be the one whose brilliant discovery sent her to prison.

For the present I took another course and followed her upstairs. The stairs creaked under my feet but they felt solid, like they would last another hundred years and another hundred beyond that. The stair carpet had been ripped up and remnants of it remained attached to tacks like tiny growths of fungi. On the landing, a shred of carpet remained near a bedroom door, but the rest of the floor was bare boards that had been painted black along either side at some point to disguise the fact that the carpet had not been wide enough for the space to be covered.

I turned the corner and came to another shorter flight of stairs. To my left was a bathroom from which the door had been removed and ahead was a bedroom similarly denuded. The bathroom was newer than some other parts of the house that I had seen, but sported an avocado suite, the type that had once been popular but which was now so dated. In the front

237

bedroom was silhouetted the figure of Steph, immobile and staring out of the large, cracked window. I felt like an intruder. The sun streamed in, catching an aerial cavalcade of dust that circulated. I came closer to her. Even when a floorboard creaked she didn't turn. I was going to ask about the photographs, or if anything had triggered a memory, but she turned and I could see she had been crying.

'This is the place. This is where I killed him', she said.

Chapter Eighteen

Shortly after that we went our own ways, Steph and Wilson to the police station and me to my hotel. She was distraught. Now that she could seemingly connect her long-held feeling to an actual crime she felt totally crushed rather than jubilant. What a terrible end to the affair; her *'peace'* could only lead to torment of a different kind as she spent years languishing in prison thinking about the fact that she had taken a life.

There was more to come of course. From the outset we had both known that it wasn't simply a case of annotating her name alongside that of the murder victim and then slinging her into a cell. They would need to establish the whys and wherefores, answer all those questions that I had posed right from the beginning. The who, what, why, when, where… One of those had been answered; the body was here, the *'where'* question settled beyond doubt. As for the rest, well there was still much to be done in my view.

On a personal note the two most important aspects of the fateful trip to the house had been that Steph's immediate and unequivocal admission of guilt seemed to obviate the need for further enquiries. Had she still been unsure there was a chance that our false memory theory still held water. The second personal aspect was that she had dropped me at once. The establishment of guilt had rendered me surplus to requirements. When I rang Billy that night, he had used the phrase, '*superfluous to requirements*', a deliberate redundancy of great cunning and subtle wit.

'So, what are you going to do?'

'Nothing. I am not due home for another couple of days, but she doesn't need me, so that is that. I might just have to hang around. I'm a bit shocked.'

'I bet you are. None of us saw it panning out this way. They still have to check out the forensic evidence and so on I imagine, or at some point in the future this will be an unsafe conviction.'

'I reckon. All the same, having someone confess to a crime is the biggest single step you need surely. Apart from anything else, the forensic link you require is right there sitting in front of you, you're not scouring the country looking for them.'

We chatted for a while. It was raining in Belfast he told me and the police had broken up a rave which had been taking place in an agricultural shed on the outskirts of the city; no greater abuse of the lockdown regulations had been seen thus far.

For a while I lay on my bed and watched the blue sky fill with grey clouds. It had to happen. This had been the sunniest spring on record. Watching the weather change, I tried to assemble my emotions into one cohesive feeling that would explain the sudden malaise that had fallen upon me. Various elements played a part. Despite everything, I actually liked Steph, that was one thing. There were the drugs and that stupid party and some odd behaviour perhaps, but essentially, she was a decent enough person, who could have had a great life with children and holidays. She'd made mistakes but everyone deserved a second chance. She wasn't evil like Hitler or British Gas. The thought of this attractive, intelligent woman spending years in prison didn't really 'sit right' with me.

Steph going to jail was a waste, but I was also considering my own sudden redundancy and not just in terms of whether or not I would get paid. One minute I had a job, a challenge, a purpose in life and the next, nothing. With my other jobs finished, that meant I had nothing to do. I'd get by. There was money in the bank and something would come up, but right now I was unemployed in a practical if not legal sense.

When Georgina rang me that night, I felt able to discuss the case in greater detail simply because it was now concluded as far as I could make out. She was, as you might expect, shocked.

'Where are you now?', I asked her.

'In the conservatory.'

'I don't remember a conservatory.'

'It isn't attached to the house. It's a brick building with a glass roof in the back garden where he goes to smoke weed. It's probably not really a conservatory but that's what he calls it.'

'How have things been?'

'Fine. He's eased off on the great husband act – he can never keep it up – so we're just slipping back to normal, but he's drinking at home instead of on the way home.'

'I'm sorry.'

'No need. It was my choice. It wasn't an arranged marriage. So how is she bearing up?'

'Not well. But I haven't seen her since. The minibus dropped me off at the hotel and they all went to the station. That's it. She doesn't need me now and it feels strange, like a rejection, a bit like a bereavement. If she had been unsure about it that would have been a different matter, but she was so certain that they just assume they have the right person.'

'I suppose that's how it goes. In the first instance if you get someone who confesses to the crime then you take that as a given.'

'I reckon so. Up until then nothing but nothing had triggered any sort of recall and then all of a sudden as she looked around the house something happened and that was it. She knew that she had been to that place and had killed that man. After all these years walking around with just blanks, she suddenly had the evidence she needed to find herself guilty of murder. I don't know what it was she saw or how it came to her, but it was a sudden change. Christ knows how she feels now.'

'And all the false memory stuff?'

'Dead in the water. Events have moved on. I really thought that was it.'

'But being in the house could be the thing that triggered the false memory couldn't it? Wasn't that part of the theory you were working on?'

'True but she has told the cops that she killed this man. She is convinced of her own guilt so that is the end of the matter and she doesn't want me there. She doesn't want a solicitor, nothing. Once they match her forensics to his forensics it's job done. Shocking.'

'Shocking.'

'So, what are you going to do with yourself tonight?'

'Watch telly. There is nothing else. There is a petrol station nearby which is still selling food so I will go across there and get some stuff for tonight.'

'I can picture you now, sitting on your bed surrounded by wrappers and crumbs from your jumbo sausage roll.'

'All too accurate. A pathetic scene. If I had a car and it wasn't lockdown, I could drive out to a seedy bar and hang out with the other PIs like they do in the films. But the best I can hope for is some Coronation Street and a bag of wine gums.'

She laughed and I wished that she was here with me. That would have made a difference to my life at this moment. I felt a little bit down and in part it was because Steph didn't need me any longer.

A light rain was falling as I made my way across to the petrol station. I selected my food – including the obligatory *single man away from home* sausage roll – and paid, briefly chatting to the young Polish or Ukrainian woman on duty behind the Perspex screen, before I shuffled back to my room for a lonely night with the TV and the reproduction canvas of a man standing next to a boat looking longingly out to sea. It was a nice enough picture I supposed but the fact that it hung in every room in the hotel sort of killed it for me.

I was in limbo now. Steph didn't need me. Wilson didn't need me and presumably had to make arrangements for me to get home. Sturridge, that one-man detection machine, would be glad to see the back of me. What did the likes of him need with the likes of me?

The TV was the usual crap and away from my house I now longer had recourse to Netflix to save my sanity. That left me with BBC crap; history programmes with tales of old re-done with a socialist slant, quiz shows with prizes with a lower value than your basket after an hour's shoplifting in PoundlandWorld. The worst BBC offering, apart from their left-wing politics shows, were the sitcoms with canned laughter. Without it there was no way of knowing which bits were supposed to be funny.

ITV was less bad, but the night's viewing was constantly broken up by advertisements for things which now more than ever seemed useless; shampoos and cosmetics with made up ingredients like pro-zambotic cellulose replenishment oil or Arse 30 mineral powder for unbeatable results. Everything was approved by the British Made-up Shit Foundation with a 78% approval rating from the clinical trials carried out on some fucking morons they paid to comment.

Worse than that you could buy a drink which was filled with bacteria guaranteed to reach the gut alive. What these fortunate bacteria were supposed to do when they got there wasn't mentioned but the consumer didn't have to think about what they bought; the marketing men had done the thinking for them. The main thing was that they bought it. You could buy hand-held cordless everythings, life insurance, the cost of which was worked out as a tiny daily amount but which added up to a small fortune, and you could sell part of your house to bastard sharks in suits who then legally stole your children's inheritance in return for enough money to buy a Nissan Micra, a burglar alarm and a hearing aid just in case you ever went deaf.

Perhaps I just wasn't in a TV mood.

Later I watched an Albert Hinchcroft (Billy) film, a classic and thought it was crap. The plot was outlandish, the acting good but the twist was weak and involved a nun. I mean, a nun?

I slept badly that night. The bed was comfortable, the temperature was perfect and the corridor outside my door was quiet. I hadn't had coffee since breakfast and only a can of diet Sprite from the garage to drink in the evening, so there was no physical reason for me to sleep so poorly I wasn't quite ready to give up on the psychiatrist and her attempts to cure Steph. The matter was out of my hands; Steph wasn't even a client any longer and yet from my personal point of view we had given in too easily. I wasn't the one with the feeling of having committed murder, so the choice about how to come to terms with it was hers. It just seemed brutal that it should end this way and that her chance of innocence could be curtailed with the suddenness of the guillotine blade falling on her neck.

Eventually I dozed off but it was much later than I had planned, and to make the problem worse, I was awakened much *earlier* than I had planned too. My phone said 0655 as it buzzed uncontrollably on the bedside cabinet. I swore, fumbled for the light and then pressed the phone to my ear as I sat up.

'Yo.'

'It's Steph. I need you to come to the station.'

'Now?'

'After breakfast. They know you're coming.'

Which was nice since until that moment *I* didn't know I was coming.

'Fine. What's happened?'

'I don't think I did it.'

'That's good.'

'Inspector Sturridge won't think so', she said.

'We'll cross that ostrich when we come to it.'

'What?'

'Bridge. I meant bridge.'

I tried to go back to sleep but it just wasn't possible and at 0745 I got up, showered and shaved ready for my trip to the cop shop. The helpful chap at reception rang a taxi for me explaining they were charging extra for the risk involved in carrying passengers at this dangerous time. I didn't care; Steph was going to pay for it.

My driver turned up promptly in a maroon Mercedes saloon, spotless inside and out. There were worse places to spend your day than behind the wheel of a car like this. I told him my destination, he gave me an approximate price and we set off through sparse traffic until we came to a monolithic red-brick station that must have looked ground-breaking on the architect's drawings in the 1960s but which now looked like some government-run torture centre.

My driver looked south Asian but his name was Andy, which I took to mean that he was trying to westernise himself. Being from Northern Ireland with its florid Celts of varying persuasions, I was not an expert on Asian culture as it occurred in mainland Britain. He did his job without fuss and didn't overload me with handy facts about the local area, his views on Brexit, the BBC and the government's handling of the plague. Andy cleaned down the door handles and seats when I had paid.

Andy the taxi driver. Job done.

The desk sergeant made note of my name and then rang though to the CID office.

'Inspector Sturridge is on his way in. Would you mind waiting?'

'Of course not.'

'I think someone will text him that you are here.'

'Thank you.'

I took a seat on a chair made from hard, orange plastic beneath a poster about how the police were continuing to operate under the new lockdown regulations. I didn't read it before I sat. I have to say that the chair looked like it would have made a potent, if unwieldy, weapon for a drunk passer-by had they decided, on a whim, to drop in and abuse the police on warm Friday night. Had it been my police station, I would have bean bags scattered around.

Sturridge was going to be a hard nut to crack. For his chief suspect to try and snatch back her innocent status was going to be a blow. Already he would have boasted about cracking the case in record time, adding to the legend of *Sturridge of the Yard* or however he saw himself. I guessed he was going to be furious and when he blasted in though the main door, I could see my prediction was correct.

'Fucking bitc...', he cut his diatribe short when he noticed that I was sitting there waiting for him. The sergeant behind the desk at whom the comment was directed, looked bemused as if relishing his superior's discomfort.

'Right. You'd better come through. She'd be better off with a solicitor', he said. If I had stood closer, I might have heard the words, *'she's going to fucking need one'* reverberating in his head.

'Is Inspector Wilson coming too?', I asked but the question clearly annoyed him. We were still in the public part of the station.

'Why?'

'Just wondered', I said glibly. Me being glib wasn't going to help so I vowed to say as little as possible from now on.

He shook his head dismissively. He had no time for amateurs like me, but I had seen his type before on so many occasions and knew that they always met their just desserts in the end. For him I foresaw a divorce, alcoholism and dismissal but that trio of terrible of outcomes probably stemmed from watching trailers for too many gritty crime dramas in which the police protagonists are always outsiders with a dark past, maverick working principles and great anger. No one in the office ever cracks a smile and everyone is angry all the time. It must be exhausting.

Our passage through the station took us past the communications room and a dozen offices. We entered an interview room occupied by a female officer and, sitting, Steph. The latter stood and gave me a hug as I came in. Sturridge rudely dismissed the constable with a head gesture.

'What's going on?', he asked as he sat.

'I don't think I did it. It all came to me yesterday but during the night I woke up and I realised that although some of it seemed familiar to me, I had never actually been there.'

Sturridge stared at her with absolute contempt. Much as I disliked him, I could see his point. Because I knew more about her circumstances than he did I was inclined to believe her but, had I been Inspector Sturridge, I would have assumed that, faced with the enormity of the consequences which were likely to stem from her confession, she was getting cold feet. Such a view was perfectly logical but since it was still my belief that she hadn't killed anyone, my inclination was to accept her new version of events.

'So, you're saying that the house was familiar to you but you have never been there, is that right?'

'Yes.'

'How could that be?'

He had managed to fill every word uttered with the greatest contempt he could muster. I could imagine him talking to his children's teachers in the same way at parent's evening when they said that one of them needed to make greater effort in Food Tech or BTec Sociology, which weren't proper subjects in any case.

Steph looked over at me and I gave a supportive smile. At least I hoped that's what it was. We both knew in that instant that her trying to explain about false memory syndrome was going to do down like a lead baboon. I scratched my head which did no good whatsoever.

'Can I explain?', I asked.

'Not really. I'd like my suspect to explain if you don't mind.'

I smiled just to piss him off, but he did have a point.

'So, if you could explain, Miss Kuler?', he said. The 'miss' part of the sentence was very pronounced to show that he didn't go for any of that PC stuff. He was making the point that he didn't care to two people who didn't care that he didn't care. The merry-go-round of life, eh?

This was going to sound ridiculous to him and when she began it did sound exactly that.

'It's a false memory triggered by a traumatic event which has made me think that I murdered someone.'

Sturridge rubbed his eyes in a gesture straight from the BBC's *Guide to acting the part of world-weary detective, interview room section.*

'So, could this traumatic event be *actually* murdering someone?'

'No. Well, not in this case.'

'That's convenient. How do you know that the traumatic event which triggered these memories *isn't* you killing someone in the house we visited yesterday?'

'I just know.'

He took a deep breath.

'If it wasn't carrying out a murder, what was it?'

'I don't know.'

'You don't know… Can you see why I met be a little bit sceptical? What I don't get is why the traumatic event which makes you think you have murdered someone can't be that you have *actually* murdered someone. Wouldn't that make sense? You have a memory of murdering someone because that's what you did? Added to that is the fact that you confessed to it yesterday. This makes a pretty good case against you. You will have to stand up in a court room, having sworn on a Bible and tell the jury that you didn't murder someone, you just think you did. They will already have heard about your visit to a house on Waring Street as was – they're going to call it something else once the new estate is built – and the fact that you admitted your guilt.

'Apparently you have been saying for years that you killed someone and now that we find the person you killed, you decide that it never happened after all. It all sounds bit suspicious, as if you suddenly got cold feet. The reality hits you. You realise that this isn't a game anymore and that you are likely to go to prison for many years, and then you discover to your and everyone else's amazement that you didn't kill this person after all. Everything so far is pointing towards your guilt and then… nothing. It sounds like rubbish to me.'

Sturridge slumped back in his chair in a gesture that said that he had said his piece. His view that it all sounded like rubbish was hard to dispute. Steph had royally fucked up by admitting to the murder, but I knew that she couldn't have prevented herself from doing so. When it came to her 'feeling' she was compulsive and emotional.

A silence fell on the three of us. To say that it was an awkward silence really didn't do it justice.

'I'm not changing the paperwork', he said at last. 'You can discuss the matter with your friend here – your representative – but nothing is going to change from my point of view. You confessed. That's it. Nothing you have said this morning is going to change my view on that. I'll leave you two to chat but my advice is that you need a solicitor. You *desperately* need a solicitor.'

251

He was halfway out of his seat when Steph spoke.

'I was seeing a psychiatrist about these false memories.'

He sat again and said, 'maybe you were, Miss Kuler, but everything I have just said stands. I'm not going through it all again. You confessed. As far as I am concerned it is for you to convince a jury of your innocence.' After a brief pause, he stood once again, the legs of his chair screeching across the floor.

'Have a chat', he said with a nasty smile playing on his lips.

Once he had left the room, I reached across and squeezed her hand. It wasn't social distancing but she needed some physical reassurance.

'What am I going to do? It's bad isn't it?'

'Maybe not as bad as you think but you do need a solicitor.'

'Can you organise that?'

'I'll get on to it.'

I sighed heavily unsure how to ask the next question.

'What?', she prompted. I blurted it out.

'What's the truth of the matter? Did you genuinely realise that you hadn't killed that man?'

'Genuinely. I still think that I killed someone, but not him or at least not in that house. In the house it all seemed to come together but alone with my thoughts that entire semblance just fell to bits again. That's the truth.'

'Right. The first thing is this: until we get you out of this predicament, I would totally drop the whole *feeling about having killed someone thing.* Just don't say it and avoid any reference to it. If you look at it from their point of view, you are saying that you killed someone and they have a body found near a place where you lived, and when you were taken to that place you confessed to the murder. You get what I am saying? Now is the time to drop anything that suggests guilt.'

She nodded. We, or rather Steph and her solicitor, were going to have a job restoring her reputation as a sound witness to her own actions.

'Next thing is that things might not be as bleak as they appear. Now that you have retracted your confession, Sturridge is going to have to make a watertight case against you and that means having evidence which proves you did it. If you didn't do it then that evidence doesn't exist. He was going to have to do that anyway. It does mean that you are stuck over here until it is all done. Unless they let you back to Northern Ireland but you will be on remand somewhere as far as I know.'

'And the psychiatrist?'

'I think that will be on hold for a while. She did say that her dealings with you did not constitute evidence that you were innocent, so we wait until this is done.'

My phone vibrated in my pocket as I spoke to her but I ignored it for now.

'How long will all this take?'

'Honestly, I have no idea. The best thing would be if some evidence came to light which cast doubt on you as a suspect. But how long that will take I couldn't say.'

Steph looked utterly crestfallen. No matter what Sturridge might think and how things looked and what dirt the prosecution, if it got that far, might dig up on her, I was pretty sure that she was innocent of nothing more than some form of mental illness brought about by God alone knew what and exacerbated perhaps by the use of strong, illegal drugs. The problem with that was, who gave a damn what I thought?

Chapter Nineteen

I met Wilson as I left the station and we spoke briefly. He was too polite to express dismay at her *volte face* but I could see that he didn't really believe her amended story.

'It sounds like shit, I have to admit', I said.

He said nothing.

'She wants me to get her a solicitor.'

'Good idea', he said. 'We're going to have to go home now. They are obviously going to keep her on remand and there is no point sending her back just to bring her back here at a later date. So, I suggest you organise that while I book our flights.'

'They still have to find evidence to link her to the murder', I said.

'Yes. If they don't find any then she's off the hook.'

'How long?'

'Maybe hours, maybe days. If Sturridge doesn't find the evidence one way, he will try another way. He's not just going to let this drop. It has to go to the DPP of course and they will look at his case to see if it goes to court. But as for time, how long is a piece of string?'

When we parted company, I checked my phone. A text from Billy told me that Curt Johnson's body had been fished out of a river in Hampshire. Maybe Bill and I had got it wrong. This news didn't really fit with any of the theories we had come up with.

***

I was alone in the hotel after my taxi ride back from the station and had just laid down on the bed when my phone vibrated again, this time with a call. I suspected, rightly, that it was from Wilson.

'We're on a flight back to Northern Ireland at six pm.'

'That's fine. I can sign out of the hotel and be out by twelve but if I can be picked up from there?'

'That's fine. Make it four-thirty?'

'Great.'

'Don't forget that solicitor. I just had a chat with the inspector and he's bloody furious. Off the record, but he's going to try his damnedest to pin this on her.'

'In a way, I don't blame him. I didn't exactly warm to the man but from his point of view she is just messing him about.'

'Hard to argue with that. Just make sure she has a good solicitor. If there is so much as a shred of evidence, he will make the most of it. See ya later.'

I used the hotel WiFi to find a solicitor and then rang.

I briefly explained my requirements to a receptionist and was put through to someone by the name of Robert Cartridge. I kept it brief, if you'll forgive the pun. He listened and then agreed to take the case on. I told him which station she was in and told him that Inspector Sturridge was leading the enquiry. He grunted at mention of the name, which encouraged me because it told me that they had butted heads previously.

'Leave it with me.'

'It's not straightforward.'

'Murders are often complex. This one is a bit different but Sturridge will have to come up with the evidence just like any other murder. He's good and he knows it, but he can't conjure up evidence out of thin air. This lady is aware that you are getting a solicitor for her?'

'Yeah. The penny has dropped. I am going back home this evening but obviously she'll go through the whole thing with you. It started off with me acting as her investigator and led to this. The truth is she's innocent but bloody mixed up. You'll have to be very direct with her, otherwise she will lose her resolve. She always thought she had murdered someone and it had got to the point where she was coming under the care of a psychiatrist – I'll let her explain – but now we are in a much more complex situation.'

'Sounds like a challenge but if she didn't do it then we'll get her off. I can keep you informed if she is agreeable to that.'

'I'd appreciate that.'

I had confidence in Cartridge and I hoped that Steph would too, for she was in a fragile state.

That left me with four and half hours to pass before the pick-up. Thankfully the sun shone and I was able to buy a scurrilous scandal rag newspaper to pass the time. I located a public park and an open shop with toilets. Lunch was a prepacked sandwich and Mars Bar purchased at great expense from a corner shop. It was adequate. I was actually looking forward to just being back at home in my own house.

The paper had the usual stark warnings about lockdown transgressions and general doom. People were taking the easing of lockdown too literally and acting as if the crisis was finished by gathering on beaches and attending parties and barbeques in which the spectre of social distancing had been vanquished, at least in their tiny minds. There were other problems in the world too, which required protests and here too the participants collectively laid waste to the regulations concerning distancing.

By some godsend the minibus arrived early, relieving my utter boredom. The plane was waiting for us and the flight uneventful. We set off about ten minutes ahead of schedule because the few passengers were all seated in good time, and managed to shave off another five minutes from our return journey. Billy would have explained that it was downhill from England to Northern Ireland, thus the time saved.

Back home I watched the news, eager to hear the BBC's views on the lockdown breaches. They no longer provided plain news and had at some point extended their remit to telling us how to think. For rabid, angry socialists the transition from information to propaganda dissemination was either welcome or unnoticed. For anyone else including moderate, democratic socialists it was something of an outrage. For me, it was just another way to exercise my right to switch the TV off. I'm not sure if the truth existed any more.

Before I switched off, I wondered if the story of the Barton murder would come up but it didn't. Murder wasn't a big deal nowadays, or not until someone decides to sensationalise it. The media made the news, forming it around a tiny kernel of truth like an oyster making a pearl from an irritating grain of sand. A corpse turning up in a house on the point of being demolished just didn't make the grade. Maybe when they found out more about the suspect and the odd events that had surrounded her it would be worthy of a few sentences.

I texted Billy, arranging to see him in the office tomorrow in relation to Curt Johnson. My thoughts on the matter related to telling the police about the trail we had followed to track him down. I wasn't sure if we needed to bother. That done, I texted Georgina but she didn't reply. I let it go. Her situation was complex enough without me pestering her, although that didn't stop me worrying that she had come to harm.

***

The sky was clearing when I got to work. I noticed a message on the door of Strainer's Gym excitedly announcing that they would be reopening on the 1st July. It seemed like a futile gesture since no one would be able to see the notice on an internal door but that was their problem. I could picture people taking a sneak peak in their Lycra drawer at home in anticipation of the great day. Fine by me. They would soon be clunking and gasping away, burning those lockdown calories in an attempt to get the beach body they required for the holiday they couldn't have. I should have respected them more for their efforts and yet there was something ridiculous about having to exercise to develop and retain the body that nature had given us to track and hunt animals. Our lives had become too easy and we suffered for it.

The malaise which had crept up on me continued and I sat for a minute as the kettle – did I mention it was chrome? – boiled for my second, and second-best, coffee of the day. I couldn't get going and part of the problem lay in the simple fact there was little for me to be getting on *with*. It felt like there was a lot but even a cursory examination of the facts indicated otherwise. Steph was in the hands of the law over in England and Curt Johnson, until now my other remaining case, was faring even less well, presumably residing in one of those big drawers inside a morgue.

When Billy arrived, I spoke to him about it.

'A bit tricky', he said. 'It's down to the police now. The stuff I came up with about the SRR is presumably wrong. It might be right, I suppose, but we can see a more obvious reason for his disappearance. Beyond mentioning that we were investigating on his wife's behalf we haven't got much to say on the matter. He obviously didn't get to Hong Kong.' Billy paused as if unsure of himself for a moment.

'The only thing I can think of is that we give them details of what she told us. Whether that is of even the slightest use to them…', I said.

'Do you want to leave it with me and I'll ring 'em.'

'If that's okay?'

'I'll get on it.'

Billy switched on his computer and then assembled the information we had on Johnson before ringing the cops. It was typical of him to have every scrap of info ready for them if they asked. If it wasn't there in front of him, he could simply tell them that he didn't know and leave it at that.

I was a little bit concerned about Georgina by this point. She hadn't responded to my text of the previous evening. Normally she would have been able to do so in the morning with Ron at work and just her alone with Jess in the house.

An instinctive reaction would have been to text again but if she didn't respond last time why would she now? Without a reply, my anxiety levels would be increased without any consequent improvement in her situation. I was edging towards a troubling conclusion: Rod had checked her phone and picked up a text conversation between us. That didn't seem right somehow. I guessed that she was far too savvy to be caught out in that way and when I thought back to the content it was all pretty innocuous. Or was it? I really couldn't think what had passed electronically between us. Maybe it didn't have to be explicit, just the fact that she was communicating with another man being enough to send him into a towering rage.

There were other explanations. Perhaps her phone had fallen into the dishwater, or the battery had died, or she had lost it, or driven her car over it. I remember a friend telling me about a time when his wife was struggling to close the boot on her car. When she slammed it down it sprang up again so she slammed harder with the same result. She did it a few more times and then decided rather belatedly to check what might be causing the problem. Her phone had dropped from her bag into a recess in which the bottom section of the locking mechanism sat, and now it lay in smithereens. Maybe Georgina had done that.

The remaining possibility was that she'd had enough of me and just hoped that by ignoring me I would go away. If that was her plan it would work but it didn't quite fit with the nature of the person I thought I knew. I tried to dismiss these thoughts from my mind but they wouldn't go.

I could text again, or I could go round to the house. Either of these might make the situation worse. I could send Billy round there on some pretext. Or I could get Billy to text. I looked over at him. He was working away on the computer. Now, if it was his number which appeared on her phone then that would be okay since he was not obviously connected to me. Quite what I expected him to say wasn't too clear in my head. Maybe it was a stupid idea,

It was then that I made a decision.

I was going to prevaricate, and I was going to start at once.

My first action in this new plan involved me walking over to the window and gazing out at the city. The traffic was building up on the bridge like it did before the plague, but the two big Krupps gantry cranes, Samson and Goliath, had not moved for weeks and still spelled out a letter 'M'. A tanker lay moored in the lough and a single small aircraft took off from George Best Airport. I could just make out the Titanic Centre, sitting like a stone-filled ice berg. The car park was empty. I was restless now and worried. A wave of relief hit me when my phone vibrated in my pocket but it was only a text to win £10,000 in a draw. Each text back cost £2. I had once accidentally texted the wrong codeword in and still been charged my £2 with no chance of winning.

There was still no word from Georgina. I looked at Billy again but doing so did not give me inspiration.

'I'm going out', I announced.

'Anywhere nice?'

'I told you about Georgina?'

'No. Maybe.'

'Well, I haven't heard from her for a while and I am worried.'

'A jealous husband on the scene?'

'That might be the problem.'

'You'll get your fingers burned.'

'I'm surprised that you don't have another body part to drop into that expression.'

'I can do that if you want. You tell me the body part and I will put it into a sentence for you. I could even make up new sentences.'

'No, it's fine Billy. I'm going round there for a look.'

'Can I suggest an alternative course of action? Why don't you just text her?'

'I thought of that. What if that makes the situation worse? What if he has locked her in a room and taken her phone from her?'

'What if *I* text her?'

'I thought of that too. Might even make it worse than worse.'

'Right, I will mind the fort. Do you want me to send a message to Mrs Johnson?'

'Asking for payment?

'I was thinking condolences.'

'Not sure. Go on. I suppose it is the right thing to do.'

I was heading towards the door when my phone went off again. I was relieved to find an incoming text from Georgina asking if I would ring her. Playing it cool, I rang at once.

'Dropped my phone down the loo. It was in a bowl of rice all night.'

'You know that you can't eat that rice now?'

'It's safely in the bin. Were you worried about me?'

'No.'

'Liar.'

'Okay then, I thought Rog had killed you, cut you up into pieces and put your remains into the drains.'

'Nice.'

'Well you did ask. That's what I thought had happened or that's one version of it. I considered the toilet option and low battery or driving over it in your car.'

'Why would I drive over it on my car?'

'Time of the month?'

Billy fired a look at me suggesting I move the conversation on quickly.

'So, what can I do for you?'

'Where are you?'

'The office.'

'Can you get out?'

'Yep. Do you fancy bumping into me in the park?'

'What time might you be there?'

'I could be there at eleven-thirty.'

'I thought soldiers used the twenty-four-hour clock.'

'Okay, I can be there at eleven-thirty *hours*.'

'Better. I can bring a picnic if you like. Any requests?'

'What sort of crisps do you have?'

***

In fact, I was there at 11.25. Georgina came at 11.32. You see how words paint a picture?

'What have you brought for us to eat?'

'I will show you.'

She had cheese sandwiches and, as requested, I had jam. Jam sandwiches, not just jam in a pot. Raspberry, if you must know. Some people think that jam sandwiches are for children only but I don't care what those people think. Crisps, Lucozade Sport and strawberries finished off the meal which she laid out on a thin picnic rug.

'This is a real mix of healthy eating and incipient diabetes.'

'Thanks. Variety is the spice of life. Now the reason I have requested this meeting is because I wanted to talk to you about our mutual friend, Steph.'

'Okay.'

'Well one of Rod's friends is a geneticist. She works in research at the university and has become a sort of acquaintance/friend of mine. She knows Steph and, to cut a long story short, she was asking me how she was getting on. She knows about this obsession with the murder and so on.'

'I see.'

'You know where this is going?'

'Absolutely not but please carry on.'

'Well, she has a theory that she would like to test on Steph and it something to do with genetics and that what she is experiencing is inherited from one or other of her parents.'

'Oh.'

'You don't get it?'

'Is this biology?'

She laughed.

'Yes, I suppose it is. If you need to classify it as that for the sake of clarity in your own mind, then definitely biology.'

'Okay then. Photosynthesis, nucleus and MRS NERG.'

She looked puzzled.

'What?'

'I am summoning up my entire knowledge of biology in case it comes in useful in the conversation we are about to have. I got a 'C' in my 'O' level but it was over twenty years ago.'

'Twenty?'

'Thirty.'

'Right, well I'm not sure if any of those words will crop up but let me explain to you as best I can. I'm not sure that I fully understand it either but here goes…'

'I'm ready.'

'Good. First of all this lady – Anne with an 'e' – is more or less trying to disprove this theory.' I pulled a face but didn't interrupt. 'That is because she has a theory of her own and one way to give credence to her own theory is to disprove someone else's.'

'Go on. You haven't lost me yet. Getting close though.'

'Right, so there is a theory about genetic memories and these are things which you have not experienced for yourself but which have happened to ancestors and become part of your DNA.'

'Deoxyribonucleic Acid?'

'Fucking hell', she said in an unladylike manner. 'How do you know that?

'It sticks in my head like diarrhoea.'

'Diarrhoea sticks in your head?'

'Just the spelling of it. Would you like me to spell it for you?'

'Can you save it for a romantic moment? Maybe a candle-lit meal.'

'You'll have to remind me.'

'Oh, I will. Not going to miss that. Anyway, this means that theoretically Steph remembers a murder not committed by her but by a member of her family.'

'But this woman, Anne with an 'e', doesn't think this is the case?'

'Correct.'

'Carry on', I said, feigning a thirst for more scientific knowledge.

'That's more or less it. She didn't go into much more detail than that. I think she has a simplified version of the story for people like you and me.'

'Interesting.'

'So, what do you think?'

'Interesting. I just said that.'

'No, I mean in relation to Steph.'

'As an alternative to the false memory idea?'

'I suppose so.'

'The only problem is that things have moved on since last night. I tried texting you but your phone was in the toilet. She withdrew her confession.'

'Which is good.'

'If they had just accepted her at face value, but having confessed to it they aren't about to let her off. She's over there now.'

'Jesus.'

'The thing is she was a gift horse to the cop who was investigating. He is going to make it stick, or try to.'

'Will he be able to do that?'

'I suppose it depends on whether or not she did it. If she did it then there will be forensic evidence and that will be enough for a conviction I would have thought. If she didn't then you would think there'll be no evidence. It's not quite so simple but she's got a solicitor now. When this is all over then she might be perfect for this person's case study but that could be weeks or months away.'

'My God.'

'My God is correct.'

Georgina looked stunned for a moment or two.

My stomach rumbled.

'Shall we eat?'

The sandwiches were good. I know what you're thinking but not all jam sandwiches are equal.

'This is good. Thanks.'

'It's not much.'

It seemed as if Belfast wasn't staging any sort of protest about any current global upsets. I couldn't honestly attribute this to the great common sense of the Belfast public, many of whom in the past had taken part in huge protests and many of whom would do so again. They protested about things which had happened in their country and which affected them, so I'll concede that point but there were some over-the-top demonstrations and protests over the years. The worst was marching season where it had become the custom for wooden pallets to be provided for burning for cultural reasons. The cultural reasons were to do with hatred and the maintenance of division within society. Many otherwise sane people lost their marbles around marching season.

'Are you still there?'

'Did I drift off?'

'You did.'

'I was thinking about the many ecological problems facing the Kaibab plateau in Arizona.'

'Yes, it's a worry isn't it?'

'If only more people understood the problem.'

'Where do you get all this stuff from?', she asked, smiling.

'My head is like the women's jumper shelf in Primark at the end of a Saturday's shopping frenzy. Stuff everywhere in random piles.'

'It doesn't sound that way when I talk to you about anything.'

'No, I can actually organise it quite well and pick out the bits I need. But when I am dormant there is all sorts of stuff going on.'

'Dormant!', she said laughing at my use of the word.

'You know what I mean. I could tell you how many machine guns a Lancaster bomber had.'

'Phwoar, keep talkin', big boy.'

'Eight.'

'Eight?'

'Eight guns.'

'Fascinating.'

'I usually keep that for a first date but we have never really had such a thing.'

'Some day', she said wistfully. 'I suppose these are like dates. We just take each moment together when we get them.'

'That may not be enough for you someday.'

She pulled a face.

Around us couples and the usual office workers socially distanced and chatted over lunch or brunch, seemingly uncaring of the deadly microbe that circulated among us looking for victims that would keep their primitive species going.

'It's odd to think that the most sophisticated living things – that's us – can be felled by the least sophisticated. Here we are at the top of the tree. We can send people to the moon, build computers, invent plastics, transplant body parts and yet an unthinking virus can get into our bodies and fell us like an old tree. It's not even David and Goliath; the difference in size is a million times greater.'

'Cheery. It won't last forever.'

'It might. We might get a vaccine for it only for it to mutate and make the vaccine redundant. That's why we are never protected against the flu. A new one comes along each year.'

'I know that.'

'But it could be the same with this virus.'

We finished our meal and then lay back in the sun.

'What's next?', she asked

'Well, I'm guessing that Andrew Lloyd Webber will want to make a musical about it. He'll call it 'VIRUS!' God knows when they'll be able to put it on.'

'I meant for Steph.'

'Oh. I have to wait and see what the police do with her. The solicitor says he will keep me informed. I think he is doing that because it was me who hired him and is paying for it but he will still need Steph's permission.'

'Do you want to speak to this woman Anne?'

'If you can arrange it, suppose so.'

'She is keen to do it. I think she's ambitious. She wants to make a name for herself.'

'You don't really like her, do you?'

'Nah. She's one of those people you just get along with, but she doesn't really like me and *vice versa*. Unspoken and unacknowledged mutual disregard, I would call it. Ambitious people worry me. I think she would trample over people to get where she wants to get. She doesn't do that to me because I have nothing she needs.'

'Those people exist in every walk of life. I'm lucky. There's just Billy and me and neither of us is out to do the other down. You'd like Billy. He's a real one off. I like that phrase of yours, by the way, *'unspoken and unacknowledged mutual disregard'*. I might use it and pretend I thought of it.'

'She talks a lot I should warn you.'

'That is a common thing. People who talk a lot are usually talking about themselves, I find.'

'You've mentioned that theory before. That's her okay. Well, if she isn't talking about herself, she's talking about genetics.'

'That could be tiresome.'

'But bear with her for she might be useful to us.'

'You reckon?'

'If the theory turns out to be true, then that helps Steph.'

'I believe you. Arrange it and we will go round there. We get to spend a bit of time together.'

'But we mustn't make it obvious; she's a friend of Rog's', she said, shaking her head with disdain. It prompted her to further assassinate her husband's character but I listened patiently, wondering if the same fate would someday befall me when she had tired of my wit and charm.

'He's also a boring bastard who likes to talk about himself', she began. 'He likes everyone to know how much he gets paid, and what sort of car he has, and where he went to school, and that he played in the School's Cup final in 1999.'

I smiled and said, 'he's a great guy for sure.'

'Yep. Sees himself as a regular hometown hero. Not sure why.'

In the distance a siren sounded. Something made me think it was for the fire service and I felt as if our *rendezvous* was coming to an end. Always, I wondered if I had been witty enough or complimentary enough, but I was getting used to her now and she to me. When she stood, she straightened her dress and I noticed for the first time that there was a bit of a 1960s thing going on, maybe Jackie Kennedy but prettier.

'You look good.'

'You look adequate', she replied.

'I'm glad you noticed. I have practised this look of adequacy in front of a mirror.'

'I'm worth it.'

'Without a doubt. Text me when we're going to see Anne.'

'I will.'

'And don't drop your phone down the toilet.'

I wanted to kiss her, but for at least two reasons, chief of which was the public opprobrium it would attract, it was not possible to do so.

We parted and I made my way back to the office. Billy had gone but a note on my computer informed me that he was sending a card to Mrs Johnson, rather than a text. That was much better. Billy wasn't a total savage.

Chapter Twenty

I didn't like the sound of Anne but if she could help Steph then I would give it a go. Of course, by this time, Steph had bigger problems but I was thinking long term and there was the added bonus of being able to spend time with Georgina. Was that part of her plan? I hoped so. The arrangement was that we would meet at Anne's because we still had to socially distance. There were still three or four hundred people dying in Britain every day, more than died daily (on average) in the war, and I was still taking it seriously.

But we had amended the plan slightly. Georgina drove to my place and we travelled together to see Anne who lived in between the big smoke and the much smaller town of Holywood, a town in which no films were made and no stars lived. Holywood could be summed up with the word 'unremarkable', which was practically a compliment for a town in Northern Ireland. If it had a tourist information bureau at all it must have been a forlorn little place, probably only carrying leaflets for Belfast or maybe something about Bangor, further down the coast. You know the Smiths' song which mentions the *'seaside town they forgot to close down'*? Well, that could be Bangor. Bangor people reputedly believed themselves to be better than anybody else, but that might just be racist slander and not something I would repeat.

But some people did say that.

Anne's house was built on a hill and had high gateposts which were slightly too close to make driving in and out a comfortable experience. The house was larger than the space between the gateposts would lead you to believe, a bungalow with a double garage, palm trees in the garden and a fish pond. A large carp floated on its side on the surface. It was either dead or sunbathing. The grass needed to be cut and a battered Citroen hatchback sat on the driveway.

'She's divorced, isn't she?', I whispered as we made our way to the door.

It sprang open as Georgina reached out to knock and before she had a chance to ask me about my excellent detective skills. This fact only confirmed my suspicions for it was obvious that she had been waiting behind the net curtain watching out for our arrival, one old car on the drive, grass uncut… I took a last look over the distant city before I stepped inside. It wasn't Chicago or anywhere much but I loved that place.

A terrier dog of indeterminate breed leapt from the bottom step to greet us and then carried out a micro-piss on an elderly piece of carpet which had been laid there for that purpose. Which came first, the pissing, or the piece of carpet? It struck me that she was training this animal wrongly, but it wasn't my concern.

Anne was a larger than life character who emanated joy and happiness to such a degree that neither of these emotions actually applied to her. She wore a floaty floral frock which disguised the many bulges on her torso by making it appear like one huge bulge. Anne's hair was a mop of dark curls and she was bedecked with dangly jewellery that really didn't improve her appearance. She had long, painted nails on her hands and feet which made her look utterly gruesome and an ankle bracelet designed to make her look a bit *boho*. Everything about her spoke of QVC, loneliness and depression. I should have felt pity but I just didn't like her much, even in those first few moments.

Already she was gabbling away about God alone knew what. Georgina introduced me and she said a brief 'hi' but that was a cursory, throwaway greeting for she didn't give a damn about me and just wanted to witter away to her friend. She gave a lie to the old adage about being oversized and cheery. The cheeriness was forced and she wanted all the attention to be on her. This character assassination took place in my head in the first ten seconds of being in her house. I am quick to judge but I knew I was right; subsequent events were to prove that.

She led us through to a living room that was stuffy and smelled of unwashed dog. Two huge velour sofas, shit brown in colour, dominated and sat at right angles to a fluffy rug that looked as if it might have soaked up its share of dog piss in the past. A lava lamp, inactive, took pride of place on a fake stone plinth on one side of the dusty fireplace and a chipped fire dog was similarly situated on the opposite side. She had a paltry collection of vinyl and a few tapes on a shelf above a CD/tape/radio combination entertainment centre. In my mind, all of her records were those made by Demis Roussos, solely because she looked like him.

The net curtains lay untidily across the top of a free-standing shelf unit which supported a selection of coffee table books on psychiatry and general shit like that. I felt the need to hire a skip and gut this room and probably every other room in the house just for the sake of making the world a better place. I had the uncomfortable feeling that no matter where I sat, a dog's grubby sphincter had been there first.

The preamble to the actual business of the day took a while and Georgina shot me occasional apologetic glances when she could. When Anne left the room to make drinks she managed to speak.

'How did you know she was divorced?', she asked in a stage whisper.

'Are you going to tell me she's *not?*'

'It's sad really.'

'If you say so.'

She returned with three cups of tea in mugs badly stained with tannic acid and a plateful of Marie biscuits. This was Anne's version of pushing the boat out- in this case, the Titanic.

She chatted some more about all the things that were getting on her nerves at the minute including how confusing the PM's guidance on lockdown was, how unfortunate it was that we were leaving the EU and how terrible it was that that 'black man' – she didn't seem to know his name – had been killed in America. She rattled off these regrets and insults to her intelligence like a litany as if she had been programmed to feel offence and to express it in a certain, unthinking way. Had I shared even one of her views I would have found myself shying away from mentioning it simply because her beliefs were so robotically unshakeable. Anne was intelligent, and educated to within an inch of her life, but I wondered if she ever really thought about anything outside of her closed world of genetics. Everything, it seemed, was black and white and she assumed that disagreement with her chosen view was unthinkable.

After some minutes of this intense carpet-bombing of views had passed, I could see that Georgina, who had barely spoken, was getting a little weary. Personally, I thought our presence there was a mistake and an increasing waste of time. She – Anne – didn't really want me there but I was going to turn the conversation in the correct direction for my purposes whether she wanted that to happen or not.

'So how did you get into the field of genetics?', I asked. I had a fair idea that the answer was along the lines of went to school, did 'A' levels, went to university, stayed on for master's degree, spell in call centre, PhD, then through fortuitous timing, a job at the university.

'I studied biology at school and really got into the genetics part of it. It just fascinated me. It is the most important part of biology. Everything in biology is connected to genetics because it explains how the different characteristics turn up in the offspring of a species. It applies to me and to you and to the cabbages in the garden.'

I was thrilled. Cabbages. Who would have thought?

'So, this project of mine is all about genetic memories. I am writing a book on it.'

I had almost switched off by the time she actually got around to the point of our little gathering. I looked at my tea and took a sip but I ignored the biscuits. Dutifully, Georgina drank her tea and nibbled on a Marie, whilst smiling politely and nodding occasionally.

Had she not been talking about her favourite subject and how brilliant she was at it she would not have bothered speaking to me at all. I was hoping that Georgina was going to steer the conversation in the right direction and she obliged after another few tortuous minutes passed.

'So, you want to *disprove* the theory of genetic memory?', she said.

'It's not a theory exactly but it is an area of study that I personally don't believe in. It's rather Lamarckian in its approach.'

'Well, he's been discredited really, hasn't he?', I offered. You've got to admit that *Gongle* is a wonderful thing. I wasn't trying to close her down but the look of astonished distaste her face made it worthwhile. I mean, how dare a humble *whatever I was*, encroach upon her field of expertise? Luckily, she picked up her thread without difficulty, for I had shot my bolt with that one statement. She went on to explain the differences between the theories of Lamarck and Darwin.

Despite myself I was interested. There, I've said it.

From the corner of my eye, Georgina was giving me a disapproving look but that single piece of mischief had been hard to resist. To prick her balloon when she had already made her mind up about me had been a compulsion, more than a simple off-the-cuff remark.

'It shouldn't really be possible for such a thing to occur. Our DNA is the code which gives us all our characteristics whether they relate to personality, our appearance, our abilities, our intelligence, whatever. As we go through life other things affect us and it can be hard to pick out whether a certain characteristic is learned, for instance, or inherited.'

'Nature versus nurture', said Georgina. But she was allowed to speak. Anne smiled indulgently and said;

'That's right.' You see Anne had already designated Georgina as an intelligent person and me as a dense one. It was no easy matter for her to shift me into the same category as Georgina and, let's face it, she probably lacked the will to do so.

'George Best', I said. 'Gifted but also practised to make himself better.'

'Possibly', she said. Anne didn't care about football or my opinion.

'Now, we get mutations occurring in the DNA and these give rise to different characteristics, or versions of them. The mutations can be harmful such as cancer or mostly they have no effect at all. But...'

She held one finger in the air to emphasize her next critical point. I wanted to snap it off and poke her in the eye with it.

'Sometimes these mutations give rise to a new species. An example would be the giraffe.'

I looked over at Georgina. She was either rapt or doing a good impression of being so. I think she was doing her damnedest not to make eye contact with me.

'Millions of years ago, there were only giraffes with short necks. They lived on the plains of Africa and ate the same food from the ground as all the other herbivores. Every now and again a giraffe would be born with a mutation which gave it a longer neck and these giraffes had an advantage over the rest because they could eat food straight from the branches of the trees. In other words, they had a unique supply of food that they didn't have to share.

'Over a period of hundreds of thousands of years, they became more successful than the ordinary short-necked versions of the species. The short-necked giraffes were competing for scarce food with lots of other species and began to die out, leaving the long-necked giraffes to reproduce and eventually take over. Nowadays all the original types of giraffe have gone and only the long-necked versions are left. This is an example of competition, or of survival of the fittest. The best-adapted members of a species live long enough to reproduce and eventually they take over.'

Anne looked pleased with herself as though she had proposed this theory rather than Charles Darwin.

'Now, the relevance of this to genetic memories is the fact that it takes many generations to take effect. It was Charles Darwin who came up with these theories of evolution through his studies of Galapagos finches but he couldn't explain the exact biological mechanism because the work on that didn't really take off for another eighty years or so with the discovery of DNA.'

'Watson and Crick', I said.

Anne gave me a withering smile.

'And Rosalind Franklin', she added making the point that she was the expert and I was just someone who had checked a few facts on the internet. I think she was also letting me know that my omission of Franklin made me a sexist pig and her inclusion of same made her a feminist.

'The mutations which gave us a new species of giraffe happened in the DNA which is the chemical which gives us our chromosomes, which are long strands of DNA which contain genes. The genes are packets of information for every characteristic we have. A human being has forty-six genes. A cabbage has ninety-two.'

What was it with cabbages?

'The chromosomes are found in the nucleus of almost every cell in our body and that means that in theory you could take any cell, extract the nucleus, extract the DNA from it and then make a replica of that individual.'

'A clone', said Georgina.

'Precisely', said Anne, beaming. Yes, Georgina was allowed to say clever things. I was not.

'Around the same time as Darwin there was another scientist called Lamarck and he was studying essentially the same thing. He came to a different conclusion, again using the giraffe as an example. In Lamarck's version of events, the giraffe stretched its neck to reach the food on the low branches of the tree. In its lifetime its neck got a bit longer and it passed on this characteristic to its offspring. The offspring stretched its neck and passed this on to its offspring and so on.

'This was a great and very logical theory but neither man knew about DNA. Eventually Lamarck's theory fell by the wayside and now we know it could never have been correct because even if the giraffes had acted as he suggested this would not have brought about a change in their DNA. In other words, they couldn't have passed on the changes to their offspring.'

She smiled and took a breath.

'And the reason this is relevant is because genetic memories should be impossible in this way. Something that happens to a person shouldn't be able to alter their DNA and therefore they would not be able to pass it on.'

'So, in the case of Stephanie Kuler, she isn't carrying a memory of something that someone else in her family has done?', asked Georgina.

'That is what I want to prove.'

'But if nurture is part of it, why can't that happen?', I asked.

'Merely witnessing or taking part in an event doesn't cause a mutation in your DNA and therefore you can't pass it on. If you are born with a mutation then *that* might be passed on, but equally it might not. But she is claiming to have murdered someone and one theory is that, in fact, someone in her family did this but left her with the genetic memory of the event which makes her feel as if she actually did it. What I am saying is that is impossible.'

I knew that I was going to sound thick here and add weight to the status she already assigned to me but I was confused and I wanted clarity. Continuing through the rest of the evening with my mind stopped at a mental roadblock whilst everyone else drove on, continuing their journey of discovery, was not satisfactory for me.

'But mutations do occur in the DNA. So, if an event could cause it, then why couldn't it be passed on to Steph maybe through generations.'

Oddly, she was a little bit more accommodating this time as if I had asked a reasonable question which hinted a small degree of hitherto unnoticed intelligence.

'It would have to affect the DNA in every nucleus of every cell. Cells make new cells and pass on the DNA each time, so every cell with a nucleus has the complete blueprint for the entire organism. When an organism reproduces – and we might as well use a human being for an example – there are only half the chromosomes passed on in the egg and the sperm. When the egg is fertilised by the sperm you have half the chromosomes coming from one parent and half from the other. So, you're a mix of both parents.'

I opened my mouth to speak but she cut me short, correctly anticipating my next question.

'The mutation which gives rise to the genetic memory would have to occur in the egg or the sperm for it to be passed on. The chances of this happening are so slim as to be not worth considering.'

Georgina said, 'couldn't that account for the fact that situations like the one Steph has found herself in are so rare? Maybe one person in every hundred million, say, has a parent with this mutation just in the egg or sperm?'

'That would fit nicely but for one thing.' Anne looked smug.

'Go on', said Georgina.

'Mutations don't happen in that way. Mutations are caused by things like chemicals, exposure to radiation or sometimes they just happen for reasons which we don't understand and have no particular cause. That is why I don't subscribe to any theories regarding genetic memories at all and that is also why I am carrying out this study. Stephanie Kuler is the perfect guinea pig for this. She has a feeling that she has killed someone but no memory of any facts pertaining to it? It is only natural that someone assumes she is carrying a genetic memory of a family member who *has* killed. It wouldn't have to be a murderer; it could be a soldier in the war who killed a German, or someone who killed a pedestrian with their car, or even just someone who witnessed someone else being killed.'

'Okay then. If you used Steph in your case study and you were able to prove that she didn't have this genetic memory of someone else having murdered or just killed someone, what would that mean for her?'

'It might mean that she really had killed someone.'

***

That was more or less it. I think we tacitly agreed on Steph's behalf that she would take part in the study so long as a few conditions were met, the first being that she wasn't languishing in jail for murder. If that was the case, then the last thing she needed was for someone to add extra possible evidence of guilt. Another consideration was that Steph would be willing to take part, and in a fit condition to make a rational decision about her participation.

But I came away with the feeling that none of this benefitted anyone but Anne, who was really just out to make her name in the field of genetics. I don't think she even strongly denied this being the case. We didn't leave at once for she wanted to show us her huge garden shed which she was having fitted out as some sort of tantric crystal bullshit healing facility. When she told us about it, I genuinely had no idea what she was on about. For someone so keen on science, so grounded in it, this just sounded like utter tripe. I think the bottom line was that she needed the money.

Georgina tried to refuse the offer of a glass of wine but succumbed and we sat there for a further ten minutes talking about God knows what until my companion successfully made her excuses. The offer of wine didn't extend to me. I was driving and I was teetotal in any case but I wasn't even offered an alternative like another cup of tea. Sometimes I wondered if people just forgot I existed.

'It was lovely to see you', she said as we left, slowly withdrawing from her hall, onto the porch and then backing away towards the car. Anne was desperate to keep talking and I was equally desperate to get away. I could still smell dog piss and general staleness, so either these odours had suffused into my clothes or they were carried out from the house on a gentle breeze.

Anne was still waving as we reversed out.

'Thank fuck, that's over', said Georgina through a fixed smile. She was waving as she spoke. 'What a boring bastard.'

'She's the sort of person who keeps a chocolate orange in the fruit bowl.'

Georgina snorted with laughter but kept waving valiantly.

I edged onto the road and then turned for home.

'But, unless I misread the signs, you have a free tantric healing session there when her shed is finished', I added.

'Don't. Did you see that thing in the box?'

'No, what was it?'

'A massage table.' Georgina feigned throwing up. 'No way is she getting her hands on me.'

'We could stop off at mine on the way back', I suggested. I was at a junction waiting for a Nissan Leaf driven very slowly to pass by. The driver might have been trying to set an endurance record in their electric car.

'Your house isn't on the way back', she reasoned.

'That's true. I was only offering a coffee and some mouthwash to get rid of the taste of her tea.'

'I could do with some Shake'n'Vac to get rid of the smell from my clothes.'

'I think I have some. Would I have to vacuum you afterwards?'

'That's generally the idea. Quite kinky.'

I pulled out onto the main road, heading back to the city. I overtook the Nissan. It can't have been doing much more than twenty-five.

'Okay, back to yours then', said Georgina brightly. 'Shake'n'Vac, not coffee.'

Chapter Twenty-one

'Look at this', said Billy holding up the newspaper. We were in the office and the wind was battering the building. An orange carrier bag flew past the window at speed. Billy's paper had an article about Madelaine McCann, the toddler taken from a Portuguese apartment thirteen years previously.

'They have a German suspect in the frame now. He was there at the time living in a campervan. In jail at the minute but due out shortly.'

'A friend of mine had a theory about that whole thing', I said.

'Same. That wee girl is dead for sure. Bloody terrible.'

The office phone rang and when I answered it, I was speaking to Robert Cartridge.

'How is she?'

'Not too bad. Worried and upset but I have explained the ins and outs of the legal process to her and seen the evidence and what have you.'

'If it went to trial now what would happen?'

'Hard to say. What a jury would make of it is difficult to speculate on and how she would behave in court is another factor. She's not your typical murderer perhaps: well spoken, well turned out, quite likeable actually. Our legal system isn't bad but one jury might acquit her and another might find her guilty. I should tell you that they have found some DNA which links her to the body.'

'Oh shit.'

'Yes and no. It isn't a perfect match but the body is in bad condition. There is no DNA anywhere in the house that exactly matches hers.'

'Is that unusual?'

'A bit. Normally in the act of moving a body and burying it there would be DNA in the house but this isn't the case here. None of this is fool proof in any way. A partial DNA match could mean that a relative killed the deceased.'

'Is that likely?'

'At this stage anything is possible and nothing is likely. This is far from straightforward. Now, interestingly, they have said that the body is at least fifteen years old. In other words, Stephanie was seventeen or less when he died. They are doing tests and they might find out that it is much older than that.'

'But not less old?'

'Not according to Sturridge. This works in our favour hopefully since we can look at where she lived up to the age of seventeen. But that doesn't mean she isn't guilty. I think the angle Sturridge will take is that since she was in care this was an abuser that she decided to kill. But if he goes for that angle, he has to discover a carer/abuser that has gone missing and there is no obvious person for that. Also, we have a possible identity for the deceased. He is either someone called Alwyn Crow – sounds like a seventies progressive rock band – or

Harold Compton. Both lived in the area. One disappeared in 1978 – that's Crow. Compton disappeared later but no one knows exactly when because he was something of a recluse and was rarely seen out and about. It is hard to get someone to even remember when they might have seen him last but probably mid nineteen-nineties.

'Obviously, Sturridge needs to know which dead person he has got and then make a link to Stephanie. He also needs to find out who Stephanie actually is. She spent her entire life in care and at present no one is too sure who her parents are.'

'Could the dead person be a parent then? Her dad obviously – I'm thinking of the DNA match.'

'Again, anything is possible. I don't doubt that something along those lines is on Sturridge's mind. Here is a possible scenario for him. Steph decides to find out who her dad is. Discovers him, finds out she doesn't like him much, or is frightened by him or something, then kills him and buries the body in the house. That all fits but they would have to know if she had access to that house, otherwise you'd expect the residents to notice a distraught child burying a dead man under their stairs.'

'You'd think so.'

'But that just leads to more questions. Why wasn't his disappearance noticed? Where were the witnesses who saw him in the company of his long-lost daughter et cetera? It all quickly falls to pieces. This is supposition on my part. I am trying to think it through as Sturridge would. We just have to wait and see what transpires and take it from there. I am cautiously optimistic.'

'Good. Well thank you for what you are doing and if you see her just tell her I said to keep her chin up.'

'I will do that. I'll probably know a little bit more by mid-week so you can expect another call from me.'

We said our goodbyes and I sat back in my chair thinking about Steph.

Billy looked over and said, 'she's an enigma wrapped inside a conundrum. Who said that?'

'Kevin Costner in JFK.'

'Wrong. Churchill.' Billy tapped on his keyboard gongling the exact quotation. He looked over as he read from his screen, '*It is a riddle, wrapped in a mystery, inside an enigma.*' He was talking about Russia.'

'So, you got almost everything about that quotation wrong?'

'I think of it as an inadvertently unique quotation. Probably should get it copyrighted but I'll let you use it.'

'Ta. What about this one? *Unspoken and unacknowledged mutual disregard*'.

'I do like that but I suspect that you didn't come up with it.'

'Georgina. She has given me permission to use it. Or rather I said I was going to use it and she didn't object.'

'Can I use it?'

'I'd have to check with her first. I don't think you would ever need it, if I am being honest. Who do you know that you could apply that to?'

'Lots of people. You'd be surprised.'

'Did you ever ring Della again?'

'Yes.'

'And did she answer this time?'

'Yes.'

'These are very good answers Billy, but if you feel like adding any detail to them by using extra words or anything, just go ahead. I'm thinking in terms of making the conversation flow a bit rather than me asking you a question and then you replying with a one-word answer.'

'Okay.'

'Is that it?'

'Okay, thank you.'

'So, I take it she blew you off?'

'I think you mean blew me *out*, but no that did not happen. She said she was stuck at home. She's shielding because she has had chemotherapy in the past.'

'I didn't know that.'

'Cancer. That's why she left the cops.'

'You just never know. She's okay at the minute?'

'So she says, but she has a weakened immune system so she isn't so good at fighting off infection.'

'You know what you should do? Send her a big box of chocolates and flowers.'

'Done it already.'

'Good man.'

'You haven't asked why I am in the office today when we don't have a case at the minute.'

'Billy?'

'Yes?'

'Why are you in the office when we don't have a case at the minute?'

'I'm glad you asked. I have been asked to look into something for someone.'

'Okay.'

'That's it. Well, I'm sort of wondering if you are okay with that. It's like doing a homer or something.'

'It's fine. You go ahead. You're on a casual contract, if anything, so you can do as you please. In fact, if you need any help or need to use the office just go ahead.'

'Good. That's okay. I didn't want to seem like I was going behind your back.'

'So, what are you looking into? You don't have to say if you don't want.'

'It's a bit delicate. It can't go out of this office.'

'Fine by me.'

'Right, this person that I know has asked me to find out about this other person that *they* know. This other person has been up to no good but it seems as though the Feds are not very interested in chasing this up.'

'Informer. Stinks of it.'

'Yep. That's what he thinks too. He just wants me to do a bit of digging.'

'Is this to do with drugs?'

'And other stuff too.'

'And the Troubles?'

'The tail end of it. I know what you are going to say; steer clear.'

'I was going to say be careful. I would tread very lightly with this one. I know you know these people Billy but there are plenty of *wrong'uns* on both sides, no matter what they might claim nowadays.'

'I know. I keep them all at arm's length and that has worked for me my whole life. Never had any bother.'

'I think you are worried about this.'

'A bit. I'm getting into territory I have always avoided. For whatever reason, I have always known what is going on but I have never been drawn into anything. It's as if they sense that I am above all that.'

I could tell that he was worried just by the sincerity in his voice. Plus, these were things we had never discussed at all.

'I suppose the option of saying 'no', has gone?'

'It wasn't a full option but I agreed to it before I knew what was involved. This might even get me into trouble with the other side if I mess it up.'

'Just take your time with it and keep your options open. You might even find that what they think has happened is not the case at all.'

'That would be the best result for me.' Billy pulled a face. I knew slightly more about Billy than he thought. I knew his dad had been a middle-ranking terrorist on the Protestant side and I knew that he had a gun hidden away somewhere in his house. But it was easier to simply not mention these things and so I never did.

Chapter Twenty-two

I was starting to get the coronavirus blues. With no case to investigate I didn't even have a reason to go into the office and so I sat at home either watching Netflix or looking for a new series to watch. But I was fine really. There had been worse times in my life. Being at a bit of a lost end didn't constitute a personal crisis for me.

I didn't subscribe to the notion that the war-time generation was better than this one necessarily. It was all a matter of perspective. They had to endure what they had to endure and there was nothing that could do about it. Life was, generally speaking, much harder in those days, so the transition from not having much spare in the way of food to having even less wasn't pleasant, but it was manageable, and an unintended consequence was that people ate better and stayed slimmer. Lockdown didn't really compare.

We had to endure what we had to endure and we could only properly compare it to the lives we had led before, which in my case was much the same. A clip of a famous singer apparently breaking down in tears at his home had gone viral. It seemed to gain him no sympathy whatsoever, which was fair in my eyes. My question was this: why did he bloody film it in the first place? I would have been mortified if it had been put on there by accident.

That was him and this was me. He was a superstar pop singer and I wasn't even a superstar investigator. Was I ever going to get my own reality TV show? Almost certainly not.

The one bright spot in my life – and it was more of a sun than a mere bright spot – was the presence on the end of a texting machine of Georgina. The arrangement was that she would text when she was free to do so, the logic being that I was always free to receive her electronic communication messages. That implied that I had no life. I could have been resentful in the modern fashion but for the fact that it was essentially true.

The mental impasse was broken by a phone call from Robert Cartridge the following Wednesday.

'There is a bit of generally good news to report', he said. 'It is looking likely that the body is twenty-plus years old which, if true, is making it more and more unlikely that the murderer is Stephanie. They don't have the identity of the man but it seems like he was around six feet tall and was killed by a blow to the head. This blow came directly from above which makes it likely that he was hit on the head by someone of nearly equal height or someone who was standing on a box or maybe a bottom stair. Stephanie is five foot six now and fifteen to twenty years ago would presumably have been less. Also, the blow completely smashed the top of his head which indicates huge force being used.'

'That sounds good. Not that he was hit on the head…'

'It is good but she's not out of the woods. You would think that the police were refining their search to someone of the appropriate height and with a fair bit of physical strength, probably not a teenage or younger girl but Sturridge has the bit between his teeth. He had Stephanie bang to rights once and he isn't about to let her slip away. It's a matter of pride that he can pin this on her but I am beginning to wonder if he is a bit autistic too. He can't let go of this, and all because she confessed. You know, if she hadn't done that, he wouldn't be considering her at all.'

'Yep. If she could just have held off. She's impulsive.'

'His latest pet theory – this is the one he's going to use if he can't get her for the murder – is that she was a witness to it but never said anything. He is trying to use the false memory angle for that. He's getting desperate.'

'From my inexpert view it sounds like he'll have a job making any of that stick in court.'

'I agree. Like I said we're not out of the woods yet but even if he implies that she was a witness or an accomplice, she was only a minor when it happened. A jury isn't exactly going to be baying for her blood. And he has to think of his reputation too. He's getting close to the point where he is going to make himself look like an idiot.'

'A spiteful idiot', I suggested.

'Agreed.'

'How is she doing?'

'Okay really. I think I have persuaded her to drop the whole *feeling that she has murdered someone* business. She is aware of how unhelpful that will be if she brings it up in court and they *will* ask her about it. If she says in court that she still has the feeling that she killed someone they will probably stop the cross examination right there and let it hang.'

'*No further questions*, that sort of thing?'

'Exactly that. As a safeguard I was thinking it might be good if we got her psychiatrist in as an expert witness.'

'Okay. I could run the idea past her. She is private so presumably it is a question of paying her to come to court.'

'Just sound her out. Belt and braces. The more ammunition we have at our disposal the better. You have to remember that if this goes to court it isn't just Stephanie versus Sturridge. It is her barrister versus their barrister and he will have his case lined up with everything they can find. Ideally this will get thrown out before we get to that point but we have to be ready.'

'I'll get onto it. Thank you for the update. It's encouraging.'

'It is. If we keep her out of jail then all you have to do is sort out what is going on in her head.'

Which was more or less what I had been trying to do since near the beginning of the case.

I didn't like to count my lizards before they had hatched but this was good news. There was a real danger that Sturridge's superior would tell him to let her go before he made the entire police force look like utter lemons. Reputation was everything in the police. Once the public begin to lose faith and the press start stirring things up with headlines that mislead gullible readers, then you are truly up against it.

It felt like a matter of time before someone concluded that when all the known facts were added up it could not have been Steph who had killed this mysterious person.

I felt the knifepoint of frustration pointed at my chest. If only she hadn't confessed. That was the weakest part of the story that would have to be recounted if she was to stay out of prison. I could picture '*my learned friend*' coming back to that again and again, referring to the bundle of notes in his hand.

'*If what you say is true, then why did you confess?*'

'*Why did you confess?*'

'*How do we know that when you confessed you were not, in fact stating the truth?*'

'*Why should we believe you now when you have previously confessed to this crime and then withdrawn that confession?*'

'*Which version of events is true?*'

Maybe I was over-thinking it but if it got to court then they were going to go all out for a conviction. To do otherwise would have made a mockery of the legal system. Better by far that Sturridge's boss took him into his office – coffee and biscuits – and told him to give up.

'*Sturridge, you weasel, just stop before you make yourself look like an utter plank.*'

Let him down gently…

***

The text asked if I was in the office. I replied that I was not but that I could go there and if I happened to bump into anyone on the way, say in the park, then I could certainly make time to engage in a socially distanced chat.

Obviously, I set off at once and to my immense surprise I bumped into Georgina in the park! After a couple of days of rain, the sun beat down on us as it might in Madrid or Rome. Maybe not quite as hot as either of those two places but by Northern Irish standards it was hot. Sticky shirt hot. Salty lip hot. Hot enough for an Orangeman to remove his bowler hat. If you have no idea what that means, type 'Orange Order' into *Gongle* images.

'Fancy meeting you here', she said.

'It is indeed a wonder.'

There was a particular tree under which we had sat on a number of occasions and which I had begun to think of as *our tree*. Its roots had grown up as well as out and in doing so had made two low, but comfortable seats padded by spongy, nutritious earth, while above, its verdant canopy protected us from the sun and kept us cool in a green, airy jungle.

But that tree wasn't available so we sat under another one.

'I didn't bring a picnic this time.'

'It's zero nine forty-five hours', I said, making the point that it was too early for a picnic.

'Twenty-four-hour clock really gets me aroused.'

'I know. That's why I use it. Some people say that it helps avoid timekeeping errors but I haven't noticed that personally.'

'How are you keeping? I just wanted to see you.' She rubbed her forehead as she spoke.

'I'm fine. You look like you have a headache.'

'Just a bit. It'll pass.'

'You need some of Anne's tantric healing beads.'

'She can stick those…'

'Apparently so. Anyway, things are moving on with Steph's case. It is getting so that I can't see them taking her to court but I wouldn't want to bet my shirt on it. How are things with the husband?'

'Same as ever. He's begun whinging about lockdown. Doesn't want to wear a mask and all the rest of it.'

'What do you think?'

'I'd like him to wear a mask. Preferably one that stopped him breathing. If not that, just one that stopped him talking would do.'

'Hmm. Lockdown is never going to end if people don't start playing by the rules again. We'll be doing this for the rest of our lives. What are you going to do about him? Are you going to stay married and hope that things get better?'

'I don't know. You know how people say that there's a thin line between love and hate? Well, I think that is true. Two people who are too different or even too alike can love each other but hate each other for some of the time and it can flip between the two until they can't bear to be in the same room almost.'

'That's you and Ron?'

'No. I just hate him all the time.'

'Oh.'

'I can't remember what I ever liked about him. I can't remember ever loving him or finding him funny. I can't remember thinking about him and getting that little tingling sensation in my tummy or going for autumn walks hand in hand and just feeling pure contentment. I don't think any of it ever happened. It feels like it has been a totally hollow experience right from the beginning.

'I'm sure there was a time when he melted your heart.'

'There must have been something but honestly I can't picture any events that we enjoyed in that way. I can't remember loving him. I can't remember even liking him. He reminds me of a PE teacher: brash, thick, a bit of a bully but thinks everyone loves him. He is totally self-absorbed but doesn't realise that most people just think of him as a boorish twat. His mates are the same.'

'Ah well, that is the problem then. If you surround yourself with people who are just like you, you never really get a fresh perspective on your own position. It's like these diva singers or film stars who have an entourage and make wild demands everywhere they go. No one ever tells them the truth about their behaviour, so they just carry on and on in the same way thinking that everyone adores them.'

'He just lives the bachelor life with his moronic mates who all think he is funny and edgy and a bit cool.'

'Maybe you should bite the bullet and divorce him. In most cases the mother gets custody of the child.'

She sighed.

'Okay, the last thing I will say on the subject is that I can help you. If you need grounds for divorce, I can probably help you to find them.'

'It seems wrong.'

I nodded but didn't point out that meeting here and talking this way was even wronger as Billy liked to say.

304

'Just have a think about it.'

Our conversation, already in its death throes, was cut short by the presence of a fattish man in jeans and a red T-shirt which said 'I am a keyworker' on it. He walked past us, a little too close really, his head held high and his gaze fixed at some point way ahead of him. He had become, through the medium of Covid-19, a cut-price man of destiny with the T-shirt to prove it.

'Can you buy those or has he had it made?', asked Georgina, waspishly.

'God knows. People are beginning to assign themselves legendary status over this, just because they have decided that overnight for no good reason other than doing their jobs, they have become heroes. It's getting a bit unbearable.'

'Do you go out and clap the NHS?', she asked me.

'I live by myself in a very short street. I would feel like a complete dick standing in my front garden clapping. I'm pretty sure no one on the street has bothered. I'd look like a mental patient. I bet Rog does? I can picture him putting down his beer bottle and clapping away, maybe a few whoops thrown in.'

'We all have to do it. A few of our neighbours join in. It gives Rob the feeling that he is really contributing to the fight. In fact, he has never contributed to anything in his life, except the size of his waist.'

She looked at me and said, 'you aren't fat.'

'I'm older than him though.'

'But you aren't fat.'

'If we lived together you might find plenty of things to hate me for.'

She smiled sadly. I don't know if it was a wistful smile for something that would never happen or an acknowledgement that I was correct. Either way, her sadness communicated itself to me and I recognised that this relationship we had was never really going to develop. More likely in fact was that it might wither and die.

'We just have to take the good times and be together when we can', she said.

'And when it rains, we can't meet in the park. We won't be sitting here in December, in the rain, on the wet ground.'

'You have made me think of Christmas Day. The fire in the grate, snow falling outside, the tree in the corner, Bing Crosby singing, 'White Christmas', a glass of glühwein, opening our presents.'

I smiled. It was a nice scene she had painted but I didn't bother to point out that she had a child who appeared nowhere in this portrait of seasonal happiness. Jessica, her daughter was an inconvenience for her in that respect. That's not to say that Georgina didn't love her but rather that she couldn't dream of a future in which she risked losing her to her husband. That was my interpretation of it anyway.

We parted company and I drifted back to the office to check my emails. I hadn't intended to go in. I stopped briefly at the little grocery shop thinking I might buy something for lunch but moved on when I saw and heard two women – one of them wearing a mask – arguing about the distance between them. The gist seemed to be that one of them, without a mask, had strayed into the other's personal exclusion zone on a number of occasions during their shopping trip. Ironically, they were both almost toe to toe as they argued. The unmasked woman was enormous with a shock of wild ginger hair and the other one much smaller, neat and fastidious-looking. If it turned into a fight it would be slaughter.

Some people weren't coping well. I decided to give the shop a miss so that I did not get knocked out in the exchange of punches. In case you have never experienced it, let me tell you that an exchange of views between two angry Belfast women was never pretty. There was little decorum, much blood.

Chapter Twenty-three

'Good news' said Cartridge. 'They're letting her go and dropping the charge against her.'

'Thank God for that', I said.

'The case fell apart. I'll let her fill you in on the details but the single basic problem was that the deceased was killed before she was born, which rather got her off the hook. Even Sturridge had to accept that she couldn't have killed someone before she had even been conceived.'

'When does she get back?'

'This afternoon. Getting into George Best Airport at half-two. She has money to get a taxi but she'd appreciate a familiar face being there for her.'

'Of course. If you can get a message to her, tell her I'll be waiting for her.'

'I will. I'll send you my bill in the next couple of days.'

'Please do. Thanks for what you did.'

'It wasn't much in the end but I did point out a few relevant points to old Sturridge. Hopefully I made him think about what he was doing but you never know with his type. They have yet to establish the identity of the dead man by the way but they are still working on it. He doesn't appear to be

308

either of the men I mentioned the other day. Also, they have been unable to establish an identity for Stephanie. They gave her the surname Patterson but she was dumped outside the children's home with no clue as to her identity.'

'She's an enigma.'

'For that any many other reasons. There is just one other odd aspect of this. You remember the DNA match – the partial match?'

'I remember you mentioning it.'

'Well, all things being equal that would have put Stephanie – and I hate this expression – that would have put her in the frame for it. Not conclusive proof but it would have been hard to explain how this partial match was possible if she had never been there or was not involved in any way.'

He had mentioned it before but this reminder left me puzzled.

'So how can that happen?'

Cartridge laughed and said, 'if he was her father.'

We wound the conversation up shortly afterwards and I checked the clock; not yet time to fetch Steph from the airport. I sat there in my executive part-leather Argos swivel chair, feeling like an extra in a new series of the *Outer Limits*. If only it had been so simple. Had we been filming the *Outer Limits* Steph would have travelled back in time to kill her father before she had been born. The scriptwriters would have had to come up with some conveniently freakish occurrence in which she had still been born without her father having been around. That was the thing about science fiction, you could just make anything up: a special key that unlocked a cupboard, or a magic crystal, or the intervention of an all-powerful alien being.

But since we weren't filming the *Outer Limits*, I was going to assume that none of those things listed were possible. I wondered if writing things down would help? I had a spiral bound pad and a selection of Biro™ pens, kept especially for situations like this. I might as well tell you I had the works: elastic bands, a stapler, Tippex™, pencil sharpener. You name it. Literally, you name it, I had it. But I just didn't think this frankly astonishing stationery array was going to help me to get to the centre of this conundrum; Stephanie had been born years after her father's death.

This couldn't be true.

***

She looked fine as she came through, maybe pale and thinner in the face but, essentially, she was in good health. It wasn't as if she had spent ten years in a far eastern prison on drug smuggling charges, so there was no reason to suppose she had been starved or beaten.

'How are you keeping?', I asked as I took her bag.

'Fine. Glad to be out of there. That bastard Sturridge was very pissed off with me.'

'Poor man. Very frustrating for him.'

'Mr Cartridge was nice, though.'

'Good. He didn't like Sturridge. When I realised that they had encountered each other before I knew he was a good choice.'

'He helped keep my chin up.'

The airport was almost empty like the set of a zombie film. The zombies were outside just waiting to get in obviously, but a quick-thinking security guard had locked the electric doors. We would have to stay inside living off food stolen from the vending machines: energy drinks, flapjacks and crisps. The novelty might wear thin quite quickly.

In reality the electric doors slid open as normal and the forecourt was inhabited by a single taxi and no zombies at all. I was beginning to think that Belfast's zombie population was a *fig roll* of Billy's imagination.

The car park was virtually empty and my car was close at hand as a result.

'Let's go.'

The roads weren't empty but emptier. I wouldn't have noticed a reduction in traffic had I not been looking for it.

'Did you grow up round here?', she asked.

'Other side of the city. This part is called Sydenham. There was a big aircraft factory here and the shipyard further on. This wasn't an airport. It was a small RAF base. Very different in those days. Lots of soldiers about. It's all history now. I can't quite imagine it as it was.'

'Before my time', she said.

'There's a generation of people who know nothing about it.'

'Was it bad?'

'At times. It came and went. Some days – probably most days – no one got killed, and other days maybe three or four people got killed. Now and again lots of people got killed.

Looking back, it feels as if someone got murdered every day but if you look at the numbers of dead that wasn't the case. Not even close. And as for how bad it was, that depended on where you lived. Some people had to put up with intimidation from their own side and threats and God knows what.'

She nodded and fell silent, seemingly deep in thought. She stared straight ahead.

'Which side were you on?', she asked out of the blue.

'That's a good question. I was a Protestant even though I didn't go to church or anything. So, some people would say that I was on that side but there are shades of *side-ness* – I know that's a made-up word. For someone like me there was never any doubt that I wanted to be British but I personally stopped far short of supporting terrorism to ensure that happened. And on the other side there were people who wanted to be Irish but who didn't support the IRA or the INLA. There were nationalists and republicans, unionists and loyalists. Shades of opinion, shades of what lengths you would go to in support of your beliefs.'

'Confusing.'

'It is. I understand it because I grew up with it but for an outsider it's confusing. Things are much better now. The division still exists but for most of the time we can all just more or less get along. So long as we don't talk about politics then everything is fine. The Catholics would still like to be Irish and the Protestants still want to remain British but no one has to die. But the truth is, a lot of people miss it. Some people need a cause and the violence that goes with it. Others can only find fulfilment by depicting themselves as urban guerrillas.'

'I don't get it.'

'Well, first you need to get people to hate other people. Somehow or other there are unseen powers at work. The media stoke it up. It has happened throughout history. There was a time when the workers of what was then Ireland almost came together but then someone injected a little bit of politics or religion into the mix and split them up again into Protestants and Catholics who could be primed to hate each other more than their bosses. The same thing happens today. The media spread half-truths and set gullible people off on protests, then run stories on their disgraceful behaviour.'

'You sound like you need to live on a desert island all by yourself.'

'I have actually booked myself a retirement bungalow on the Moon. I find the world a dispiriting place sometimes.'

'You know the feeling that I talk about?'

'That you killed someone?'

'Yes.'

'You still have it', I said. 'But that is what we can work on. We know that you didn't kill that man in Barton.'

'Okay.'

***

We didn't talk much for the rest of the journey and when I dropped her off at her house, she looked a forlorn figure as she made her way to the front door. Although she wasn't going to prison, the torment continued in a slightly more relaxed format. It was strange to consider this fact after everything that had happened. We were no further on. True, we had some possible courses of action to take, but essentially Steph was still battling the same demons that had plagued her for much of her adult life. Certainly, she had made mistakes, but who was to say that these didn't stem in part from the difficulties she was experiencing? This thing that she described as a 'feeling' was more like a disability and just because we had established that she didn't kill this man in Barton that didn't mean her paranoia was in any way diminished.

For now, the best I could do was to get that next psychiatrist's appointment organised.

As I drove home, I felt uncomfortable with... everything. I felt uncomfortable with the world. We could send people to the Moon but not exist side by side. No country had been more divided than mine, so God knows I am an expert in the matter of manufactured fear and division. Anti-Semitism was on the rise. How, after the events of the mid-twentieth century could that ever be? And now the lockdown regulations were being flouted by protestors whose actions threatened to kill many more people than the one they were commemorating. People still acted without thinking.

I found it depressing.

It was one of those nights when I craved a drink. It was a mild craving, if such a thing exists. But I maintained my abstinence via the usual route available to me – the house was devoid of alcohol. I had a bottle of hand sanitizer that I had panic-bought prior to the pandemic hitting our shores, along with seven hundred toilet rolls, three quarters of a tonne of noodles, four hundred packets of Nice biscuits which I could slide under the door to myself if I had to self-isolate and a bag of Quavers so what if I drank the hand sanitizer? What could be the harm? I had survived Saddam Hussein's missile attack, how bad could the effects of a bottle of hand sanitizer be?

Maybe in the morning the world would have given itself an almighty kick up the arse and people would understand things a bit better or take time to consider alternative points of view. But I went to bed sober and thinking that things would be just the same the following morning and for every morning thereafter. It was peculiar to think back to the Cold War when we had lived our lives minutes from destruction and to remember how safe the world was then. Talk about a paradox; those times were much simpler.

And the internet hadn't existed to spread lies that fed our fears.

Chapter Twenty-four

'Are we doing this thing with barmy Anne?', she asked.

'Not sure. Steph is back with the psychiatrist today.'

'Are you dropping her off?'

'Yes. She needs the company more than the lift. I won't go in with her or anything. I just think we need to give this a chance before we strike out in another direction.'

'She'll be disappointed.'

'Anne or Steph?'

'The former.'

'Well, yes. But it is just tough shit. In actual fact all she is doing is exploiting someone for her own ends.'

'You sound very militant this morning', joked Georgina.

'I'm just pissed off.'

'How about I come to visit tonight?'

'Only if you bring some of Anne's organic healing crystals.'

'Orgasmic?'

'Even better, if you have them.'

'What about your neighbours?'

'No, I don't want them round, just you.'

'I meant, what if they gossip?'

'It's not my neighbours you have to worry about, it's yours.'

'They won't notice.'

'Okay, just come when you're ready.'

She turned up looking stunning as usual despite the need to leave the house dressed in no particular style. Checked shirt, jeans, white trainers, hair tied back. Simple. If you can pull it off you can pull it off.

'This is the first time I've been here', she commented as she came in. 'What are you doing?', she asked.

'I am making sure that no one saw you arrive by sticking my head out of the door and looking up and down the street in a really obvious way. I saw someone do it in a film.'

'Fair enough. Good idea.'

'We have to stay two metres apart, you know.'

But she was already pulling me towards her as I kicked the door shut. Her body was warm against mine, comforting and soft. We stayed like that for a while until I said, 'I'm just popping out to feed the alpacas.'

It did no good.

'Feed 'em later.'

I didn't feed them later.

I didn't really have any alpacas.

**

Steph had chatted about inconsequential things as we drove out of the city towards Cedar Woods. In part I think she didn't like silences – some people are like that, but not me – and in part to hide her nervousness. I don't think she was at ease with seeming ill-at-ease, if you get me. Confidence was the name of the game, always cheery, always smiling, life and soul et cetera. But this other feeling that lurked within really ate away at her.

'I'm not going in with you today.'

'I know. It's fine and thank you for taking me.'

Doctor Patel came out in person to collect Steph for her session, cheerily saying hello and putting the patient at her ease.

'Good luck' I said as she stood and followed the doctor in a corridor. For the next hour I sat reading a pristine copy of Autocar that had been left on an *occasional* table for non-patients like me. Today was one of those occasions by the way – the occasional table was a table today. My guess was that being a table was actually a regular thing. Not so the humble commode which I would class as an *occasional* toilet. Some people don't think about things like that.

The chairs, I noticed, had been spaced out to allow social distancing; unless you were going to stand right next to someone on purpose then you were far enough apart. The place was a chapel of wellbeing and contentment as opposed to a production line of coughs and sneezes which might characterise your local surgery. There were those who despised private healthcare but there were plenty of plus points for all concerned, not just the patient. For instance, someone using private healthcare was still *paying* for the NHS in their taxes but not taking *anything out*, thus leaving more doctors, nurses, physios, cleaners, ambulance crew, receptionists, porters, radiographers, healthcare assistants, theatre technicians, security guards and managers for everyone else. Any objections to private healthcare, therefore, had to be purely on grounds of principle.

If the same logic was applied to life in general then we would all buy shoes of a certain value, cars, underpants and so on. None of it mattered really.

When Steph reappeared, she was beaming, quite the opposite of how she appeared when I had picked her up from the airport. Doctor Patel looked pleased too and it seemed clear that a major breakthrough had been made.

They parted on warm terms like old friends and I chatted to Steph as we left the hospital.

'Cured?'

'I don't think so.'

'Oh. Things looked better.'

'I feel better but I am not cured. She has given me hope that it can be sorted and a few things I can do when I feel anxious about it. We ran through it and it all seemed to work.'

'So, you're going back?'

'Definitely.'

'What did she say about your feeling? Does she think it is a false memory?'

'That is the sort of angle she is taking.'

The journey back to her house was easy, the traffic with green lights at every junction.

Back at her house by late morning she asked me in for a coffee, but I chickened out of having to explain that I wasn't interested in being with her in anything other than a professional capacity. I was glad that she didn't look disappointed.

'I have another appointment next week', she said, simply.

'You would like me to pick you up?'

'Please.'

'No problem. Listen I am glad this is starting to work out for you. The false memory thing has got to be the answer. I think she'll work it all out and then you will know how it happened and what it actually relates to. In my mind, once you are at that point it can never affect you in the same way again.'

We were sitting in the car but she wasn't trying to create a deliberate delay.

'It's hard work', she said. 'It's always been hard work. There are times when everything has been okay and times when everyone has looked at me and not realised what is going on in my head. But most of the time I live with this horrible guilt. Up to now it hadn't been something that I could just rationalise away. It has felt so real that it is impossible to think anything other than that I have actually done it. It's like telling someone with depression to cheer up – it just doesn't work in that way.'

'But with Doctor Patel, it's different?'

'I think so. I feel encouraged. She isn't just telling me that it didn't happen but giving me new ways to think about it. She asked me if my rational self thought I had killed someone and for the first time I was able to say 'no'. The feeling remains and it can be crippling but I can remind myself that it is just in my head which gives me some respite.'

'I suppose we can say that you are on the road to recovery. There is another thing that Georgina brought to my attention…'

'Georgina?'

I shouldn't have mentioned her name, of course. Why would Georgina, whom I had met at a party on one occasion be getting in touch with me about anything? How did she have my number? I had to improvise quickly.

'From the party. She called by the office and told me about this mutual friend, Anne, who is doing a study on genetic memories. She's actually trying to disprove that they exist but in doing so she might well discover that the opposite is true.'

She still looked puzzled by my relationship with Georgina.

'I'm not sure', she said.

'This isn't instead of Doctor Patel. This is something you could consider. To be honest I didn't really warm to her but if you thought it would help..? I would just leave it on the back burner if you're not sure.'

I said nothing more on the subject but was unsure if the idea had really registered.

***

Her recovery continued over the coming week or two and it wasn't long before I was no longer required. As I sent the bill to her it was with a feeling of something like regret. Maybe I would miss her more than I expected or maybe – and I thought this more likely – I felt that my assistance had been marginal. The real help was coming from Doctor Patel and she could have arranged that for herself. In that respect she probably lacked resolve or initiative. The condition was crippling. I think that it was the combination of doubts and worries I have just expressed which made me consider Anne's idea, or whatever you might call it, a little bit more seriously.

She had pestered Georgina about it for weeks since we had first gone to see her and it was obvious that not having Steph involved was a major blow to her great, world-beating theory. She was totally self-centred. Georgina gallantly deflected her increasingly insistent enquiries until, her thoughts on the matter converging with mine, she agreed to ask Steph if she would give it a go.

'I don't mind doing it but I thought since you were in charge of that sort of thing…'

'That's fine. It isn't going to cost her anything except a bit of time in the company of Anne and her diminutive piss-hound. Does she know her?'

'Not well but she knows her a bit. Do you think she'll go for it?'

'It's worth a try. She has nothing to lose. She was a bit taken aback when I mentioned your name before so we will have to tread gently. All in all, she will take a dim view of it. It's none of her business but things don't always work out that way. So, what do we do next?'

'Just sound her out and get back to me.'

'Leave it with me.'

'Is she bearing up?'

'The trips to the clinic are helping but it is just giving her ways to cope and get things off her chest. The whole idea that she killed someone is still with her. I think that the most worrying aspect is if this never leaves her. It's got beyond the point where anyone else believes it. She is the only one who still thinks that.'

We chatted for a little while longer, but in my mind it was obvious that I was finished with Stephanie Kuler. Whether she went to see Anne or not was her business and not mine. It was not even the case that I was the intermediary; essentially that was Georgina. Again, I was gently assailed by a pang of regret. It was like coming to the end of a weird adventure undertaken with friends, who you would never see again and who had shared your innermost feelings. It was, in fact, like when Mystery Inc split up in Scooby-Do, but in real life.

Regardless, I rang her that night and we chatted like friends before I mentioned the business with Anne.

'I don't really like her.'

'I didn't warm to her myself. Her house stank too. Have you ever been?'

'Not had the pleasure.'

'She has a side line in tantric healing. It's all going on in her garden shed.'

'A garden shed?'

'It's quite a big shed. Plush. But still a shed.'

'I don't like the sound of that. What is this thesis of hers?'

'Well, if I've got this right, she is trying to disprove that our genes can be altered by events that are experienced by relatives.'

'Parents?'

'Not sure if it has to be just parents. Maybe other people but ones you are related to. The genes mutate and then you get the feeling that the event which caused the mutation applied to you.'

'So, someone in my family murders someone but I feel as if it was me.'

'In your case that is the obvious example but it could be something else. And it wouldn't have to be murder. So, if your grandfather had been in the war, say, and had been a soldier, and had killed someone, then if that altered his genes, he could have passed that on to your mum or dad and then they passed it on to you. You feel like you are the one who did the killing but actually it happened long before you were born.'

'Okay. You know that I have no idea about my family. Not one single family member is known to me.'

'Yeah, so you can't exactly research it but it could still be true.'

'I'm confused about something. How would this help me?'

'It might not but it might be something else to go on. The other slightly awkward aspect to it is that she is trying to *disprove* this theory. In other words, she wants to find out that what we have just talked about has *not* happened. The bottom line is that you just don't have to do it.'

'It sounds like she is just using me.'

'She is. I would only do it if there was a chance that it would help. If not, she can bugger off.' You don't have to decide now', I said. It sounded as if I had got her hooked on the idea which wasn't really my intention.

'In one way I am intrigued and in another I really feel as if she is taking the piss. I want this feeling to go forever but I can't picture what she can do about it.'

'I presume she has tests she can carry out to determine if the faulty gene is there.'

'But she can't operate to remove it.'

Which was exactly the point she made when we went to visit her the following day.

Chapter Twenty-five

Georgina had been a little put out when I explained what I was doing and I understood her minor grievance completely. Going to see Anne had been her idea and yet now I was hijacking it.

'She wants me to go with her', I explained, 'but she knows that you set it up. If you want to come along, you can'.

'She has a thing for you.'

'I put her straight on that and it isn't a thing any longer. She probably thinks I am gay.'

Georgina laughed at that thankfully because I was obviously the very definition of someone who was not gay...whatever that means.

'Probably.'

I frowned.

'Why don't you come round tonight, afterwards?'

'I'm not sure. It is tricky. He is going to start wondering what I am up to if I keep going out. For one thing, strictly speaking there is nowhere to go.'

'Sorry. It's easy for me to say it but much more difficult for you to do it.'

We agreed on principle to meet but it was never destined to be a satisfactory arrangement.

***

Steph was ready, if not eager, when I called for her.

'Are you having second thoughts?', I said as she got into the car.

'Second, third and fourth. I don't want to go to her house, I don't want to be a guinea pig and I don't want to be exploited by her.'

I started the car and pulled out into the traffic, of which there was plenty. It did make me wonder where all these people were going when everything was shut, but of course they might have been thinking the same thing about me and about why I had someone in my car who was certainly not two metres away. People were either getting angry about other people flouting the rules or getting angry about the lockdown not being lifted. Or something else.

'Well, let's just give it a go and if it isn't for you, then we can tell her so. I don't think it can make the situation any worse.'

'I can't see what she is actually going to do. She's not a surgeon.'

'From my vast knowledge of the subject, gained through minutes of study on the internet, I don't think there is an operation for it anyway. If the genes have been affected by past events – other peoples' past – then that means that all of them have been affected.'

***

Which, as I stated earlier, is more or less what Anne said when we turned up there. The dog pissed on the carpet and she provided a lavish meal of tea and plain biscuits. She was definitely a Happy Shopper type of gal.

'If the gene has been affected that would mean that the same gene on the same chromosome in every nucleus would be affected and there wouldn't be anything we could do about that. That's the amazing thing about our genetic code', she said, her eyes gleaming with the thrill of inheritance, 'it is so complex and yet it is present in every cell. DNA provides the blueprint for that living thing. Everything about you is contained in this microscopic twist of chemicals and yet despite the huge amount of information contained therein, it is replicated billions upon billions of times over. Not only that but your cells are constantly dying and being replaced and each replacement contains the code and each cell lost takes the code with it.'

That was more or less her introductory speech, the preface to get you salivating like a dog, yearning for more.

'So, what are you actually going to do?', asked Steph. She smiled politely. As expected, Anne was fawning over Steph, her glamorous and worldly subject, and ignoring me, the uneducated oik from Belfast who thought he knew everything just because he had dared to look it up on the internet. That was life – filled with prejudice. People make snap judgements, myself included, but the trick is to let new judgements form as appropriate.

'I am going to ask you about your experiences and then link them to your past and to the past of your ancestors. I should point out that I am trying to disprove a theory. I don't actually think that events carried out by our forebears can change our DNA. It doesn't really fit with the principles of heredity. So, if someone gets cancer, for instance, that is when the genes have mutated and caused a tumour to grow. A tumour is a bunch of cells that don't serve any function but can stop other parts of the body from working properly. The tumour can break up and move to other parts of the body and do the same thing there.'

I knew the rest – cancer can be caused by radiation, certain types of chemical or sheer bad luck – but I said nothing. Thanks, Dr Gongle.

'So, something like cancer can be caused by things that happen as we go through life, like smoking. However, what does not happen is the cancer being passed on to our children.'

'Aren't some people more prone to cancer?', asked Steph. Anne, already with fire in her belly, was delighted at this question.

'There may be a predisposition towards cancer in the family but that doesn't mean that you will automatically develop cancer without one of the stimuli mentioned before and it certainly doesn't mean that you have caught cancer from your parents.'

Did this explain that it was impossible to carry a genetic memory? Not to me but I didn't feel confident about challenging Anne.

I looked over at Steph and smiled encouragingly. She didn't look especially encouraged but she smiled back and cast her glance round the living room in which we sat.

'So, if I took part in this experiment what would I do?'

'It would be like genetic counselling and certainly not a surgical procedure or anything like that.'

Steph looked blank. I presumably did too.

'Genetic counselling is where you look back over the family of a person and make links that might give an idea about their chances of developing an inherited illness or the likelihood of them developing cancer and so on.'

'How far back?'

'Either as far back as we need to, or as far back as we can.'

I thought I knew what Steph was thinking; her family was untraceable. She didn't say anything.

Anne continued. 'So, if we went back for three generations to find the event which gave you the genetic memory then we wouldn't need to go back any further. If we went back that far and found nothing, then we would try to go back further.'

'And if you still found nothing no matter how far you went back?'

'Eventually, there comes a point when you can't find any more records because they don't exist. And then it is evidence that the genetic memory doesn't exist. Of course, if you find it then it is evidence that it might exist.'

'Might?', I queried.

'You couldn't say for certain that a genetic memory was attributable to that event but it is evidence that it there might be a link. To prove it you would have to isolate the genes in question and test them, to show that they had mutated in such a way that this genetic memory had been created. And we're not quite there yet. Some day that might be possible but not at present.'

Steph asked the next question. Something similar had been troubling me.

'If you go way back, isn't the feeling likely to be diluted by the time it gets to me? So, say my great grandfather fought in the First World War and he experienced the horrors of the trenches and saw death at first hand. Then he passes that to his son, my grandfather, and then it is passed to his son, my father...'

'It doesn't work quite that way. It is a more of an all or nothing situation. You either get this genetic mutation passed on or you don't. It doesn't become diluted, just rarer. Genetics is very complex and lots of factors play a part but when males and females produce gametes, which are the sex cells, they only pass on half of the chromosomes. A sperm has twenty-three of these, and likewise the eggs, and this allows for the offspring to have a mix of characteristics from both parents. Fifty-fifty.

'That would make it seem as if half of the offspring would be likely to have it in each generation but there are other aspects to consider. The fifty-fifty split is, at best, a statistical measure. It might not work out that the mutated gene is carried over half the time. Also, it depends on whether it is a dominant or recessive gene that we are talking about. If it is recessive then the characteristic, in this case the genetic memory, is covered over by a dominant gene which masks its effect. There is a chance that you would pass on that characteristic without suffering the effects. You would be a carrier in other words.

'If it is carried on a dominant gene then the characteristic is expressed if that gene is in the egg or sperm.'

I nodded. Steph nodded. I was only partially lost but I was confident that Steph followed the whole discourse quite successfully.

'There is one last thing to say. If the characteristic is carried on a recessive gene then it will not be expressed unless that egg or sperm is fertilised by an egg or sperm which also has a recessive gene in the same place.'

Now I was lost.

Steph said, 'so it is more than likely carried on a recessive gene?'

'Either that or some of your forebears also suffered from the same thing.' She smiled. 'But you don't know much about your family, do you?'

'Nothing actually.'

'So, it could be that they did suffer what you have been suffering but you aren't aware of it?'

'Yes. I had never thought about that... Well, I wouldn't because I have always been convinced that I actually did it, not that it was a memory belonging to someone else. But you don't believe this anyway. What is to stop you just not going back far and then deciding that there is no evidence for the genetic memory theory?'

'It would be bad science for one thing. Other scientists have to verify my work for it to be considered valid. If I didn't do it properly then I would be leaving myself open to claims that my theory was rubbish. Science is a very cut-throat business. There are plenty who would like to see me fail because they are pushing theories of their own.'

Office politics, I thought. Even in the pristine, sterile world of science there were people working to their own agendas. Anne was one of them.

Steph sighed heavily and I knew it was a sign that she was about to give her assent to the procedure.

'Okay', she said, apparently happy. 'Let's do it.'

Anne looked pleased.

'I'm glad you said that because I have made a start.'

Steph looked aghast and I thought that Anne had gone too far with this. There had to be laws governing what you could and could not do in the field of genetic research (if that was the correct term) without the subject's permission.

'I have some forms here which you fill in with your basic details and another form which gives your consent to the research. The second one has to be witnessed.'

She looked at me and I smiled obligingly. Perhaps this was the start she had been talking about; merely assembling the relevant paperwork.

Steph was reading the documentation but she looked up and asked for a pen which was duly handed over. The gleam in Anne's eyes had returned and she resembled a hungry dog waiting for a bone which was coming its way.

'Someone might ring you to confirm the details, Steph, or they might not. But I can get going at once. It's very hard to say how long this will take. Sometimes it is days or weeks and sometimes it is months.'

'Do you need a sample of DNA?'

'Possibly but not at the moment. I might have to ring you about other matters if that is okay?'

'Yeah, fine.'

'In that case, just leave it with me. I'll be in touch. I presume you will want to see what I find out, who your parents were and so on?'

'I've come this far, so that makes sense.'

***

We drove back to the city in near silence.

'Over there', I said pointing, 'was a little boatyard where a man built boats out of concrete.'

'Concrete?'

'I'm not sure if he ever sold any but they sat there for years. You could see them from the train.'

After dropping that fascinating piece of information, we barely spoke until we reached her house.

'How do you feel?'

'Fine. It's all a bit too much. The thing is I really like Doctor Patel so I am inclined to favour her treatment. I don't like Anne and I sort of resent the way she is doing this and how she goes about it.'

'She is the only one not getting paid for it', I pointed out.

'True and yet she seems the most mercenary.'

'That is a strange but true fact.'

'Do you want a coffee or anything? You've never actually been in my house.'

'No, but I tried to get in once. After the party. You don't remember it.'

'Oh God. I'd forgotten that. How humiliating.'

'Water under the bridge. There may be other clichés available. So as for this coffee. I will come in on one condition.'

'What is that?'

'That you don't ply me with cheap Rich Tea biscuits.'

'It's a deal. Come on.'

She led me up the path and then unlocked the door. Memories of that night came at me unbidden: trying to get her out of the car and then trying to get her back into the car, the feeling of frustration and annoyance.

'Aha. This is what it's like on the other side of the door.'

'So embarrassing', she said. 'But you're in now. I'll get the water boiling. Have a seat.'

I took my place in a wingback chair and surveyed the room which even to my inexpert eye was very nicely done out, especially considering she hadn't lived here for long. A series of small paintings was arranged above a Victorian fireplace with ornate tiles and a blackened iron grate. There were no ornaments and few embellishments of any kind, but the room was homely for all that.

I commented when she returned with the drinks.

'Thanks. It was the first room I did when I moved in. It was in good order so I just had to redecorate. Some of the other rooms are a bit tatty but it was all good enough to live in.'

'The paintings look good. I'm not an expert on things like that.'

'Thank you. I did them.'

'Really? Can I take a look?'

'Help yourself.'

I stood and took the few steps to the mantlepiece. I sensed her next to me. One was signed SK and the others SP.

'These are brilliant.'

'Thank you. My one and only talent apart from history.'

'Where are these places?', I asked.

'I don't know. I just make them up. That one I did in America, so it might be some sort of amalgam of various places or things I have seen and the others, who knows?'

'So, these aren't even from photographs?'

'No. I just make it up. They could be real places, I suppose. No idea.'

Each of the paintings depicted a street scene of some type. The first was a row of terraced houses, very neat, red-brick and populated by just one person, a tiny girl who stood staring at some unseen object *out of shot*, so to speak. The next one along was of an old-fashioned US gas station, with two pumps and again one single person, an older man in overalls staring at something we couldn't see.

'These make me think of Edward Hopper', I said. 'A little story being told but each person who looks at it will have their own version of it.'

'Thank you. Quite a compliment.'

The third one had a little girl alone at a school gate; satchel, forlorn look, forbidding red-brick school in the background, green railings. It could easily have been a cliché and yet, to me, it wasn't. The child was seven or eight.

'Is this you?', I asked turning towards her.

She shrugged. It was the sort of shrug which suggested that she had wondered the same thing, which was odd since she was the creator of the art in question and therefore, presumably, had control of the characters she depicted. Did she really not know who the child was? It didn't seem to matter then but her lack of knowledge on this point was an anomaly.

The last picture was of a car, rather the back of a car. I would have said it was a Sierra in red and the engine was running; a trail of exhaust fumes came from the exhaust pipe. It was my least favourite and it was bereft of a human subject, although it was implied of course that someone was in the car since it was running.

'I can't help feeling that these tell a story.'

She smiled and sighed.

'The story of me?'

'That would be a natural assumption.'

'I don't think so. Not even on a subconscious level. Doctor Patel would love to see those paintings but they don't mean a thing. I like them but I dreamt them up.'

'Out of thin air?'

'Out of thin air.'

'What era in history is your speciality?'

'The last three centuries of European history but I like all history. I know bits and pieces about all of it probably.'

'What do you know about this city?'

'Not much actually. What is its most important story?'

'James Magennis.'

She raised her eyebrows.

'You thought I was going to say the Titanic?'

'Fair play. Yes, I did.'

'When I am gone – I don't mean after I have died or anything – just when I have left your house, find out about James Magennis. It will tell you what was wrong with this country and also a little bit about what is wrong with the world.

'I will do that', she said. She looked sad.

'How are you feeling?', I asked again. I wasn't her counsellor, confidante or anything else but she did look strangely vulnerable at that point as though her confidence had been knocked.

'Okay. It's all a bit nuts.'

'Your situation or generally?'

'Both. A while ago I was in a cell and might have ended up in court and so on, and now I am being metaphorically poked and prodded by Doctor Patel and Anne.'

'They're poking and prodding in your head.'

'That's what they are doing.'

'It was a strange proposition you came to me with, you have to admit. It was never going to be simple.'

She laughed.

'All a bit fucked up. *I* am a bit fucked up.'

'Do you think this is where some of your past problems have stemmed from?'

She looked at me as if assessing what I knew about her and what remained a mystery. I knew about her child in America, for instance and now I noticed that there were no photographs of the child here.

'I suppose so. It is not the case that if someone reminds me of a past event – something that went wrong – that I can instantly pin it on my childhood or this murder which has followed me around. To me the links aren't there, but I know that when Doctor Patel is talking to me she sees the links all the time.'

She fell silent and I sipped my coffee.

'Do you feel like it is going to be okay?'

'No. I feel like I could drown under a sea of rational explanations without the feeling inside me diminishing in the slightest. I've learned not to talk about it as much, but to me it is still the case that I killed someone. It's as plain as that fireplace or that door or anything in this room. They exist and I killed someone. I don't have any idea what I would feel like not to have this thing with me all the time.'

She looked utterly despondent.

'Does Doctor Patel know this? Have you said this to her or have you watered it down to make her feel better?'

'That's funny, me trying to make the doctor feel better. But I have been honest with her.'

'So, what is her view?'

'She says to stick with it and it will get better. But she has to say that doesn't she? It won't sound brilliant if she says that it is never going to work and we are wasting our bloody time. Bad for business.'

'You'll get there. At least you're not in jail. One way or another, things will... I was going to say get back to normal for you but what I mean is that they will *become* normal for you.'

'You think so?'

'Yes. I do. I'm sure that this can be cured and I know that me saying it doesn't change anything in your head, but you'll get there. Even if it ends up being something written on a sheet of paper that you have to look at now and again or another way of thinking about things, you will get there.'

She smiled and nodded. I hoped I was right.

Chapter Twenty-six

I drove away feeling empty. Not sad or depressed but as if someone had scooped out my insides. It was just one of those things, not attributable to any particular event. I thought about Billy and wondered how he was getting on with whatever business he was tending to. I would text him later. I thought too about those paintings and wondered what they signified, if anything. I was sure they meant something and for her to think that she had created them from nothing other than a few random images formulated in her head seemed like a bit of a stretch.

When I pulled up at a junction, I spotted lots of people, mostly kids, sitting around. It looked at first glance as if they no longer felt vulnerable to the virus. I hoped they were right. For a second, I thought about Steph's paintings and wondered if they had more relevance to her than she even knew, but the lights changed and that thought evaporated as I drove off.

Back at home I made the mistake of turning on the TV news as I waited for my tea to burn. It was a mistake because what I saw infuriated me: the BLM protestors in London, daubing slogans on statues and the Cenotaph, the police in full retreat and hordes of protestors completely losing their bloody marbles. The history of Northern Ireland told me that this was no way to get things done. Why couldn't they have followed the example of Martin Luther King, or Nelson Mandela, the two men who had changed the course of history for black people in modern times?

'What the fuck', I said to my empty room. It was just depressing.

I switched off and sat back in my chair wondering when people would wake up. As I did this an unconnected thought came to me. It might well come to nothing, but I was going to ask Steph to photograph her paintings and send them to me via her mobile communication device (MCD). Maybe they meant more than she thought.

***

'Yo, Billy, how's it hangin' in the hood, dude?'

'Does that mean hello?'

'But in the talk of the Malone Road ghetto.'

'Fuckin' Malone Road. The block. Boils my piss.'

'You're are jealous of their wealth and influence. You were born in the gutter and you will die there.'

'True enough. What do you want?'

'Just checking on my oppo. Making sure that he is okay.'

'I'm fine.'

'You don't sound it.'

'Can I come to the office to chat?'

'You can't talk on the phone?'

Silence.

'Yeah, come to the office. I'll go in tomorrow. I'll stay until home time if needs be.'

'See ya, then.'

'Yeah, see ya. Watch out for those zombies.'

But he didn't laugh. If Billy was scared then I was scared too.

***

'I'm worried.'

'I can tell.'

'Not quite over my head but close.'

I nodded and didn't comment on the pistol in the holster under his jacket.

'You want some help?'

'I'm too proud to ask normally.'

'Maybe but we all need help sometimes. We're like the Three Musketeers, remember?'

'There's only two of us.'

'Is this the time to be splitting hairs?'

Despite his intense unease – I won't call it fear – he smiled. Billy was the toughest nut I had ever met and yet he glided through life in such an unassuming way you would never have known just how resourceful and, if required, deadly he was. The fact that he was so apprehensive made me fearful.

'Right, listen. If you need money to lie low for a while, you've got it. If you need someone to house sit while you get

343

out of the way, that can be arranged. There are ways and means.'

'You haven't asked what the problem is.'

'Do you want to tell me?'

'The less you know, the better.'

***

Six days passed before I met up with Steph and we made our way out of the city to get to Anne's house.

'Is this it, do you think? The big reveal where she tells you who you are and what has happened? Like that TV programme.'

'Who Do You Think You Are?'

'Probably. Nicky Walker and Rosetta McCall.'

'Nicky Campbell and Davina McCall.'

'Are they in it too?'

'Fuck sakes. They are the hosts and it is called Long Lost Family. ITV. Quite interesting for me as a historian. And yes, I do think that this is the big moment.'

'Okay.' I felt a little bit of nervous excitement that we had come to this point and, in a world which seemed to be going to hell in a handcart, that was very welcome. I just hoped that whatever Anne had come up with did the job and allowed Steph to become reconciled with her past, if that was indeed the problem.

'You must be nervous', I said pulling around a black taxi. I pointed to the taxi and said, 'when I was growing up those were rumoured to provide funds for the IRA.'

'Was it true?'

'Not sure. Probably some truth in it. I dare say the drivers wanted to make a living from it too. Perhaps they were intimidated into handing over a tithe, if that is the correct word. Protection money is a better phrase. When you are young you just believe anything you are told.'

I pointed over at the shipyard.

'Those are the biggest cranes in the world.'

'Really?'

'Fact.'

'I looked into James Magennis.'

'He's my hero. Or one of them.'

'I know why. I understand what you were saying when you mentioned him to me.'

James Magennis VC was the only Northern Irishman to win Britain's highest gallantry award in World War Two.

However, there was a problem with James Magennis: he was a Catholic. He was something of a celebrity in Belfast after the war but permission was denied for a statue in his honour because of his religion. Other excuses were probably made but that was the real reason. Northern Ireland was a Protestant country for Protestant people. Someone like James Magennis could not be allowed to seem better than the Protestants who had served in the war. He was a bit of a rogue but a brave one.

He could have claimed oppression or that he had been held back but he did none of these things.

'His story tells us what is wrong with the world in many respects – discrimination – but he didn't make a big deal out of it. He moved to England. He sold the medal, which I find very sad. If I had won a VC, I would never sell it.'

We arrived at the house just as the bins were being taken away. The bin men wore masks. Bearing in mind the job they did it might have been a wise precaution all along.

'We'll all be wearing those soon. We might never go back to how we were. This is history', I said pointedly. 'Write a book about it.'

'Lots of people will be writing books about this.'

'Then write the best book.'

She smiled.

'I'll start tonight.'

'Tonight, you will either be drowning your sorrows or celebrating.'

'Hopefully the latter. Will you join me?'

'Well, social distancing…'

'You can bring Georgina. She has told me.'

'Ah.'

We stepped out of the car and made our way to the door, where, as usual, we were expected and ushered inside with some kind of supressed excitement. It had to be good news.

This time she didn't even bother with the shitty biscuits or tea.

'I know who you are and what happened. I've got the whole thing. It just needs confirmation but it is only right that you see what we are trying to confirm before we go ahead.'

'We?', said Steph.

'My team and I.'

'Okay.'

'Sit, sit.'

We sat as ordered.

'You have no name.'

'Ah.'

'You were left in a basket outside a hospital when you were a few days old.'

'Cliché', said Steph, sardonically.

'Pardon?'

'Bit of a cliché. Left in a basket. I bet it was a box.'

Anne looked annoyed at her story being interrupted but she carried on.

'Obviously you were straight into the care system from that point and when you were old enough you were shipped off to the first of several foster homes.'

'I remember.'

'Shortly after that a lady was arrested and charged with fraud. She was attempting to claim benefits for a child who didn't exist. She was charged, tried and found guilty and sentenced to a jail term. As part of her processing for jail, she underwent an examination. The examination revealed that she had, in fact, recently given birth. She wouldn't admit that this was the case even though this was medical evidence. She never admitted to having had a child and therefore she never gave away the whereabouts of the child.'

Steph pursed her lips but said nothing.

'You think you know where this is going but you don't. Not quite, anyway. She was never charged in connection with anything to do with the child she couldn't, and wouldn't, account for. What did happen was that when they tried to find her husband to ask him about this missing child, it transpired that he too was missing.'

'Jesus', I said.

'Only recently has the truth come to light. This woman was tracked down. She is nearly seventy, living in constrained circumstances near Oxford. She was in and out of jail, for fraud, prostitution and drug dealing amongst other things.'

Anne paused. It was for effect.

'The lady was called Karen Merchant.'

'She was my mum?'

'She was your mum. But there is more. The man in the house in Barton?'

'Was my dad?'

'Brian Merchant.'

'Okay.'

'Well, here is the bit which may be the last part of the puzzle. Whether this is an answer or simply the stimulus for more questions, I can't say. Karen is dying of cancer. She has nothing left to lose now. She has admitted to killing your father and when she did so...'

'She was pregnant with me?'

'Correct.'

Chapter Twenty-seven

Sometimes small talk just doesn't cut it. We drove back in silence and Steph was spared any more snippets from my vast catalogue of knowledge of Belfast and general wit. Some might call it inane banter. Whatever, it didn't matter. It was better for her to be alone with her thoughts, for only now could she really come to terms with her past and a possible reason for the thought (singular) which had plagued her all of her life. She had been given answers that she had never sought. Her dad was dead, killed and buried like a dog under the stairs. Her mum was not only a murderer but a generally unsavoury character in every possible way you could imagine. But that wasn't the worst of it.

The worst of it was that her mum had killed her dad whilst she was pregnant with the child she couldn't be bothered to name and who she gave away.

Then again, that was just my view. Maybe the old boy deserved it and then Steph's mum couldn't live with guilt and felt that she would be a bad mother as a result. Who knew?

Was this the reason for the false memory? After all, Steph, in the weirdest way possible, had been present when the murder was committed.

Or, had her genetic make-up been altered by her mother's actions? Not according to Anne.

We pulled up outside her house but she didn't immediately get out of the car and sat staring straight ahead.

'How do you feel?' It was a question I had asked her countless times.

'Shocked at the very least. I don't know where to begin with it.' Steph rubbed a hand across her mouth and her eyes glistened as if she might cry. 'The funny thing is, this feeling of having murdered someone seems to have gone for now. I can only presume that it has been overwhelmed with everything else I have felt. I think it will come back when I settle down a bit. It's been with me forever so I can't imagine how it would be for it to be absent. It might be like a bereavement but a good one.'

'I think I understand. Do you want me to come in? I could make the coffees. I'm really good at switching a kettle on.'

'You have to put water in it too', she joked with a sad smile.

'Oh, I didn't know that. Better not risk it.'

'Listen, it's a lot to ask but could you be on standby to come round tonight? I want time to think about all of this but I might want to talk later.'

'Well, I was going to paint the inside of the garage but for you, I will sit next to the phone,'

'It's a mobile phone; you can take it with you.'

'I know. And sit next to it.'

She laughed, and why wouldn't she with such a titan of comedy next to her? With a sigh she got out of the car and I walked her to the front door.

'Such a gent.'

'I know. There are only about two billion of us left.'

Comedy gold.

'Take it easy and give me a ring. You're not going to do anything…'

'No. Nothing silly. I feel as if things might be getting better. Genuinely this could be the start of a better life.'

She pecked me on the cheek, potentially passing on the virus.

When I drove away, I couldn't help thinking that she was still vulnerable in some way but I couldn't quite picture the future for her. Thinking purely of myself, Anne's news was a lot to take in. Rain started to fall and the wipers ran across the windscreen with a noise like sludge being shovelled out of a ditch. The sky seemed to have clouded over in great haste as a natural backdrop to my sombre mood.

Back home again, I lit the fire for comfort as much as for heat. I longed for the glass of whiskey too; somehow the two went together, or was that just because of the so-called peaty taste of that particular spirit, as the marketing men insisted?

I texted Georgina but there was no reply. I texted Billy and the same thing happened. When I set my phone down it was clear that I had very few friends. I mean, two calls and I had run out of people to talk to. It was ridiculous but the truth was that I didn't really mind; fewer funerals to attend and all that.

I was having investigator's block. I have mentioned it before and there is probably no such thing but here I was with nothing for my mind to work on other than a case that might well be solved but which didn't make complete sense to me.

The wind cast rain at the window and I reached for a blanket which I kept draped over the arm of my favourite chair, pulling it around me as an extra layer of protection from the world. A tree in the garden of the house across the road swayed and shuddered in the breeze, slowly pulsing to an irregular beat. I marvelled at the unseen forces which bombarded the planet's surface and wondered how we survived on the thin skin of this red-hot orb which span on its axis at speed, even as it drifted round the sun and travelled further and further out into hostile space. I had long been of the opinion that none of us mattered, me especially. Literally no one on earth gave a damn about me.

I was not sinking into a slough of depression by the way. It didn't matter to me that I didn't matter, if you follow. It was just a fact of existence. I was as important as a single corona virus.

But even though I didn't matter, I was still pleased when Georgina rang me.

'Can you talk?', she began.

'It appears to be one of things I can do.'

'Excellent. Just had a call from Steph and she wants to meet us tonight.'

'Us. You and I?'

'She knows about us. She, you and me. Her place. Can you make it?'

'Well, there's a really good show on Netflix…'

'See you there at eight.'

'Do you want a lift?'

'Better not. I could drive to yours but then I still couldn't drink. I might as well meet you there.'

I agreed to that even though it sounded like the brush-off. If it was, then *que sera* but I didn't really feel so blasé as that.

Billy texted back with one word.

'What?'

We had a brief textualized communication session (TCS, obviously) in which I expressed my relief that he was still alive. He confirmed that he was but that he couldn't talk right now. I left it but that did not prevent me from worrying about him. This time I think he had bitten off more than he could chew. It was most unlike him.

***

She didn't exactly look as if the weight of the world had been lifted from her shoulders but she had made an effort with the room and bought some bits and pieces for us to eat and drink. Georgina was already there and gave me a coy little hug when I came in, which reassured me about that aspect of the evening if nothing else.

'How do you feel?', I asked. It was the obvious question.

'Violated, confused, angry. But that other feeling? Not there. At the minute I do not feel as if I killed someone. I'm waiting for it to come back because I can't quite imagine life without it, but for now, apart from those other feelings, life is good. And something else. You remember when you told me to stop the drugs and all the rest of it? I haven't touched anything since then. Hardly had a drink actually.'

We engaged in small talk of course but it was only ever a preliminary to the main event which was tucked away in the air somewhere like a cloud of intent, watching over us for a cue to join in and take over. I was a bit of a spare part as they discussed women's things like jumpers and wine.

Actually, I can't remember what they spoke about and was happy enough to let them get on with it. I enjoyed being out of my own house and neither woman was bad company.

Eventually Georgina looked over with her fake sympathetic face and asked if I was okay.

'I'd rather be talking about football, politics and dog racing but it's fine. Some things are more important. Handbags. Men might like handbags too.'

'Some men do', said Steph.

'Exactly my point.'

'But we haven't come here for that', she added. 'I think I just need to talk to someone and try to make sense of what we are doing. Not that, actually. Make sense of who I am. Do you know what I mean?'

'It sounds as if you need to talk and we need to listen', suggested Georgina.

'Well that's about it really. Where do I start?'

'Start with how you feel about your mum and what you want to do next. That's what I would do.'

She nodded.

'I want to visit my mum', she said after a moment's deliberation. It came out sounding like an admission, that she was pleading guilty to something a bit like a crime, maybe just an indiscretion. Perhaps she thought it sounded like an unwise course of action or that the woman didn't deserve it. Either of those could be true.

'Do you know where she is?'

'Hospital. I know where and so on. They won't tell me much because as far as the hospital is concerned, I am not related to her. I can't actually prove that I am. She would be on remand awaiting trial for murder but for the fact that she isn't going to survive. I need to go soon for that reason.'

'Will she know who you are? I mean, if you explain?'

'I don't know. She might not be conscious. She might not be alive when I get there but she is my only relative at the minute. She is the person who caused the pain in my life. I feel as if *not* seeing her might make it last forever and seeing her *might* make it go away. Can't be sure either way of course. Can I get you a drink Gina?'

The use of the shortened version of her name startled me slightly.

'You could stay over. You both could.'

'Thank you but I will have to go back to Rob. He's looking after Jess which always makes him feel like a bloody martyr as if I never do anything. Anyway, forget him. Let's get you on a flight over there and car hire and so on. We can book it tonight.'

'I don't know if it is the right thing to do. What if it makes things worse?'

'I doubt if it will but I think you have to take the chance. She isn't going to be around for long and she is a part of the puzzle. You can't risk not seeing her in those circumstances', said Georgina.

She nodded.

'And how do you feel about your dad?'

'I think I need to find out more about him. It will all come out in the case I suppose. I don't know if they try someone who has died but surely they have to piece together the crime and what have you. As for how it makes me feel about my mum, if that is what you were asking, then I don't know. I can't feel hatred or disgust for someone I don't know and I can't feel bereaved about someone else I also never knew. It's like a reading about any murder in the paper. You know it is wrong but you don't feel any direct connection to it.'

'It's peculiar. Do you feel there is a link between his murder and your memory?', asked Georgina.

'I'm not sure yet. I think I still need a bit of processing time. It will be good to explain it all to Doctor Patel. It is the first firm thing I have had in relation to this. Until now I knew nothing. My priority is to get to see my mum. It isn't for an explanation I have decided, because she might not be in a fit state to offer one, but since she is the person who caused this... I don't know, I just have to see her.'

'So, your mind is made up?', asked Georgina.

'Yes. I have to do it.'

'What I would like to know is whether this is the false memory caused by being there, even though you were in the womb, or if it is the genetic mutation caused by being there. If this was something that had happened generations beforehand then you would have to look at the possibility that the genes were altered at the moment the act was carried out, and then passed down. But if I understood Anne correctly that shouldn't be possible, if our current understanding of the subject is correct.'

I saw them both nod in bemused agreement with my summation of the situation.

'However. If you were actually there, albeit in the womb, then doesn't that make it more likely that the DNA was altered on the spot?'

'More likely but it all depends on whether or not it can happen in the first place. According to Anne, if the event was capable of altering the DNA and it being passed on then it would have to happen to the egg or sperm, and that would mean *before* I was conceived, and the person killed couldn't actually be my dad…'

'This is too much like *Back to the Future*. I hate to sound glib but I am lost. If I sounded knowledgeable a minute ago then I wish to retract any false impression that I might have given about knowing what the hell is going on.'

They laughed politely.

'They do say about babies listening to music and voices and so on in the womb and then recognising them when they are born. To me this sounds like you remembered this event in some way and it just stuck with you. Maybe it was the voices or the sounds, or just the chemicals that were flowing through your mum's blood as she did it. Hormones – fight or flight – what do you call it?', said Georgina.

'Adrenaline?'

'That's it. Could that have left this shadow on you? Who knows, but since we are in uncharted territory here it makes as much sense as anything.'

'It's got to be something like that. I am looking forward to hearing what Doctor Patel says.'

'This is a set of circumstances that can only have happened a few times ever. Most pregnant women would probably feel too incapacitated to kill someone', I said.

'They might have the urge', said Georgina, wryly. 'Anyway, let's get those flights booked.'

'Will you come with me?'

'Who?', I asked.

'Both of you. I'll pay. I just want some people with me when I meet her. I don't know how I am going to react and I'd like some moral support.'

'Fine by me.' I looked at Georgina.

Steph said, 'you'll have to run it past Rob first.'

'Fuck him. Let's get over there. He can be childcare superman for a day or two. This is more important. Where's your computer?

Chapter Twenty-eight

The journey across was trouble-free. Security had cleared away all the zombies from the main entrance and we boarded the plane without difficulty, sat miles apart, and got off at the other end. The car hire worked more smoothly than at any time I could ever remember and after Georgina had signed two forms we went outside, picked up a Hyundai hatchback and set off for the hospital. Social distancing inside the car was tricky; we're not talking about something the size of a Cadillac limo here but by that point I think we felt sure that none of us was infected.

The car had a satnav which duly led us to the hospital. We parked at huge cost for, not being local, we didn't know which side streets might be available. An elderly lady wearing a mask – a hospital volunteer – was able to direct us to the correct ward, and we set off on a lengthy journey down a corridor which was segregated according to direction of travel. It was like apartheid. Why couldn't I mix with the people going in the other direction? It was blatant *directionism* and called for a protest.

'What are you smiling at?'. asked Georgina as we thinned out to let a trolley past.

'I'll tell you later. Just one of my moronic observations on life.'

We moved on. Almost everyone wore a mask. I wondered if they would become mandatory soon. It would be great for bank robbers. They could travel to and from their robberies on the bus and no one would bat an eyelid.

At the entrance to the ward we sanitised our hands and then filed in, but didn't get far before being stopped by a nurse who explained that the bays were limited to two visitors at a time. When Steph explained who she was, the nurse led her away and pointed us to a small waiting room with horrible plastic chairs and a broken TV that looked ready to drop off the wall. Georgina and I sat there alone with our thoughts, neither of us quite sure what to make of these strange times. I studied a poster about Covid-19 without taking in any of the details and then spent a moment gazing at the yellow rawl plug that seemed to be the only thing keeping the TV attached to the wall. At least if it fell off and brained someone they were in the right place for treatment, but I couldn't help thinking that removing the dangerous item might have been a better idea. No doubt there was a procedure to be followed in these cases, which involved filling in a form, carrying out a risk assessment, putting up tape and warning notices and then ringing for the handy man to come from NHS Handyman HQ, Handyman House, Dringly Court, Leicester.

I'm not sure of the post code. In fact, I made the whole thing up but it would be something along those lines if someone wanted to take the TV down. Gone were the days when you could just decide to act on your own initiative. Having been a soldier, even in the dim past, I baulked at the lack of common sense that existed. A soldier will see what needs to be done and just do it. If not, an NCO will come along and tell him to do it. It's not a bad system.

'I wonder how she feels now?'

'God knows. This would be peculiar under any circumstances but add in the fact that the woman she is going to see killed her father and abandoned her and then consider all the things that happened to Steph as a result…'

'Imagine if that hadn't happened, how different her life would have been', I said.

'And we would never have met.'

'I'm glad we did. I thought you were giving me the brush-off yesterday when you didn't want a lift. It's got to happen someday, but I wasn't ready for it.'

She smiled sadly, silently acknowledging a distant truth. Neither of us wanted to think about this eventuality.

Perhaps ten minutes passed before Steph returned. There was nothing in her demeanour to indicate that anything, good or bad, had occurred in the time she had been away.

Georgina asked the question.

'How was she and how are you?'

The three of us were in the tiny waiting room. Around us a hushed routine was carried out by the nurses and doctors in their masks and gloves.

'I'm fine. She is unconscious and dying. Sorry for sounding so matter-of-fact about it but it has left me feeling nothing. No regret or sadness. She is as much a stranger to me as anyone else on the ward. God knows, I looked down at her for long enough trying to feel something but there is no connection. I don't doubt that she is my mother but whatever biological link there is between us isn't strong enough to make me care about her. How odd. You'd think I would feel something.'

'Nature versus nurture, I suppose', said Georgina, standing, ready to leave. 'You have the nature part but not the nurture part and you feel no connection to her. That's good feedback for Anne. Maybe nurture plays a bigger role in defining us than anyone ever thought. Maybe the nature accounts for very little.'

'What next?', I asked.

'I want to visit her house.'

'You have the address?'

She held up an orange Post-It note for confirmation.

'That obviously isn't the address in Barton?'

'No. This house is where she lived for most of her life but no one knows if *I* ever actually lived here. It is possible that I was born in the house. They just don't know. It actually belonged to my grandparents and they passed it on to her and my dad. When she came out of prison – God, how awful does that sound? –it was there waiting for her.'

It was a short drive and I recognised part of the route.

'Near Barton', I commented.

'I remember this road.'

We turned right at a petrol station with a short queue of traffic lined up and into a modern estate in which the architects had managed to cram hundreds of identical houses with no consideration given to any aesthetic adornment whatsoever. Row after row of red-brick semis lay before us like a huge urban maze designed to trap the unwary visitor who might never find his way back out and die of hunger and thirst in the orderly gutter.

'Ideal starter home', said Georgina. 'That's how the estate agent markets these. Plasma TVs and Nissan Qashqais. Upward mobility. Selling us a lie to keep us compliant.'

'Up the revolution', I said feigning agreement. 'This is making plumbers and electricians feel like they can join the middle-classes without going to university. Someone needs to do something about it.'

However, no one did anything about it and we took another turn to the right, following a road which led us past older houses, the remnants of a village and a duck pond in village green. A few isolated picnickers sat eating curly sandwiches and drinking middle-class fizzy drinks in bottles, pretending that the world wasn't going to hell and that we weren't about to be run over by a combined army of zombies and professional protestors.

The news was full of stories of protest, the rhetoric of BLM given over to a struggle with anyone whose views might differ. It was peaceful protestors versus right-wing thugs. The press and the television media had created the story they wanted and now it was just a case of ensuring the protagonists acted it out for them. And yet these thoughtless people ate sandwiches when they should have been out defacing war memorials in the name of race relations.

'Bastards', I said.

'What?' asked Steph from the front seat.

'I was just thinking out loud.'

'Have you got Tourette's?', asked Georgina.

'Twat!'

'Pardon?'

'I don't think so.'

The sat nav was directing us right again. I had made a mental note that when it came to extracting ourselves from the maze we just needed to keep turning left and we would find ourselves back on the main road or somewhere else.

'Down here', said Georgina, driving.

The nicely kept houses of the village gave way to a tatty street with narrow, terraced houses that once stood as a symbol of working-class solidity and decency, but which had become another type of symbol completely, a reminder of social decay. When we stepped out of the car, we all noticed the smell of weed immediately.

Actual weeds grew from the gaps in the pavement. Ancient cars lined the pavement, BMWs with blacked-out windows and 'modded' Vauxhall Corsas or Golfs. A skip sat outside one gutted house at the far end of the street and actually looked better than some of the vehicles present.

'Which one?', I asked.

'Fourteen.'

The three of us strolled down to the correct house. I noticed a yellowed lace curtain twitch here and a ghostly face pressed up against a net there. One house had a set of what Billy always called *venereal* blinds but these were shut and remained so.

'Do you wish you had a key?', I asked. We had congregated at a battered wooden door, painted blue. The doorstep had been painted grey in the distant past and needed to be redone or sand-blasted. The window frames were PVC and in better nick, but an air of desolation hung around like smog.

'It would be nice to look inside and see if anything was familiar but I have a feeling that it would be a waste of time. I don't know what I expected to see or feel.'

'Well, since you were here anyway, it was no problem to visit. Who knows how you might have felt?'

I sighed and turned to survey the street as one might when coming to the end of an adventure when you realise that things will never be the same again and that the people you shared your time with would soon be strangers. In a sense life would go on, but it would be lacking something.

Except that when I turned something caught my eye. I frowned. Just a private frown, not a stage frown like for a silent film.

It was *déjà vu* (*not again*, Billy would say), or some close relative, which beset me now. There was something familiar on the street, some phantom presence made real, an object that belonged in my head and not in any actual, physical situation. It was a car.

I was dimly aware that Georgina and Steph had stopped talking and I could sense their eyes burning a hole in my back. A metaphorical hole.

The car. It was a red Ford Sierra, a bit of a wreck but a runner. One front wing was blue, but the rest of the car was red. The tyres looked low on air but not flat. If it would start, you could have driven it, put it that way.

'What are you staring at?', asked Georgina. And yet as I began to walk towards the old car, almost in a trance, I couldn't quite bring myself to break a spell that had fallen upon me. A red Sierra. I was six feet from it when I retrieved my phone from a jacket pocket. I stopped now. I was standing in the road, my eyes still fixed on the car but I tore them away and clicked on the 'photos' button of my Chinese phone.

This car was the one in the painting above Steph's fireplace, the only one of the four which I hadn't liked. I changed angle to align the photograph she had sent with the car in front of me and was surer than ever. My heart thudded in my chest. What did this mean? After everything we had been through, after every avenue we had explored, what did *this* mean?

I turned again and beckoned Steph over to me.

'Recognise anything?', I asked.

'No. I don't think so.'

Georgina followed behind, perplexed.

'What is it?', she asked.

I handed over my phone to Steph, pressing a button as the screen began to fade. I pointed.

'You might not recognise anything, but you painted that car.'

She pulled a face.

I paused and frowned again, or possibly extended my original frown. Taking a step back it became clear that this was, without question, the street she had painted. Pristine in her painting, tatty now after years of neglect, but recognisable nevertheless. I knew then that she had been here before, that the painting in question was not just a product of her imagination. Why did she paint this scene? Who knew?

I could not fathom what bearing this new knowledge had on recent events. There suddenly seemed to be a connection between the art she had been so dismissive of and the street she had brought us to.

A further thought occurred to me. It seemed unlikely that we would find an American-style gas station in these environs but...

'Is there a school around here?'

'A school? I have no idea. I've never been here before', she said. I fired a quick glance at Georgina who had remained silent. She gave a tiny shrug as if to distance herself from my thought processes. She had no idea what was going on and nor did I really.

'Let's go for a walk', I suggested.

'We have to catch our plane', said Steph, sounding rational and unperturbed.

I checked my watch.

'It's fine. We have time. Just a few minutes, that's all.'

I began walking and thankfully my two companions followed. I was on a mission now but I hoped that I didn't have to walk far before my point was made. In twenty seconds, we had come to a junction and instinctively I turned right, an inspired directional choice, for shortly afterwards I had taken my little posse to a set of iron railings, painted green, behind which sat a red-brick primary school. I turned and smiled at my companions and then led Steph to a gate, where we stopped. Leading her gently by the shoulders, I moved her through ninety degrees until she was facing the school.

I didn't say anything for a while, letting her reach her own conclusions. It was almost silent on the street, as if the atmosphere had been vacuumed up for effect. A shiver tickled my spine.

We were joined by a perplexed Georgina, but she respected our silence, leaving me to break it.

'You painted this too, Steph', I said. Her response was a heavy sigh, coming after a tense second or two had passed. Impossibly, the silence deepened, the clocks that run down our lives stopped, nothing moved. I could almost sense the weight descending on her shoulders once again, crushing her anew. Her despair infected me at once and a ring of pressure formed around my diaphragm, leaving me just slightly nauseous.

We returned to reality when her mobile phone rang, jarring us back to the present and to things which were possible, things which really happened and could be explained rationally.

'Hello?'

I turned away, unwilling to overhear her conversation even unintentionally. Georgina gave me a quizzical look but I shook my head as if to say, *I'll explain later.*

Few words passed between Steph and her caller, but it was bad news, and I could guess what form of bad news. She continued to face the school, the phone clamped to her ear, her gaze fixed on that forbidding building, ochre reflected from the walls and through the railings to her tear-filled eyes. Like an automaton she signified the end of the call by letting her hand drop to her side and I thought she might release the phone from her grasp.

She didn't speak for a few seconds. Georgina had just opened her mouth to ask what had happened when Steph abruptly ended her period of mute reflection.

'That was the hospital. My mum is dead.'

***

'You realise that you will probably own that house when your mother dies. You might not feel like it, but you should make some claim on it.'

'Hadn't thought about it.'

'So where does all this leave you?'

'I don't know. I feel cured. Honestly. This weight has been lifted off my shoulders.'

I believed her – sort of – but I needed to double check. Events outside the school had clouded the issue terribly.

'You're not just saying that?'

'I have always been honest about it. Whether it lasts or not, I don't know but right now, I feel… right. I think this is how I should always have felt. I have nothing to compare it to but I feel happy or something. Ready for the future.'

I wanted to believe her.

'So, what about the car and the school and the street?', I said casting a glance at the paintings on the fireplace.

'God knows. I might mention it to Doctor Patel but other than that it must have been a coincidence.'

When we parted, I wondered if I would see Stephanie Kuler again. But Belfast was a small city so you never knew. I

370

drove away thinking about this and thinking about the paintings too. Who painted the back end of a Ford Sierra, for instance?

I thought about something else, something which had troubled me for reasons which had not initially been clear. It was something she had said. *My mum is dead.* Not, my *mum has just died.* Maybe I was looking for a slip where that wasn't one, but *my mum is dead* is too matter-of-fact, too past tense.

So what? Well, her choice of words opened up a huge possibility, a horrific one. What if she had already been dead when Steph left her room that day? What if... I don't even want to think about it... but what if Steph had exacted her revenge on her mother for all those years of torment?

What if Steph had only foreseen the murder she felt she had committed? Could she actually *become* the murderer she thought she was by killing her own mother years later? Was the feeling that plagued her for so many years actually a premonition?

But who believes in premonitions anyway?

Epilogue

Whatever the truth, the matter was concluded for all concerned. My doubts remained but they were locked away in some tiny mental compartment labelled, 'case closed'. Georgina and I continued to see each other now and again. For the meantime the arrangement suited us both. We were content, you could say. If I had to choose between contentment and elation I would take the lesser emotion every time simply because it endures. No one goes through life elated, not even Timmy Mallet.

My big concern was Billy. Something was up.

Billy was the person you turned to in an emergency, the sort of man you can rely on no matter what. When Billy was nervous. I was nervous.

But Billy wasn't nervous. He was terrified...